Bad Marriage

BAD MARRIAGE

~~~~~~~~~~~~~~~~~~~~

John Tagholm

Friday November 13 09

To dear Helen,

who has a better pension
than me! Enjoy!

x John

Quartet Books

First published in 2009 by
Quartet Books Limited
A member of the Namara Group
27 Goodge Street, London WIT 2LD

Copyright © John Tagholm 2009

The right of John Tagholm to be identified
as the author of this work has been asserted
by him in accordance with the
Copyright, Designs and Patents Act, 1988

A catalogue record for this book
is available from the British Library

ISBN   978 0 7043 7170 5

Typeset by Antony Gray
Printed and bound in Great Britain by
T J International Ltd, Padstow, Cornwall

For Darwin

Bi-focal

Sometimes up out of this land
a legend begins to move.
Is it a coming near
of something under love?

Love is of the earth only,
the surface, a map of roads
leading wherever go miles
or little bushes nod.

Not so the legend under,
fixed, inexorable,
deep as the darkest mine
the thick rocks won't tell.

As fire burns the leaf
and out of the green appears
the vein in the centre line
and the legend veins under there,

So, the world happens twice –
once what we see it as;
second it legends itself
deep, the way it is.

WILLIAM STAFFORD

PART ONE

Two Lives

Chapter 1

When she stopped in front of the familiar porticoed building, she knew that the two conflicting strands of her life were about to be joined. The pressure of holding them apart, at times almost physically, had distorted her existence so much that she had barely been able to survive. She had no idea of what their fusion would produce but she was quite calm now and glad, at last, that she had taken into her own hands the process of bringing the two elements together. She had come full cycle, but the lanky girl who had climbed the stairs to the National Gallery four years ago was very different from the woman who now paused and looked again at those stairs and the imposing façade beyond. The process of reclaiming her life had begun.

She walked across the crowded entrance to the gallery with the certainty of someone who had done it many times before, threading her way through the scrum of people littering the curiously anonymous portal to the capital's most important collection of art. The columned foyer contained a party of school children unaware that they were blocking the flow from the doors to the wide stairs which led up into the first of the collections. A woman with a buggy, loaded with a child wrapped against the typical summer weather outside and laden with the paraphernalia that goes with supporting a modern infant, attempted to force a passage. A group of foreign students with bulky rucksacks provided a further barrier. Outside, a cold rain was falling and many of those coming through the large doors paused to shut their umbrellas or peel off their coats, some with a dog-like shake of their heads. They were confronted by an uneven line of people waiting to leave, hesitating to go out into the inclement day as their outstretched arms pulled on brightly coloured anoraks and thick overcoats. It was a strangely chaotic scene straight out of Brueghel.

By now the woman had reached the top of the wide stone steps and passed between a pair of uniformed wardens sitting on wooden seats on either side of the archway. Although each wore an identification tag marked 'security', with their photograph and name, they were an unlikely couple. Probably in their fifties, they appeared uninterested in the irregular stream of people around them, grey figures against the grey walls of the gallery. She didn't give them a second glance. She continued her purposeful way, in contrast to the groups and individuals who wandered aimlessly from room to room, a mix of exhausted children, bored teenagers and elderly couples supporting themselves wearily on sticks. Very few of them seemed to be looking at the pictures, particularly those who held to their ears the odd-looking handsets on which they could listen to recordings about the wonderful art all around them. Why bother to look when someone has already done that work for you?

By now, she was used to this chaos and she had long since decided that the strange diffused light of the gallery and the carefully controlled climate inside, neither too hot nor too cold, too dry or too damp, had an enervating effect on those inside, inducing a sort of disorientating torpor. Or, maybe, they were simply overwhelmed by the art.

Those who watched her – and there were several who could have registered her progress on monitors in the security control room – would have seen a tallish woman, perhaps in her early twenties, wearing a baggy yellow silk shirt over dark leggings carrying a sketch pad under her left arm. What might have caught their attention was the headscarf which concealed her powder-black hair and fell over her shoulders and partly obscured her lower face. Neither a hijab nor the more severe burka, it was a home-made affair, a beautifully patterned shroud in zigzags of black and grey over a headscarf of red dots on a white background, almost piratical in style. They framed a face which immediately defined her on several levels, particularly to those who were trained to look for the extraordinary. Her origins, near or distant, were not British. The paleness of her dark skin might have told the more knowledgeable of her watchers that her roots were in Afghanistan, or Pakistan. They might even have guessed that she was a Pashtun and in this they would have been on the right lines, but the distinguished hook of her nose and the penetrating blue-green of her eyes offered more specific proof of her origins. In the bowels of the National Gallery no one possessed such knowledge and even if the sweep of her scarf had been removed, they would have been unable to tell that she was descended from the Afridis, one of the many tribes that fall under the generic title Pashtun and whose homelands are the harsh and uncompromising hills of the Safed Koh range in the north west territories of Pakistan. When she herself had learned of this background she had laughed, for the bleak territory she inhabited was in south-west London, off Tooting Bec High Street, similarly uncompromising but for very different reasons.

The fact is, no one registered her steady progress through the great rooms of pictures, or if they did, found nothing of great interest to attract them. She was just another visitor to the gallery, a mature student perhaps, intent on spending the day copying a work of one of the great masters.

She ducked under the arm of a man who had his back to the famous Seurat painting of bathers on the banks of the Marne and who was holding the information phone to his ear as though his life depended on it. Somewhere in another room a baby cried, its high-pitched insistence rising over the steady shuffle of feet and murmured comments on the pictures. When she had first re-visited the National Gallery and encountered the nomadic groups and random individuals haphazardly making their way between vast rooms of Renaissance art and Impressionist exuberance, she had thought it was a one-off, a rare busy day when the crowds, if not out of control, seemed at odds with the purpose of the building, more the bustle of the market square than the reverence she had expected. But this was her tenth visit since she had returned to the gallery and she knew by now that this is how it was. The gallery could barely cope with its visitors and the daily invasion was like a school playground full of infants but with the sound turned down. The visitors were, in the main, indifferent to the art around them and had come because they thought they should, or because they had to, or because it was merely a place to meet. They provided the perfect backdrop for what she intended to do.

Her route was familiar and she remembered the first time she had rounded this corner, just over four years earlier and had seen the picture at the entrance to the next hall. Although tiny, it had stopped her in her tracks, for the face it depicted, intense and handsome, held her immediately with its mix of fear and defiance. She had felt that she was a privileged observer of a man in crisis, called upon to dig deep into his resolve to conquer what lay before him. She was enthralled by his look, at one and the same time entirely modern, his long hair flowing to his shoulders and his cheeks slightly sunken like those of a very fit man and defined even more firmly by the hint of a five-o'clock shadow, and also timeless. She smiled as she remembered that for her it had been love at first sight. In that moment, she recalled, the gallery had seemed to shrink back from her, the other visitors disappearing to the periphery of her vision so that all she could see and register was the handsome face looking up at the peril that confronted him. She had crept slowly towards the picture to read the label on the wall by its side which revealed it was the face of Christ. Her reaction then had been a mix of shame and disappointment, for here, contained in one delicious rectangle of delicately painted canvas, was the confusion of her life at that time. What she saw in front of her was forbidden on so many levels that to continue gazing at the face was an act of both daring and defiance. She did and returned many times to look at the tortured face, on each occasion being drawn further and further into its spell.

Looking at the picture again now it amused her that she could have fallen so deeply in love with what it represented. She shook her head and her scarf slipped below her mouth to reveal the full extent of her long and handsome face, the set of her jaw and the graceful line of her lips. In that moment, the covering for her head, an act of modesty, seemed to have quite the opposite effect, serving only to emphasise the startling qualities of her face, as a frame would a portrait. Staring again at the small painting of Christ at the flogging column, the crown of thorns on his head and the rope curled around his neck, she lowered her eyes and allowed herself the briefest of recollections of what had happened in the weeks that had followed that first encounter. She opened her notebook with a flourish of her right arm and immediately broke the thought. She took a few steps backwards to a leather block where she sat and looked across to the picture, the scarf now restored to her face. Inside the pad were several drawings of the anguished face in pencil and crayon and she began to add to them. Her eyes, though, betrayed the purpose of her visit. She noted again the single camera above the far door, disguised in the same grey colour as the ceiling. She registered once more the two attendants who by turn wandered around the room, before returning to their seats, a ballet they repeated at odd intervals throughout the morning. They were not the couple who had patrolled the room the previous week and she assumed that, in an attempt to relieve the undoubted boredom of their job, they were regularly assigned to different rooms in the vast gallery. Alongside one of the chairs was a CCTV monitor, divided into six sections, each showing the output of a different camera. Every five seconds or so the images would change and from where she sat she was able to watch this Battenberg cake of views blinking up and then disappearing, knowing that it was difficult to make logic of what they were showing. The woman with the loaded buggy trundled by, her child asleep amongst the baggage, one armed raised in front of its face as if to block out the huge picture of St Thomas which loomed above.

What would her father have thought if he could see her now and known the purpose of her visit? Would the tired old man sitting in the half-light of his front room, the curtains drawn against the sharp sun and the roar of the traffic in the high street, have accepted the course of her actions? Towards the end, his face had sunk into itself but the fierceness remained. She had always thought that her father's looks belied the severity of his manner since the lines on his face seemed set for a permanent smile, the slight upward tilt of one of his eyebrows appearing to confirm a look of benign amusement. When he spoke, though, his voice could often be without warmth, his tone sharp and unforgiving so that his cold sonority would ring through the house as a warning to wife and child alike. Part of her was just like him, she realised now: singular and unremitting.

She walked up to the picture as if to examine some detail in the smooth texture of the small painting. She moved first to one side then the other, glancing down at her pad as she did. What she was confirming was not the minute and masterly brushstrokes, nor the finely graded flesh pinks of the face, but the mounts of the picture, just visible towards the top side of the frame. She noted how it appeared to be hung on two stainless steel pins secured to the grey wall. She stepped back, as if to sketch further, her eyes moving up the paper to take in the flickering CCTV images, knowing by now that she would appear in the bottom right-hand corner of the divided screen. And there she was, for five seconds at least, standing in front of the picture, an art student intent on capturing something of the brilliance of a post-Renaissance masterpiece. She walked slowly backwards from the painting, like a courtier leaving a queen, before turning and heading in the direction of a pair of enormous open doors which led through to the adjacent collection. In this room hung a series of large and lugubrious paintings, heavy with dark paint and meaning, semi-naked Christs and prophets from the Old Testament in the midst of death and damnation. Many of these great canvases seemed to have no virtue except size, saved purely for their antiquity and attractive only to pedants and art historians. The largest of these hung towards the far end, in a sort of giant domed anteroom and didn't declare itself until you walked into the space to discover its brooding menace looming over you.

She counted the number of paces she took from the small picture to the large, confirming that it was the same as the day before. The painting, over four metres high, was hung on a giant chain just visible as she walked into the five-sided room. She waited for a moment or two, studying the enormous picture, which emphasised its bulk by leaning slightly towards her, and watched people arrive in the domed space. Some regarded it as a full stop and turned back, whilst others looked blankly around them, barely registering the massive tribute to some obscure story in the Bible, before moving to an open doorway in one of the other walls. They were like characters in a video game, working their way through the gallery and hoping the next exit would bring them happily to the conclusion of their journey. She looked back into the main salon and could see the lone CCTV camera above the big doors staring in her direction. She knew that it covered the whole room because she had seen its output on the monitors and noted that it appeared to have only a wide angle. She turned her attention back to the giant painting and puzzled at the culture which could have accommodated and revered such a gloomy statement. Then she moved through the open doorway, which led on to a small corridor from which she could see the entrance to the connecting bridge that took visitors through to the new wing of the National Gallery. She looked at the sweep of the second hand on her watch as she covered the twenty paces in about the same number of seconds. As she retraced her steps she felt entirely in control and quite calm, so very different from that summer which, although only four years earlier, seemed so long ago that it belonged to another age and to another person.

She left the building unhurriedly, her sketch pad conspicuous under her arm, her headscarf back in place so that just her eyes and part of her nose were visible, skipping down the wide stone steps and gliding between the endless muddle of the foyer and out into the cold air. She passed the staff entrance to the gallery, her head down against the cold wind, and was glad to turn off the wide pavement up the narrow passage that led along the western edge of the building towards Whitcomb Street, which sloped down from Soho, thus linking the two extremes of culture in London. She had taken the flat a month before on another rainy day when the wind had rattled the sash windows on the top floor of the small terraced house that had seen better days. The agent had been surprised at the speed of her decision, for a flat in this position did not come cheaply and the rent was extremely high for a shabby kitchen-living room, small bedroom and tiny bathroom. When he had left, his highly polished black shoes clumping down the narrow wooden stairs, she sat by the window and looked out at the back of the National Gallery. The first part of the puzzle was in place and from here she could fill in the rest of the pieces.

And now she shut the door on the rain and climbed the stairs, just as the resolve rose in her. Tomorrow she would do it. The girl who had fallen in love with the painting no longer existed. She had been enchanted and enthralled and in that moment she had been broken and discarded. The woman who now contemplated her future held those memories with an even detachment, as if she was examining a specimen under a microscope. If these disconcerting echoes from the past were driving her forward, her momentum was fuelled from somewhere deep inside herself, from a place she chose not to examine.

She knew, though, that tomorrow would be the beginning of the rest of her life.

Chapter 2

In the hot summer of 1997 Habiba Popals looked and acted much older than she felt. Tall and slim, she wore tight narrow jeans to emphasise her height and her black hair was cut short and slicked down with two large flattened curls, like scimitars, as sideboards. Her defiant nose made her appear both haughty and intelligent, of which she was certainly the latter, even though she often chose to disguise it.

'You have absolutely no idea about heat,' her father told her. 'In the mountains in summer the air, if you could call it that, was so hot there seemed no oxygen in it at all. Those who were not used to it would move their mouths like fish out of water.'

When her father began to talk like this, Habiba knew that it was best to let him flow on uninterrupted, particularly if she had something difficult to ask him, as she had now.

'We would sometimes climb the White Mountain in search of the cooler air but it was a difficult equation balancing the toil of the lower hills against the pleasures of the upper slopes. And we would not have worn anything as ridiculous as those trousers.' He ended his admonishment with a familiar rasping cough which seemed to roll through him like the ominous warning from a soon-to-be-active volcano.

She hesitated to tell him they were jeans, for something told her that he was deliberately goading her by using the wrong word. It was the Saturday of the second week in July and the sun beat down on Tooting Bec, laying bare its shabby ugliness, glinting cruelly off the cars and revealing the foul, grey air of the low-lying and unloved suburb. Although their house was on a turning just off the Bec, it was the first in the terrace and the noise of the main street was with them the whole time, even during the night, the buses grinding along in low gear to the soprano accompaniment of the ever-present sirens. In contrast, the Popals kept a small and immaculate house which smelled of rose petals and lavender, its coloured walls and multi-patterned rugs an oasis from the outside world.

'You would not have considered taking one pace in those trousers,' he gestured dismissively towards her with his hand. 'Wholly inappropriate.' He considered the rest of her wardrobe with the same distaste: the black sleeveless T-shirt, the jewelled belts and the ridiculous green-and-white American trainers. Latif Popals' eyes conveyed his displeasure at his daughter's appearance, a cold and dismissive appraisal. Habiba had, in fact, dressed down for this meeting, leaving off the heavy mascara she had recently been using to elongate further the almond shape of her eyes and the white ankle boots patterned with chrome studs. Her father was in his usual outfit: a brown jacket over a white shirt and caramel v-necked sweater with black trousers. But for the sandals he wore over his bare feet, he was dressed for a mildish autumn day with, perhaps, just the hint of winter to come. He coughed again, a deep rich, liquid cough, a midwinter cough on a fine summer's day.

'If your mother could see you now,' he concluded, with a shake of his head. Habiba's mother could not see her now, for she had died two years earlier of a cancer which lay undiagnosed for too long, partly because of her fear of doctors and, in the end, because of their indifference to her. She was never seen in the street without her shalmar kameez and if her untimely death had any positives at all, it was that she was spared her daughter's drift into clothes and behaviour that she could not have tolerated and which would have shocked her to the core. Habiba regarded her father and bided her time for she knew that he had not finished, the faraway look in his eyes a prelude to further reminiscences.

'The snow leopard knew how to conduct itself, moving north in summer and south in winter,' as if somehow comparing the behaviour of the animal with that of his daughter. Habiba was very familiar with stories of the snow leopard, which her father had told her regularly as she was growing up. When she went walking with him on Mitcham Common, hand in hand over the flat, scrubby grass, she would secretly hope to see one, a flash of brown or white, depending on the season, disappearing towards the distant chimneys of the recycling plant across the marsh. Since the death of his wife, her father had begun to talk more like this, recalling the family stories and telling them again and again until Habiba had stopped listening. By now she had realised that snow leopards do not inhabit the land between Beddington Park and Tooting Bec Broadway.

'I have something to ask you,' she said tentatively, trying to inject a confidence into her tone which she singularly lacked. When he merely looked at her and said nothing she realised that, like an animal, he had already detected trouble on the horizon.

'I have been asked to go to London,' she said.

'You live in London,' he replied.

'No, London, the centre,' she rushed on. 'It's an art course organised by the National Gallery . . . '

She watched his big, dark eyes give the slowest of blinks as he prepared himself to respond, but she continued before he had the chance.

' . . . and it lasts a week and we can stay in one of the halls of residence at London University.'

'To do what?'

'To learn about art and to copy some of the masterpieces. It's what I want to do.'

Again, the slow blink from the still face. 'And who would you go with?'

'A group of us from my class.'

Latif Popals could see them now, a collection of over-painted young girls, exotically dressed and noisy – why were they always so noisy? – alone in the centre of London and looking at pictures which his own parents would have thought wrong and dangerous. He stared at his daughter and saw the eagerness and the fear in her face, her eyes pleading with him to consent.

He coughed and breathed in through his nose, giving himself time before his reply.

'You are very young,' he said ominously.

'I am nearly eighteen. And it's educational.'

'You are seventeen. And will you have a chaperone?'

She was caught for the moment, unsure how to respond. 'Not as such,' she said. 'There will be an expert provided by the gallery and we'll spend most of the day there.'

'And at night?'

How Habiba hated this constant questioning, as though she was unable to control her own life. She could only shrug.

Her father considered her response. He had sent her to a private all-girls' school, which he could barely afford and although she was surrounded by girls from families more wealthy than hers, at first it had seemed ideal. Only lately had the problems arrived thick and fast: requests to stay with friends, the relentless pressure to dress like them and to follow their behaviour. She was still a child, despite the jewellery and the fancy clothes and the clever language.

'I cannot allow it.'

There was no softening to his response, no 'I'm afraid' or 'on consideration', not even the familiar 'for your own good'. It was an abrupt and final decision, a closing of the case. There could be no appeal. This is how it had been with his father, who as a parent and an elder, had to be obeyed without question.

At this moment, Habiba hated her father, a state that she had found herself in more often than not recently. Respect was the closest she came to affection but most of the time she oscillated between fear and hatred. It was as if part of him was still in the old country, governed by rules and behaviour that belonged to another time and place. The sunlight shafted through the bay window and she looked at the bleached rectangles it created on the floor. She knew that he didn't want her to go to art college and that this was another blocking manoeuvre to force her to reconsider. Why did he always think he knew better? Sitting still, he was not looking at her but across the room, terminating their conversation and signalling that his mind had moved on to other subjects. She got up and left the room, glancing back as she quietly shut the door, but his gaze was still averted.

She lay on her bed in a cocoon of posters of pop stars and film actors. Habiba was wise enough to know that her father's inflexibility was traditional and handed down through generations, but she was also young enough to want to flounce out of the house and do whatever she liked. She pulled open the small drawer of her bedside table and from a small pouch she had taped underneath, she slid out a postcard. When her father infuriated her, which he did with increasing regularity, she liked to hold this picture as an act of defiance. It showed Gustave Courbet's *The Origin of the World*, his painting of a woman's vagina. For Habiba, it represented everything that she knew would shock her father to the core. She slipped the picture back into its hiding place. She was too frightened to disobey him directly and so, under the stares of the beautiful young men on the walls around her, she tried to find a way to get around her father's steely resolve. She wondered about calling Uncle Baddy, for he always made her feel better even when he took the side of her father, which he sometimes did. Badsha was a friend of the family whose warmth and generous advice to Habiba over the years had allowed him to drop naturally into the role of honorary uncle. Badsha never confronted a situation but worked stealthily around it, a born diplomat and strategist. Habiba closed her long fingers behind her head and decided she knew what he would have suggested as a course of action. It would involve her closest school friend.

She picked up the phone.

'Sharifa, it's me.'

Latif Popals sat downstairs and mourned the loss of his wife with whom he could have shared his feelings of dissatisfaction. His daughter was like a brightly coloured moth which he could not quite catch in his hands but which flittered distractingly around him. She flaunted all the rules with which he had been brought up and, though he would not admit it to her, something of her defiance appealed to him and reminded him of his own mother. Alone in the sitting room he nodded to himself, acknowledging an event way back in the history of his family. If Habiba knew the whole story, would it make matters worse for him? He considered the consequences and as he did so he was transported back fifty years, not long in the scheme of things, but to a world so different that it bore no relation to his life now. He closed his eyes and he could see the khaki-coloured hills dry and dusty from the summer heat and the road snaking up through the pass. Higher still, there was the White Mountain, snow tipped even in early summer and, in between, the villages of his childhood, as brown as the landscape, were tucked away in the valleys of the Bazar and Bara rivers. Far above, the wide-winged vultures floated on the rising heat.

He was woken by the front doorbell and he rose stiffly to his feet. He opened the door to find a pair of eyes regarding him from behind the sweep of a grey hijab. His face lit up.

'Sharifa, how lovely to see you. Please come in.' Still smiling, he stepped back to allow her to enter. This was his favourite of Habiba's many friends and he ushered her into the front room with pleasure.

'My parents send their warmest greetings, Mr Popals,' she said to him, offering just the slightest bow of her head.

'Some green tea, I think,' he said, remembering what she liked to drink. 'I'll call Habiba down.'

When his daughter came into the living room her father was

still in the kitchen. The two young women looked conspiratorially at each other and waited for the tea to arrive. When Mr Popals came back into the room, Sharifa got up and cleared a table so that he could put down the tray.

'I have some delicious fig biscuits,' he said, offering her the plate.

'You are very kind, Mr Popals. I adore figs.'

'And what are you up to these days, Sharifa?'

Sharifa loosened the headscarf and lowered it below her mouth before she spoke. 'Now that the end of term is so close I have managed to get myself a job in Boots to pay for what I intend to do in the summer.'

'Are you going away with your family?' he enquired.

'For part of the time. We will be going to Spain again.' Mr Popals recalled that they had a villa in the hills behind Malaga.

'And then I shall be doing the course at the National Gallery. I think that Habiba is part of this as well.' She continued before he could respond. 'It should be really fascinating being told about the greatest art by real experts. And it will look good on my CV.'

Mr Popals frowned. 'But I thought you were going to study law, Sharifa.'

'Oh, I am Mr Popals, but to get into the university I want you need to impress on all sorts of levels. That's what my parents think and I'm sure it's true.' She turned and looked over to Habiba. 'And it will be quite hard work.'

Mr Popals frowned and glanced over to his daughter before continuing.

'Habiba did mention something about it. Tell me more. Where will you be staying, for example?'

'There are some splendid halls of residence, on the canal by Mile End. New buildings and not far from the tube. It's a proper campus with security and everything.'

'That's not far from Uncle Badsha in Bow,' added Habiba, apparently as an afterthought.

'Anyway,' continued Sharifa, 'it is easy to get into town. And it will give us a taste of university life.'

Mr Popals saw his moment. 'And perhaps it will give you a taste of other things as well, activities that your parents might not approve of?'

It was as if Sharifa had been waiting for this response for she hardly missed a beat before replying. 'I can understand your concerns, Mr Popals. But we are sensible girls and,' she paused, looking across to her friend, 'it's not as if we cannot get into trouble here in Tooting.'

Mr Popals hesitated, his instincts fighting a losing battle against Sharifa's quiet and measured offensive.

'When Habiba first mentioned this trip to me I had my doubts, I have to admit. But I now see that it might be useful.' He paused for the importance of his words to sink in and he did not see the lightning-quick look his daughter gave Sharifa, their eyes meeting for the fraction of a second.

'I trust you to be sensible, as I know you will.'

If Mr Popals was aware of how he had been manipulated he didn't show it, even though he felt a vague unease as he heard the girls chattering as they climbed the stairs. How could he have known that his decision would change the course of his daughter's life? His low cough rumbled up the stairs.

Chapter 3

The question of right and wrong never entered her mind.

During the month she had been in the flat she had already established a pattern to the comings and goings of the National Gallery. By now, she knew he no longer worked there, and although this made what she was about to do easier, part of her was disappointed. Although it was four years since she had seen him, the image of his face, smiling, arrogant, persuasive, drove her on. Thinking about him, she felt a coldness descend on her, wrapping itself protectively around her heart and fixing her resolve. How different she was now, in ways he could not possibly understand. As she checked and assembled what she needed, her mind was entirely focused and clear of the distraction of doubt.

Even in the narrow, sheltered street the rain still managed to find a way through and slashed against the windows. She had her back to the stormy scene as she surveyed what she had prepared. The picture was propped on the mantelshelf above the small fireplace, contained in its elaborate frame, and she once again admired its authenticity. She lifted it off and carefully placed it, face down, into the shallow, rectangular wooden box, similar to the drawer of a table, but without a handle. The picture fitted exactly with barely any margin for movement. The box was painted grey, the exact colour of the walls of the gallery.

Then she began to load the buggy, laying the box carefully in the base. Around the narrow wooden edging of the grey box were strips of sticking tape, protected by quickly removable transparent covers. Over the back of the picture she placed the mattress and then, as carefully as she would a real baby, she lay the doll on top. She put several blankets over it before zipping the rest of her equipment into a baby bag, which she lodged on the shelf underneath. She added some baby wipes, a spare blanket and a bottle half-full of mixed baby milk. She pulled up the hood and stretched an elastic line of coloured figures across the opening and stood as far back as she could in the small room to assess its authenticity. She stepped closer and hesitated, arms on her hips. She leaned into the buggy and removed the doll. She replaced the blankets and took a few paces back. It was impossible to tell there was no baby in the buggy. She sat the doll in an old armchair and nodded in satisfaction at her decision.

The rain was cold, driven from the east by an unforgiving wind and it lashed the broad pavement in front of the National Gallery causing pedestrians to clutch at the collars of their overcoats and turn their heads against the stinging wetness. Some ran up the steps to the gallery for cover and only Nelson, aloof on his column, seemed unperturbed by the foulness of the day. His gaze was fixed on Parliament and a distant Spain, regardless of what was happening below.

For Habiba, the conditions were perfect and she stooped to secure the plastic weather-shield across the hood of the buggy before carefully bumping it up the steps. No gallant man came forward to help and for this she was grateful. She was wearing a black anorak and she had tightened the hood over her hijab. The throng of people in the entrance was worse than ever and this further reassured her. The smell of damp clothing filled the air and inside the mosaic floor was wet as the rain dripped from the coats of the visitors. She loosened her hood but did not push it back and she felt quite calm as she made her way into the gallery, one of many still dressed for the lousy weather. Although she knew exactly where she was going, she took a haphazard route through the collections, sometimes retracing her steps, looking at pictures for a second time, like many of the visitors. There were several mothers with pushchairs joining the usual throng of pilgrims worshipping at the altar of art, the shuffling chorus of a modern opera played out in a continuous daily performance. Only today would be different, the plot more dramatic, the ending unexpected.

She had now worked herself around the gallery and was in the room next door to the one she wanted. She sat in front of Botticelli's *Venus and Mars* preparing herself for the intensity of the next few moments. She looked up at a sleeping Mars, disarmed and vulnerable, with Venus by his side, awake and alert. How appropriate, she thought. Like Venus, she felt in charge of herself and the situation, entirely at ease. She looked at her hands, stretching the fingers in front of her, noting how still they were. She tightened the scarf over her mouth as she watched the attendant by the far doorway as he finished a slow walk around the room, hands behind his back. He was now being asked a question by an older man with a walking stick. She stood, pushing the buggy towards him, pausing just before him to take a peek at the sleeping baby. From the tray underneath she brought out a brightly coloured baby bag which she placed by the side of the buggy. She knew from previous observation of the monitor screens that this small area of the room, closest to where the attendant stood, was not covered by the camera above the door. She reached inside the bag, which proclaimed My Baby in large letters, and triggered the fuse. She had twenty seconds to leave the room, plenty of time to amble beyond the attendant, who was explaining, not for the first time, how to get from Religion and the Renaissance to Van Gogh's *Sunflowers*. As she waited for the noise, she undid the poppers of the buggy cover and brought out from the cot what looked like three bottles. As she did so, a roar, like the rush of escaping steam, came from the room she had just left. Everyone turned as the tall doorway began to fill with smoke. And then the commotion began, the calls and the cries, the running feet and the smoke alarms. All attention was directed away from her as people fled the smoke or stared in disbelief. She had at least two minutes before the smoke gun ran out and as she walked into the next collection she pulled the pin and dropped the first of the smoke grenades, which immediately began to gush a dense, red cloud. The smoke pushed her further into the room and in the red shroud she pulled the pins on two further canisters, the second in front of the small picture of Christ, whose anguished face she could just make out through the swirl of red. She waited a few seconds before the smoke was at its thickest before pulling back the covers in the buggy and lifting the picture out of its wooden casing. Resting it against the buggy, she then placed her hands on the frame either side of Christ's face on the gallery wall, and lifted the picture off its steel hooks. She laid this in the empty box and covered it with blankets before picking up the other picture and placing it on the wall.

She had calculated that people touring the gallery soon lose their sense of direction so that, in the first few seconds of panic that followed the alarms, they would begin to run in different directions, parties of school children crying out in concern and crashing into adults rushing one way and the other. It was in this predicted mayhem that Habiba was able to move to the second stage of her plan.

The whole room was now filled with dense, red smoke and she began pacing her way towards the far end, counting out the exact number of steps she needed to reach the domed room. Pushing the buggy into the short corridor beyond, she reckoned she had thirty seconds to complete her task and she did it with time to spare. She took the grey box from the buggy and walked calmly over to the bridge connecting the two parts of the gallery. She unpeeled the strips from the shallow box and placed it on the wall, a blank box on the similarly grey wall, a complement to the other boxes nearby containing audio visual equipment. There were calls from the other room but she knew if she couldn't see them she, too, must be invisible. Returning with the buggy to the corridor, she left the top open and the blankets dishevelled. Only now did she lower the hood of her coat, although her face was still partially concealed by her headscarf. She removed the black anorak and from underneath the buggy she took another bag and pulled out a stone-coloured mac and a red, spotted headscarf. She quickly put on the coat and placed the scarf over the one she was already wearing. She stuffed the black anorak in the bag and put it on the shelf under the buggy. Only then did she move towards the main entrance.

She heard an announcement about the evacuation of the building and she increased the speed of her walk in line with the other visitors around her. If Habiba had been unable to imagine beforehand what this part of the operation might have been like, it was just as new and unexpected for the staff of the gallery. Although they had practised a few drills, they had not done so in rooms full of dense smoke. Order just about dominated chaos and yet there was a degree of confusion when Habiba reached the main exit. Police and fire crews arriving from outside were met by internal security staff unsure whether to keep people in the gallery or let them out. By the time she had arrived at the doors, the bare bones of a strategy had been put in place and she could see that she would be searched before being allowed out into the rain. Even as the security man, conscious of her sex and perhaps of her religion, called over a female colleague, her quiet resolve remained in place. She gave an address that was four doors up from her parents' old home, that of an embittered couple who had steadfastly refused to acknowledge her father in all the years that her family had lived there. The woman in the dark blue uniform took down the details and apologised for what had happened. Very soon the smoke gun and canisters would be discovered and shortly afterwards the buggy, but she was out and away and the first part of her plan accomplished. When she turned up the alleyway, the wind was at her back and seemed to blow her home. She took this as an omen. Safe inside she later watched the police tour the boundaries looking in vain for clues to what might have happened.

*   *   *

There was a telling delay between observation and reaction. Brian McMasters heard the alarm in the no-man's-land between his office and the security room and his instant reaction was to wonder who on earth had ordered a practice drill this morning. There was a curious lack of logic about this, since he was the only person able to instigate such a procedure. Not only was he in the wrong place, his rusty senses had let him down. By the time he got to the control room, thirty seconds later, two of the monitor screens appeared to be malfunctioning, one showing pale pink the other a uniform light grey. It took him a moment to realise that they were recording smoke-filled rooms, by which time the noise of two different alarms assailed him: the first a general fire warning, which could be heard by the whole gallery, the second a high-pitched bleeping, which was local to the control room. It was the first time he had ever heard them ring together and the discordant tones clashed in his head, further disorientating him.

Although there were two very capable members of his team in the room, he felt on the edge of panic, as a multitude of options seem to rush towards him. One of the men was speaking into a walkie-talkie. 'Possible fire in Rooms 4 and 5. Evacuation procedure. The brigade will be here in about two minutes.' As he spoke, the second man turned to his boss.

'Motion sensor in Room 5 indicates activity around some of the pictures.'

Another walkie-talkie crackled. 'We've located a smoke gun in Room 4. We can assume similar in 5.'

Both men were now looking at McMasters, who grabbed an internal phone and, with more authority than he felt, spoke to the security desk in the foyer. 'We've located the trouble in 4 and 5. I'm going to make a public-address announcement. Institute body searches on those leaving. Stop any new entries and close the gallery.'

He composed himself and scribbled a note on a pad on the

desk in front of the monitors. One of the assistants moved aside so that he could slide into his place. He depressed a key on a small box and spoke into a wire grill the size of a tennis ball.

'Ladies and gentleman. This is Brian McMasters, head of security. There has been a small incident in one part of the gallery. There is no need to worry. I repeat, there is no need to worry. We are organising an orderly evacuation of the premises and I would ask you to walk, I repeat, walk, to the main entrance. We are sorry for this inconvenience.'

He pushed back the chair and left the room, walking quickly towards the rooms where the incidents were taking place. Room 4 was still full of white smoke, curling and tumbling, seeking a way to escape. The huge space had been reduced to a circle of about two metres around him, all the distance he could see. Above, the massive ceiling space was filled and he could barely see a picture on the wall nearest to him. He walked forward, his body disturbing the smoke which swirled angrily around him. He heard the snort of what he knew to be a foam fire extinguisher and out of the mist appeared two of his men dousing a large hold-all out of which had been gushing a steady stream of white smoke. His heart was beating fast as he approached the wall which contained the pictures covered by the motion sensor alarm. To his immense relief, all the paintings seemed in place, each coming into focus the closer he came. One of them was a picture of Christ and the look of pain on his face he was quickly able to identify with. His eyes, though, were drawn to the layers of smoke mingling in the doorway beyond, a dancing mix of red and white combining to produce the inside of a giant piece of seaside rock. He walked cautiously on into the pink haze, his left arm extended in front of him in case of collision.

The red smoke was thicker now and as he shuffled forward his foot kicked a metal canister which span across the floor, the hollow metal sound continuing into the distance even as the smoke closed around it. He followed its trajectory as best he could and, taking out his handkerchief, picked up the spent casing. He made his way to the room beyond, whose dome was now shrouded in billowing red clouds still issuing from a smoke canister. He ignored it, knowing that it would shortly stop. Keeping close to the perimeter of the room, he quickly confirmed that the pictures were all in place, before taking the smaller door in the corner out into the corridor where he found the buggy. He spoke again to the main desk.

'I want the back corridor by the domed room sealed off. There is pram here which might have been abandoned by a frightened mother or it might be what we are looking for and therefore evidence. It's not to be touched.'

He looked over the buggy which, like the *Marie Celeste*, seemed to have been abandoned in mid-use, the blankets strewn across the small mattress as though a child had been snatched up, the baby wipes ready for whatever mothers did with baby wipes. He didn't touch anything but noted the black windcheater stuffed into a bag in the tray underneath. He clicked the walkie-talkie into action again.

'I want all this morning's CCTV footage from opening until,' he looked at his watch, ' . . . until now.'

'Already under way, boss.'

He looked again at the buggy. What on earth is all this about, he wondered, cursing his luck. Alone, he leaned back against the panelled wall. He was due to retire in the summer and he was within sight of the finishing post, just like Devon Loch, way out in front, before his mysterious collapse deprived him of the Grand National. What obstacles was he going to have to clear now? Already he could feel himself building his defences against the accusations that were sure to follow: too old, too unprepared, a dinosaur in a digital age. His gloomy thoughts were interrupted as the liaison detective, with whom he had sat on many committees to discuss routines to cope with incidents just like this one, came running up the stairs. They shook hands.

'I haven't touched it. May be innocent, but somehow I doubt it. Can I leave it to you?'

'I'll get the bomb boys to look at it first. What do we know so far?' Detective Inspector Colin Tyler was already preparing the answers to the questions he would be asked the moment he left the building. Ten years younger than the head of security, he had that solid bulk that policeman seem to acquire over the years, perhaps as a buttress to what they are asked to confront.

'Come with me,' McMasters said, leading the DI back into the domed room. The smoke had thinned now, leaving a pale, theatrical haze.

'This is the domed room which, as you know, leads off Room 5 with, beyond it, Room 4. As far as we can see – and, believe me, it hasn't been far – these are the only areas affected by the incident.'

He handed the policeman the smoke canister he had picked up. 'Don't worry, the handkerchief is clean.'

As they moved through the room, the dissipating smoke became whiter until it appeared that a gossamer veil had been placed all around them. Two attendants were guarding the hold-all, which was now covered in powdered foam. McMasters nodded appreciation at the members of his team who had earlier extinguished the flow of smoke.

'Well done, chaps,' he said. 'It looks as though whoever it was left the smoke gun hidden in the bag and then moved on whilst it warmed up for ignition. Then they set off three red smoke grenades at staggered intervals, giving them a total of about five minutes' cover.'

Although this was not the time for the apportionment of blame, he could hear his comments at the last group security committee meeting ricocheting around his mind. He had been adamant that he did not want to introduce airport-style electronic detection equipment at the entrances, which many of the leading European museums had now put in place.

'This is not Heathrow,' he had announced, grimacing now at what came next. 'This is the gateway to art and we need to be civilised about our security.'

At this point, Giacomo Baldini, the deputy head of security at the Uffizi in Florence, had raised his eyebrows the merest of fractions and wondered which of the two countries could have first claim on civilisation. He was a handsome man with a square face and short, dark hair running to premature greyness. He had about him the quiet composure of a judge with a measured gaze and the air of one who weighed decisions carefully. Recently, his museum, the Uffizi, one of the most visited museums in the world, had installed electronic portcullises and although the queues to get in now stretched around the block, he believed they were an essential precaution. He had been invited to the session in London to offer his advice and discuss the implications of their introduction at the National Gallery. He had been given short shrift by Brian McMasters and his team.

And now McMasters knew that his words would come back to haunt him.

'And the pictures?' The policeman's question cut across his thoughts.

'From what I can see at a cursory glance through the smoke, they all seem to be here. We had a trembler go around one or two of them, but that looks as though it might have been people getting too close in the panic. And, mercifully, it appears that the smoke is non-toxic. Certainly the canister you've got there is harmless enough.'

'Maybe it was a prank for publicity,' suggested the policeman. 'We might find out from the press what it was all about tomorrow. It wouldn't be the first time.'

'We'll shut the gallery for the rest of the day,' McMasters said, as if he had not registered the other man's comment. But then he added: 'A stunt? Let's hope so.'

The two men set off to the main entrance in order to observe the evacuation. There was very little complaint, although one or two visitors, who had been in parts of the gallery furthest away from Rooms 4 and 5, were puzzled at what all the fuss was about. Now that any sense of danger had departed, most enjoyed the sensation of being part of a drama and were only too willing to be searched as they left. The gallery was cleared in less than two hours and the strange silence that descended on the old building allowed the noise of the traffic in Trafalgar Square to filter through to McMasters' weary senses.

They returned to examine the pictures in Rooms 4 and 5, checking each one for damage or disturbance but all seemed in order.

'Well, what was all that about?' McMasters repeated to himself and both men gave a shrug of the shoulders.

'Let's find out,' said the policeman as they went upstairs to the control room to review the footage of the morning's events. Brian McMasters lagged behind his police colleague, his tread heavy and slow on the stone steps, his mind wishing he could wind back the clock and start the day all over again.

Tyler, sensing the mood of the man behind him, turned and said: 'It's an impossible equation, you know, to let as many in as possible and to maintain security at the same time.'

It was meant to be a statement of support. It failed.

Chapter 4

He watched her enter the gallery, the tallest in a small group of girls, and he leaned forward to zoom in on the image. It was a game he enjoyed, following the pretty women, tracking them through the collection, watching them unseen from the quiet isolation of his room of monitors. The various images reflected on his glasses as he switched between cameras and he imagined he was directing an outside broadcast for live television. He tried to gauge the exact moment she would leave one room and enter another so that he could seamlessly display her progress on the main monitor. She was certainly a striking-looking girl and easy to follow because of her height and her colour. He thought she might be Indian, but she couldn't help that and he watched her tight jeans leave the frame of one monitor and emerge into another. He guessed she might be nineteen or twenty, her friends a little younger, and she carried herself with a certain authority. This was his third month on secondment from the Gallery of Modern Art in Glasgow and he was beginning to feel comfortable with the new scale of his life. The National Gallery was enormous, in a city which dwarfed his home town of Glasgow but, equally, the opportunities that he was now offered had grown in direct proportion. In Scotland he had been made to wear a uniform, but here the policy, unless you were an attendant on the floor of the gallery, was more informal and the only identification he carried was his security pass around his neck, which he could easily hide under his jacket. Sean Dunmore, it announced, and he was quite pleased with his photograph which showed the upward flicks of his dark and deliberately tousled hair above what he had to admit was a winning smile. Matinee idol looks is what his mother used to say and he felt he had to agree, even though he wasn't sure what a matinee idol was.

'You are here to learn,' his line manager Brian McMasters had told him on his first day, 'about an impossible equation: how to protect priceless works of art whilst at the same time inviting the world to see them. We'd be better off,' McMasters had continued, 'locking up the originals and putting up framed photocopies in their place. Most people wouldn't spot the difference, anyway.'

Time and tedium had worn down Brian McMasters, the head of security for the gallery, so that this introductory talk was conducted in a weary monotone. 'We have to make all the pictures accessible, touchable almost. It's madness really and it's only luck that has maintained our record to date.'

'Surely, it's an illusion,' Sean had said to his boss. 'We give the impression that it's all laissez-faire inside when in fact it is heavily controlled. We hide what we do.' There was a down-in-the-mouth quality about his boss which Sean found depressing but he had to admit that their Scottish backgrounds had helped him get the job.

'Up to a point, son. But it's a fine line, believe you me. A fine line.'

Sean was part of a small team actually based at the National Gallery but their numbers were swelled by groups of expert consultants who met regularly to review security and revise policy. Yesterday he went to a session on fire and listened to a presentation from a leading manufacturer of advanced sprinkler systems on how specific fire detection and directional sprinklers would improve the safety of the pictures. Sean was amused that the pictures came before the public but kept the observation to himself.

He continued his scrutiny of the tall Indian who had now meandered her way through various rooms in the gallery, pausing here and there to observe a picture more carefully. They were being shown round by Dr Ruth Pitts, an enthusiastic but somewhat dishevelled expert from the education division of the National Gallery, who was generally known as 'Armpitts', since she had the habit of gesticulating wildly when excited by a painting, which she often was. Right now she was explaining the virtues of a Dutch still life, and he chuckled as he watched her arms describe the delicate shapes captured by the artist, her cupped hands almost touching the shoulder of a beautifully painted vase, her fingers extended as if she were about to lift out the flowers it contained.

'Silly bitch,' Sean said under his breath and switched his gaze back to the tall Indian who was busily making notes in a sketch pad. Output from all the cameras was recorded and kept for a certain period of time and he was aware that his tracking of this visitor would be registered if the material was ever reviewed. He doubted that it would be but in these times of heightened awareness, why shouldn't he follow one of our darker brethren, a possible Islamic extremist, if indeed they did Islam in India, he wasn't sure.

Although Sean knew the geography of the gallery and could tell you how to get from the Rembrandts to the Van Goghs, he had little or no interest in the pictures except perhaps to despise some more than others. He couldn't see what all the fuss was about with the Impressionists, who seemed absurdly slapdash to him, and the big Rembrandt portraits were too dark and heavy, reminding him of the draughty Scottish castles his parents used to drag him around as a child. The collections were merely a backdrop for his interest in order and authority, ends that created a means. Unlike his boss, he was excited by the potential battleground between viewer and viewed and the technology, most of it hidden, that came between the two. He was at home in the world of vibration sensors, motion detectors, closed-circuit cameras, alarms and all the other paraphernalia that goes with security. In a way, the pictures in the gallery were like a matador's red cloth, a tease and a temptation. Part of him was excited at the thought that someone might attempt to steal them and could be prevented, if not by death, then by a series of disguised blows which he might orchestrate.

Brian McMasters put his head around the corner to enquire if all was quiet.

'Fine, boss,' Sean replied, as he routinely did. People continued to shuffle mutely across his monitors, coalescing in front of some pictures before breaking up and wandering off and coming together to pay homage in front of another masterpiece. He imagined it was something like religion and couldn't understand what all the fuss was about.

Looking and seeing are two different things, Dunmore had been told when he first got the job but it took him a few months to understand the difference between the two.

'Just look at our Peter there, for example.' Peter was the senior press officer, a man unduly pleased with himself, against whom Sean had taken an immediate dislike. 'Just look at the way he moves around the place, so entirely different from everyone else. If he didn't work here, you'd want to know what he was up to. It's like the poor old souls who come in here just to keep warm, or the ones having affairs and choosing this as a place to meet. They're easy to spot.'

As the weeks had gone by, Sean enjoyed sifting through the visitors and dividing them into categories. The regular visitors, whom he saw at specific times and whose arrival he could predict; the irregular regulars who came in often but at varying times; the first-timers, bewildered at the geography of the building and the avalanche of pictures; the tourists, ticking the National Gallery off their list; the professionals, often accompanied by someone from the gallery. And so on, until he was able to rank almost everyone who came to the gallery. At the top of his list of stratification, though, came the pretty women and from his protected eyrie he could select those he might like to pursue. He had been successful from the start, sidling up to a chosen woman and remarking on a particular picture. If he had picked well, the reaction would be the same, a certain surprise followed by a softening when they saw the accreditation around his neck and his undoubted good looks. He'd heard Armpitts rabbit on about some of the pictures and he would repeat her words adding, *en passant*, that he was part of the team that looked after the master-pieces. It was a winning combination, Sean Dunmore's matinee idol looks, laced with a touch of art history and a dash of the mysterious world of security.

The tall Indian and her group had spent time in front of a large family group by Sir Joshua Reynolds before moving on to an Henri Rousseau, which he could see Armpitts didn't like as her arms remained firmly by her side. He watched the small group take a break in the café, the young girls clearly excited by the progress of the morning. He zoomed in the camera on the Indian as she laughed, throwing her head back to reveal her long neck and white teeth. When they resumed their tour, he was beginning to lose interest and he gave up tracking them in favour of a couple of tourists, perhaps Italians, who were clearly not that interested in the pictures. It was only by chance that he came across the Indian again, standing alone at the entrance to the large room of fifteenth-century religious paintings, a collection which he found unutterably boring. She was very still, as if not wanting to disturb an animal or a sleeping child. It wasn't clear what she was looking at but he watched her slowly move forward through the large doorway into the next room, where he picked her up on the next monitor. She appeared to be staring at a small portrait, the last in a line of pictures along the left-hand wall. The rest of her party had moved on through the room and were now looking at a painting of St Thomas. It was not unusual for visitors to remain transfixed in front of a picture but he thought it was strange that she should have split off from her group. This might have been an opportunity for him to approach her, to call one of his colleagues to cover for him, but he hesitated since he knew nothing about the picture she was looking at and he felt that she might at any minute be called back to join the others. Sure enough, Armpitts came over to collect her, no doubt offering a few words of wisdom about the picture in the corner. Despite their difference in age, the young girl towered above the art expert and had to stoop to listen to what she was being told. When the group re-formed, Sean turned his attention back to the two Italian girls and found them where he might have expected, in front of Van Gogh's *Sunflowers*. Now why couldn't the Indian girl have gone there instead? He could have shown off a bit about the *Sunflowers*.

The Indian girl, like so many others that drifted across his screens, was now forgotten. Later, he wandered downstairs to find the Italians, only to discover they spoke very little English and that his observations on Van Gogh's work were wasted. He almost missed her the following morning, for she arrived by herself and walked straight through the gallery to the picture that had held her attention the day before. Again she approached it cautiously, as you might a horse, standing away from it at first and then slowly coming towards it. She was still wearing the tight jeans, but today she had on a white collarless shirt and a short, striped cardigan. He watched her staring at the picture, moving closer to it until her face was close enough to whisper to it, which is what he thought she was going to do. And then she stepped back and shook her head, turning away, returning to the foyer where she waited for her friends to arrive. Sean quickly accessed the on-line catalogue to discover more about the object of her attention, before phoning Ruth Pitts' office to enquire about the group she was escorting.

By the end of the second day, he had watched her again, increasingly drawn to the long, graceful body and dramatic face that drifted before him. He knew that she would be there for the rest of the week and he planned his moment of approach. He was at the edge of his dark web and he slowly rubbed his fingers over the scar on his right hand as she walked beneath him.

Chapter 5

The wind continued to rattle the windows, an irregular insistence of noise that was beyond her hearing. She was in a cocoon, suspended in a zone where she could not be touched, protected by the shell of her own conviction. Although there were no lights on in the small room, a spill of orange fluorescence washed the walls and marked her profile. The space over the mantelpiece was empty but in her mind's eye she could see the face of Christ, the shape of the head indelibly marked on the dirty white wall, a shroud for her thoughts. If, in these small hours of the morning, she had any doubts about what she was doing, she had only to remember the first impact the image had on her young and innocent self. She closed her eyes and saw again how the painting had mesmerised her, drawing her forward so that when she stood, millimetres away from the fine jaw and narrow lips, she had wondered if she could feel the man's warm breath on her face. She recalled the moment and began to deconstruct it, a surgeon to her own emotions, delving into the broken thoughts to piece them together as London roared on around her regardless, the tramps and the drunks aimlessly wandering the streets. He had been no better than them, oblivious of what he had taken and destroyed, severing a precious connection with wanton disregard. There would always be scars, the permanent reminder of the trauma, but on this stormy night the wound was still raw and the healing process barely begun. No, there may be two images of Christ's head opposite in the gallery, but the one in her mind served to drive her onwards. She would never again be able to capture the simple purity of the girl she had been, and for that reason she now sat alone and wide awake as the wind tapped out its indecipherable message behind her.

She got up and looked at the empty street, rubbish rolling like tumbleweed beneath her. There would be no sleep tonight, although it was not anxiety that kept her awake, but a calmly controlled impatience. Having waited so long she was now close to removing the pin which had impaled her and kept her fixed like an exhibit from life, trapped and useless. The walls of the gallery loomed anonymously in front of her, bleak and windowless, a symbol of what she had become, impenetrable, blank. She had breached them once and she would do so again on the road to a conclusion she could barely glimpse.

The wind carried a siren far into the night.

Chapter 6

When she came to, it was her father's parting words that she remembered. In that half-world between sleep and consciousness, reality takes on elaborate dimensions, distorted, intensified, simultaneously more real and yet unattainably remote. But the journey that Habiba was taking, although she was yet to be aware of it, was not from natural sleep, but from a drug-induced state where all her senses had been subdued. Through this no-man's-land, where time loses all measure and geography is elastic, Habiba could see her father looking at her, his face set harder than the stone of his beloved mountains. Although his lips did not move, she heard his words with ominous clarity.

'There are some things in this country I don't understand and I expect I never will. But I trust you to think of your mother and your mother's honour and conduct yourself in a way that she would have wanted. I have made this decision against my better judgement and I cannot say I feel easy in myself. Respect yourself, my child, respect yourself.'

Instinctively, she rolled on to her side and vomited, her body helpless as the waves of nausea rose and fell. She was still only half-conscious and uncertain what was happening to her and as her father receded he was replaced by disconnected scenes from a room full of people that she felt she should know, whose faces drifted in and out of focus. She was sick again and now she was more aware of her body and its tortured retching, and with this came the sensation of knowing something bad had happened but she could not remember what. She sank back on to her pillow and attempted to open her eyes, fearing that this simple act would reveal the truth of what was troubling her. It merely confirmed that she was in her room on the campus with the rush of water from the lock on the canal joining in with the other noises in her head. By now she was regaining her senses, about to step across a threshold which, at this stage unknown to her, would mark her for life and divide the child from the adult. Her body was empty and bruised but her mind was alive and was sending her muddled signals of caution which she was attempting to decipher. She groaned, the noise reverberating inside her head, further altering the kaleidoscope of thoughts that were beginning to assail her.

'Oh my god,' she said, as she began to remember. And then again, 'Oh my god,' as she pushed back the memories which seemed to cause pinpricks of bright light in her vision. She swung herself to the side of the bed and groaned again. Unsteady on her feet, she trod carefully across the room to the tiny galley kitchen where she filled a bucket with hot water and returned to clear up the most obvious signs of the mess her life had just become. She still could not think clearly and her forehead was clammy with the effort of trying to piece together the circumstances which had led to this calamitous awakening. It wasn't just denial that was holding back the details and as fragments of recent history began to reveal themselves to her, she sank back on her knees and began to weep.

*   *   *

By the beginning of the third day she had fallen in love as assuredly as any teenager does. The fact that the object of her passion was a picture did not seem at all odd to Habiba, for it fitted entirely with her mood of defiance and confrontation. When she dressed that morning, she took particular care, choosing a plain brown dress with a single discreet line of sequins down each side over which she wore a pale, slightly oversize linen jacket. The dress finished mid-thigh and the jacket, wide at the shoulders, also finished short, just below her waist. The outfit served to emphasise the length of her body and the shape of her legs. She would never have worn such an ensemble at home and whilst dressing she could hear her father listing his objections and condemning her immodesty. It almost gave her pleasure to rehearse this confrontation, turning in front of the mirror to flaunt her independence. The only item of dress he would have liked were her sandals, flat and open-toed but held together by a series of stylish metal rings. She declared herself pleased with the outcome.

The group had settled into the halls of residence and already the journey into the centre of London seemed familiar. She saw it as a trip through three different worlds. First, the walk along the dreary wastes of Mile End Road to the tube, a familiar world to someone brought up in a similar urban wasteland in south London. And then, twenty minutes later, after emerging from the tube at Tottenham Court Road, a second and more beguiling world, the maze of streets that make up Soho. To Habiba, this was a different world, one in which she was happy to be lost, a laissez-faire world of live and let live, where differences were not only tolerated, but positively emphasised. Although she was puzzled about who would actually dare visit a sex shop, she saw them as a reflection of this general acceptance, catering for every taste without comment. Along Berwick Street Market, the cheap saris were blowing in the summer breeze, the wind buffeting the awnings as it carried the smell of vegetables and coffee, tinged with the acid aroma of urine from the alleys and doorways. Entry to the National Gallery brought her into a third world which both beckoned and embraced her and could not have been more different from the last. She stepped into this artificial, climate-controlled world with barely suppressed excitement, feeling open to all it might suggest, finding a willing partner on her road to change. She abandoned herself on arrival, gave herself up to the avalanche of possibilities each room contained. It was a journey that provided some shocks, although she was keen to keep these reactions from her colleagues. On the first day she had seen the image of a naked man on the end wall of an adjoining room and she approached it as a cat might stalk a bird. Close to, the picture left very little to the imagination, the bulky rear of a shipwrecked sailor clambering naked from the sea, his testicles hanging below the crack of his bottom. And when she looked at this picture, she could not escape the tug of doubt, injected through years of conditioning, that this was somehow wrong. But she wanted to blot out these distant bells of warning and consign them to another part of herself, which is what she did when she stood once again in front of the tiny picture of Christ.

Habiba did not see Christ, did not want to absorb the religious connotations. Perhaps it was her deliberate perversity which swept these aside in favour of the physical, for in the shape of his face, the narrowness of his mouth and the fine line of his nose she had found a symmetry which compelled her to stare. But for the rope guard rail below her, she might have stepped forward and kissed him. Her body responded to the thought, a frisson of sexuality running through her which was both alarming and exciting.

At first she was unaware that someone was standing just behind her. His words seemed to match her thoughts.

'Extraordinary, isn't it? Tiny, yet perfect.'

When she turned around, the man wasn't looking at her, but at the picture. He had a handsome face, made more so by his concentrated look. He was wearing a smart, dark blue suit and from the tag hanging around his neck, she could see that he worked for the gallery.

'The interesting thing about this picture,' he continued, as if it was part of his job to explain such details, 'is that it was probably painted as a special commission for private devotion. I'm sure it would have appalled its first owner to discover just how public the painting has become.'

Only now did Sean Dunmore look at the young woman. He

had seen her come into the gallery, watching as she meandered between the pictures and noting which had caught her attention. From earlier observation, he had guessed that she would come to this one and from the website he had assembled a few key points about the small painting. He had assumed that she would not ask too many questions.

'It's about the size of an A4 sheet, and yet it contains so much emotion, doesn't it?'

For a moment, Habiba wasn't sure if he was part of the programme that had been arranged for her week and, in response to the puzzled look on her face, the man answered her unspoken question.

'Let me introduce myself. Sean Dunmore. I'm with the Gallery and I am aware that you're part of the group that has been going around with Arm . . . ' He just stopped himself using her nickname. 'With Dr Ruth Pitts. I hope you are enjoying it.'

His voice was calm and confident and Habiba assumed his accent was Scottish.

It seemed perfectly normal for this man to have approached her with further information and her response was enthusiastic. 'I'm absolutely loving every minute, thank you.'

He looked at her face, lit up with pleasure, the smile on her lips revealing her white teeth, the genuine sparkle in her large, dark eyes which, given they were same height, he was now looking directly into. She really was quite stunning.

'I also noticed you looking at the picture back there.' And as he said this, he turned and with an authoritative gesture of his arm, invited her to follow him. She was uncertain at first which painting he meant and was slightly alarmed as they began to approach the naked sailor. How had he known that she had momentarily stopped in front of this picture? She felt embarrassed, as though she had been caught looking at pornography on the Internet. To her relief, his tone was absolutely serious as he began to drip-feed her the few facts he had gleaned not twenty minutes earlier.

'This might have been a study for a bigger picture,' he explained. 'It was quite shockingly explicit for its time, although, of course, the display of male genitalia has happened through the years, from Michelangelo onwards.' He said this as casually as he might have commented on the quality of the foaming seas in the background of the picture. Even so, she blushed at the reference.

'He was only thirty-three when he died, more's the pity,' he concluded, indicating that he was familiar with all the artist's work.

She wasn't sure how to respond and glanced down at her watch.

'I know you have to join your party soon,' he told her helpfully, 'but if there is anything else I can help you with, you'll see me around from time to time.'

He turned and walked away from her, threading his way through the crowds, his smile concealed from her as he muttered to himself, 'and I shall be seeing you most of the time, tracking your every move.'

Habiba watched him disappear, his authority emphasised by his neatly cut blue suit and the directness of his walk through the gallery. She raised her eyebrows and wondered what all that had been about. She gave the naked figure a final glance before turning to find her colleagues.

From time to time, during the rest of the day, Sean Dunmore watched her on the monitors. By now he had in front of him the group's itinerary and he noted that their progress today would take them from Turner to Monet under the title 'The Birth of Impressionism'. He laughed at the pretence of it all, the reverence paid to the pictures and the reams of information each one produced. He was amused that paintings like these could fetch millions of pounds and he wondered at the folly of those who were eager to pay such fortunes merely to own one. Mind you, the fact that people were prepared to steal them gave him his job and his fascination lay in the intricate ways that this could be prevented. Sean Dunmore lived and breathed the sophisticated and expensive world of prevention and detection. This was the art that interested him. That, and young girls.

Habiba thought about Sean Dunmore as the story of Turner's *The Fighting Téméraire* was explained by Dr Ruth Pitts. She imagined how much nicer it would be if he could be her private tutor for the day and she looked behind to see if she could catch a glimpse of him amongst the visitors. It was a gesture Sean Dunmore registered from the control room.

'And you will see how masterfully Turner reflects the setting sun in the water so that sky and sea seemed to be one and the same. You will see later how Monet uses a similar technique in one of his studies of bathers.'

Habiba wasn't sure about the Turner, but the Monet seemed so much more accessible and she marvelled at how an accumulation of just a few separate brushstrokes could create such a wonderful and comprehensible picture. The detail of the Turner appeared painstaking in comparison. She craned her neck forward to look more carefully at the dashes of colour and from above Sean Dunmore watched the tilt of her body and the way that her dress revealed just a little more of the backs of her long legs.

A little later, as the group sat and sketched their copies of the *Bathers at La Grenouillère*, he found an excuse to pass by and share a few words with Ruth, casually nodding at Habiba as he left, a clipboard under his arm, a man with a purpose. Habiba was flattered that he had noticed her again and when, as she was leaving the gallery later that day, he suddenly came out of the staff exit, she thought it was a happy coincidence.

'Well, we meet again,' he said, his voice expressing both surprise and pleasure. 'How did you find today's pictures?'

Habiba stopped and looked at him, noting again the confident smile on his face and the jaunty quiff of his hair. He had now taken off his tie and he appeared more relaxed than he had in the gallery.

'Fine, thank you. I wasn't mad keen on the Turner but I'm not quite sure why.'

He just prevented himself from saying that he had noted that she hadn't liked it from her body language on his monitors. Instead he said 'But it's such a sad picture, don't you think?'

'Sad? I'm not really sure about that.'

'Look,' he said, pointing across the square, 'we can't talk here. I sometimes have a drink after work over there. Why don't I buy you one?'

For a moment Habiba was caught, and although she couldn't quite define them all, a series of possibilities and contradictions presented themselves to her. Was this an innocent offer, and if it wasn't, did she mind? If she could hear her father's disapproval ringing in her ears, didn't she want to fly in the face of his stern warnings? In the end, she decided to compromise.

'Look, I really can't now. Perhaps tomorrow?'

'Sure,' he said casually. 'You normally finish about five, don't you? Shall we meet in the Lamb and Flag at half-past five? It's just over there, behind St Martin's, in Rose Street. OK?'

And before she had time to reply, he had turned away, and with a wave of his arm he trotted down the steps towards the fountains, scattering the pigeons in his wake. She watched him depart, his dark figure lost behind the spumes of water, and considered the strange mix of excitement and apprehension the forthcoming rendezvous had engendered in her. As she walked up Charing Cross Road towards the coffee bar where she would find her friends, she decided, for the time being at least, to keep the details of Sean Dunmore to herself. This was the first of her several mistakes.

*   *   *

Habiba would acknowledge that she was both young and old for her age, a mix of innocence and experience, but not necessarily in the same quantities as some of her friends. In Tooting she was a minority within a minority, an Asian amongst Afro-Caribbeans, in a white working-class area. She had suffered abuse from both sides, but had developed strategies to keep out of trouble and was streetwise beyond her years. Habiba knew she was not beautiful in the traditional sense of the word, but she was striking-looking and the older she became it was these looks that both increased her experience and intensified her innocence. For most girls of her age, the meeting with Sean Dunmore would have been part of the normal process of growing up, of boy meets girl. But for Habiba such encounters were weighed down with different expectations and fears. She thought about these as she strolled over to the Lamb and Flag the following day, past the renovated façade of St Martin's. In the distance, Big Ben chimed the half-hour with the same reverberating insistence that her father issued his decrees. Things had become increasingly difficult after her mother's death, as if her father's responsibilities had not merely doubled but had accelerated geometrically. Habiba's appearance, her burgeoning sexuality, were unacceptable to her father and he wanted them suppressed, hidden. He desperately needed his wife here to help him do this, for she could have softened his displeasure, found a way to interpret his demands to their daughter. As it was, Habiba found herself caught between two extremes: the sexual freedoms of one section of her friends and the repressions and ignorance of girls from families like her own. On the face of it, Habiba appeared to belong to the former group, her clothes and appearance announcing her liberation. In fact, for the moment, they were merely a camouflage.

'Penny for your thoughts?'

He had caught up with her just as she reached the pub, almost as if he had been following her. Habiba looked at him and wondered if her thoughts might, at that moment, have been worth a good deal more than the penny he was offering. Or, perhaps, less.

Sean Dunmore had indeed followed Habiba to the pub, as he

had tracked her most of the day. He had deliberately avoided bumping into her group, in case this gave her an excuse not to see him in the pub later. From his monitors he noted with pleasure that she seemed to have dressed up for him and was wearing a necklace of round, clear beads with coloured centres, like marbles. Instead of sandals, she wore shoes with a slight heel and she carried a small shoulder bag in red leather.

The evening began badly for Habiba, but later it became worse in ways she could never have expected.

'What will you drink?' he asked, showing her to a seat towards the back of the pub. This was a battleground on which she had planted her standard several times before in defiance of her father, who had never countenanced alcohol. She asked for a white wine and watched as he expertly attracted the attention of the bar girl, who had quite clearly seen him many times before.

'I wasn't sure if you would want to drink,' he said, handing her the wine. 'Quite a lot of Indians don't.'

She looked at him, trying to detect any extra nuance in the word 'Indian' and wondering whether she should correct him.

'I am right, aren't I?' he continued, nodding at her in anticipation of her agreement.

'Actually, I'm from Tooting Bec,' she replied, an answer she had given many times before. His reply was equally familiar.

'Really? I mean, before that.'

'Well, for me, there wasn't a before that. But if you mean, where did my parents come from, then the answer is Pakistan.'

'Sort of nearby then,' he persisted, having really no idea of the geographical relationship of the two countries.

Habiba let the moment pass, but she was already beginning to pick up distant signals which cast doubt on the evening. It was as if Sean Dunmore sensed this and changed his tack.

'I noticed from your itinerary that you studied the little Monet yesterday. Incredibly powerful for an oil sketch, isn't it?'

Habiba agreed and as he continued to tell her about the painting, she looked more carefully at the man sitting opposite her. Habiba was well aware by now that she attracted men and she was beginning to realise that they fell into several distinct categories. She wondered if Sean was one of those men who wondered what it would be like with a coloured girl. He seemed pleasant enough and she pushed her doubts to one side as she listened to him explaining about his real job at the gallery. Every so often one or other of his colleagues would come into the pub and call over to him, some offering further drinks. Habiba was cautious and accepted just one more, which Sean fetched from the bar.

A little while later, she began to feel extraordinarily relaxed, her anxieties disappearing as the pub filled up with people spilling out of work. Sean Dunmore watched her as she began to talk more freely about herself, telling him a little about her strict father and her ambitions to go to art college. She spoke of the little painting which she admitted 'to sort of falling in love with'. He was surprised to find that she was not yet eighteen and this increased his excitement. The effects of the drug were beginning to work and he bided his time, expert now in knowing exactly the right moment to move to the next stage.

When he asked her where she was staying, Habiba took the question to be entirely innocent, telling him about her hall of residence and joking about the joys of the Mile End Road. She had never really talked like this to anyone before, certainly not a male, and she felt curiously emboldened. When he offered her a lift she readily agreed and as she left the pub the other drinkers appeared to be somewhat distant from her, as if behind lightly frosted glass.

That morning, Sean Dunmore had brought his car to work, an expensive decision but one he balanced against the rewards that might await him later in the day. He had an arrangement with a company whose headquarters were on the other side of Trafalgar Square. Sponsors of the National Gallery, they allowed occasional use of their underground car park to the museum's staff. Unsteady on her feet now, Habiba accepted Sean's arm as he led her down the shallow slope towards the mouth of the car park. She registered no concern as they entered the poorly lit interior and slid clumsily into the front of his car, her skirt riding up her long legs.

It was just after eight in the evening and the car park was deserted. Nevertheless, Sean Dunmore walked a few paces further into the half-darkness, looking left and right before returning to the car. He drove out of the mouth of the car park and began to head eastwards where the sky was already beginning to darken, the pink wash of the day becoming dirtier and greyer. He watched her out of the corner of his eye and smiled.

Chapter 7

It was the headline in the evening paper that ultimately cost Brian McMasters his job although by then he had already comprehensively laid the pathway to his own dismissal. By chance, a reporter from the *Evening Standard* had been in the gallery at the time of the incident and was able to write a first-hand account for the front of the final edition. So, barely four hours after the event, Londoners read about the threat to their priceless collection of art, under the title: 'Gallery Security Smoked Out.' The reporter had managed to include several quotes from the gallery, one from the director and another from Colin Tyler, both confirming that no pictures had been taken or damaged. In a daring leap of logic, the journalist had concluded that 'the fireworks at the Gallery' were nothing more than a colourful prank but one which laid bare the parlous state of the museum's security systems. It was the final straw for Brian McMasters and it came at the end of an afternoon he would try to forget but would always remember.

By the time his team had assembled around him in the control room in the immediate aftermath of the smoke bombs, Brian McMasters was beginning to seize up with indecisiveness. A pain had spread from his chest to his head and it was all he could do to watch the replays of the CCTV. When Colin Tyler said that he assumed they would be watching the replays from five minutes before the triggering of the alarms, he could merely nod in agreement. It should have been his instruction. There were six cameras that covered Rooms 4 and 5 and their immediate hinterland. These fed into the monitor by the door and were relayed to the control room where they were viewed and recorded. They were linked by time-code and could be run simultaneously at whatever speed was demanded. The four men began looking in real-time and watched as the visitors flowed across the screens, moving in and out of the static shots, some stopping at every picture, others choosing to pause more irregularly, with one or two passing straight through without looking right or left at the collections. Again, Colin Tyler spoke first.

'We're looking for something that could carry or conceal a smoke gun and several smoke canisters. We found a buggy, black with green side panels, abandoned in the corridor beyond Room 5. It might be suspect. The bomb people are checking it out now.'

Over the next few minutes, parents with buggies and prams, students with rucksacks came and went in front of them, each a possible suspect. By now, Brian McMasters' default setting had slipped into malfunction and he could barely watch the succession of potential perpetrators shuffling through the area in his charge.

'What about her?' one of his team said, pointing at a buggy being pushed into the room. They slowed down the image and observed a middle-aged woman wearily guiding a buggy loaded with clothes and carrier bags. It was impossible to see if there was a baby inside as the hood was half-lowered. Painfully slowly, she was overtaken by a pushchair, on the back of which stood a child on a small platform with wheels. The child's body partially blocked the view of two carrier bags hanging from each arm of the pushchair. Both groups inched forward until they disappeared from view on all the monitors.

'There's a blind spot in this coverage. Did you know that?' The DI turned and looked behind him at Brian McMasters, who shook his head with small, quick movements which caused him to blink in unison. When the policeman resumed looking at the monitors, the two family groups had reappeared.

'Anything could have happened in those few seconds,' Colin Tyler observed. 'We're getting near the critical time now. The alarm went at 11.31, so the next minute or so is crucial.'

Somewhere, a long way away, came the distant and muted alarms of the emergency services arriving at the gallery. At the exits, people talked excitedly about the drama that was unfolding around them. But in the control room a quietness descended, as eight pairs of eyes scrutinised the ant-like movements across the banks of monitors. Colin Tyler could hear the short, uneven breathing coming from the head of security behind him.

'Stop.' The DI raised his arm as he made the demand and the various images froze instantly. In two of the lower screens, the ones that covered the approach to Room 4, a woman was sitting with a buggy.

'It looks like the one in the corridor,' someone said.

'She's looking at the Botticelli,' added another voice, as if this was somehow relevant.

'But there's something more than that,' the policeman added, as he zoomed in to the frozen image of the woman and then activated the footage in slow motion. In a jerky series of freeze-frames, the woman turned her body to put her hand on the buggy. As she did, it became clear that her face was almost completely hidden by a headscarf.

'What do you call those things?' Colin Tyler asked incongruously.

'Aren't they burqas?'

'I think it is a hijab,' Brian McMasters said in a small voice from the far wall. His mind had already sped forward to the possibility of Islamic terrorists, beyond which his imagination would carry him no further.

'A hijab,' Colin Tyler repeated. 'How very convenient. I assume it is a woman?'

All eyes were now on the figure and as it rose it was quite clear that it was, indeed, a woman, although at no point was her face clearly visible.

'Normal speed,' he demanded.

The woman was wearing what looked like a long, black anorak

and she made her way casually towards Room 4, pausing once to look at a picture, before continuing on her way.

'She doesn't look as though she is about to create a commotion, does she?' Colin Tyler enquired of the room, not expecting an answer. 'But now we're heading for the black hole.'

For a second or two, the woman disappeared. Colin Tyler once again froze all the images. The watchers could see one of the security men at the entrance to Room 4 in conversation with a visitor who was leaning against a walking stick, but it was as if the buggy and its owner had vanished. The policeman then began to move the images forward, frame by frame, so that the figures in the screens moved like robots in a mechanical dance. The bulk of the buggy then began to nose its way into view, the woman in black continuing her stately progress as she had before, even pausing once more to glance at another picture. All seemed normal.

'Look', one of the watchers said suddenly, pointing at one of the monitors. A rush of smoke, directed from an object out of vision, rushed horizontally across the screen, filling it in seconds. Colin glanced up at the monitor with the wider angle and was astonished at the speed the large room was filling with the dense, white smoke.

'Stop and go back,' he ordered and the images were played backwards to the point where the woman and the buggy had left the seat in front of the Botticelli.

'Let's see who else is in frame.' Before, their eyes had been on the woman in black with the buggy, but now their focus was wider. Several people were heading in the same direction, two of them carrying backpacks, another, a large carrier bag.

'Who on earth would want to lumber themselves with all that junk before walking around a picture gallery?' one of the men said.

'Someone who wanted to hide a smoke gun, three smoke canisters and goodness knows what else,' Colin Tyler volunteered.

Moving one way or the other, there were at least half a dozen visitors who passed through the blind spot between the cameras and any one of four might have been able to carry the smoke bombs. He now played the sequences forward and at normal speed but even in the replay not one of the suspects appeared anything other than genuine visitors to the museum. The images they were watching were mute and so the roar of the smoke gun was lost, but they could see by the reaction of the people in the large room that it was considerable. Groups and individuals stopped and turned in unwitting symmetry. As the smoke began to billow outwards, their unity disappeared and they began to turn and move in different directions. And then the smoke began to shroud all the images, the buggy disappearing as it was enveloped on most of the monitors. Before it could reappear in the two monitors covering the entrance to Room 5 these images were lost to the red smoke of the canisters. Soon the four men in the control room were left, if not in the dark, then in its pale pink equivalent.

'Well, anything could be going on down there,' the DI said to the room. 'Call the main exit and ask if anyone has left the building carrying a baby and reported leaving a buggy inside. And then tell me exactly when the motion sensor was activated.'

One man picked up the phone, the other shouted across to him, '11.32.31, sir.' Why he should have used 'sir' at this stage, the DI wasn't sure, but it had something to do with Brian McMasters' conspicuous silence. He was *hors de combat* and his staff knew it.

Colin Tyler shuttled the time-code on the images to the exact time he had been given and paused the pictures. They were none the wiser. Whatever had happened in the fog would, for the moment, remain a mystery.

'Somebody knew what they were doing,' the DI concluded, as much to himself as his colleagues, as the phone rang in the room.

'Several people left carrying babies and young children,' he was told. 'But no one has reported leaving a buggy behind.'

'OK, let's reel right back and start tracking the woman in

64

black with the pram from the moment she arrived. C'mon, I need this to be done quickly. And as we go through the footage, keep an eye out for the other figures who appeared with her at the end. Compile time-coded sequences and I'll look at them when I get back.'

He got up suddenly and beckoned to Brian McMasters to follow him.

'What are you thinking, Brian?' the policeman asked his colleague.

The head of security was having trouble keeping up, in every sense, and as he trailed behind the DI he could only call to the other man's back the phrase he had already used several times that morning.

'But what's it all about?'

'Precisely, Brian. Let's go and look at those rooms again.'

A lingering white haze still hung in Room 4, the residue of pink slightly stronger in Room 5. In front of them were several of the most precious objects created in Europe over the previous six hundred years.

'Doesn't bear thinking about, if any of these went missing or were destroyed, does it?'

The beleaguered head of security shook his head again, as if denying the thought entry to his overworked brain. To discover that they had lost a painting might have caused him to explode, or collapse.

'Let's just go through the pictures again, to make sure that nothing's been touched or damaged. You lead the way.'

And so, for the second time, the two men crabbed sideways along the rows of masterpieces, craning forward from time to time, to reassure themselves that all was in order. Brian McMasters could not shake off the fear that pressed down on his shoulders, the ache that weighed him down and spread through his body like a virus. He didn't want any more problems and his cursory inspection was from a man wanting to believe the least-worst outcome. By the time they had concluded their inspection of the domed room, other security attendants and curators had called through on their mobiles confirming that the other collections were all intact.

Which left the buggy.

The bomb experts had given it the all-clear and Brian McMasters stood over it like an inexperienced father, whilst the DI, wearing rubber gloves, carefully excavated the layers that made up the cot and the tray beneath.

'Let us work first on the assumption that this is entirely innocent,' Colin Tyler suggested. 'Firstly, all the equipment to look after a baby appears to be here and, but for the hold-all with the other coat, nothing seems untoward.'

He leaned under the buggy and scooped out the bag before carefully extracting a black coat. He looked across at the head of security.

'It's quite logical that the mother would have snatched up the child out of concern. She would have been able to move much quicker without the pram. But it is extremely unlikely that she would have changed her coat before she did it. We'll fingerprint all this and find out as much as we can about where it came from. Go up to your boys and have them line up material from the exits from about 11.32.'

Colin Tyler wandered back into Room 5 and stood in the middle of the large open space with his hands in his pockets, turning slowly to take in all corners of the room. Logic you can decipher, he thought, unpick a train of events which had some reason to exist. A prank, or a random act of violence, was harder to understand and dissect. He wondered what he was dealing with here.

It took a further half an hour for the security team to put together a trace of the woman in black with the buggy from the moment she arrived in the gallery until her point of departure. The four men in the control room watched her meanderings through the rooms, until the point where she sat in front of the Botticelli. They looked at each other for insights.

'All seemed perfectly normal to me.' Colin Tyler spoke for them all.

'It took us a bit of time to pick her up afterwards, boss. Several reasons for that. She had switched coats and she had changed the colour of her headscarf. She looked for all intents and purposes like a different person.'

The DI looked at the security officer and thanked him for the speed of his work. The two men had put together a logical sequence in very little time.

'We estimate that there is a gap of about two and a half minutes when we don't see her at all, when either the smoke blots her out, or when she's in the corridor beyond our surveillance.'

The DI nodded his approval and then watched the figure in the stone-coloured coat and red, spotted headscarf hurry towards the exit with the flow of other departing visitors.

'Anything strike you as unusual?' Colin Tyler asked the room, as he kept his eyes on the screen. They replied as one.

'No baby.'

'And nothing else, as far as we can see. Have we got a good shot of her face, anywhere?'

'Sorry, boss. The best we've got is the exit cam, but all you can really see are her eyes.'

And he froze the picture just before the woman left the building, the sweep of her scarf over her head and the merest glimpse of her nose and the whites of her eyes.

'Is she foreign?' someone asked.

Colin Tyler was staring at the screen. 'Hard to say. It's one of those games of two halves, isn't it? Her hijab might tell us she is and then again the hijab is such a good natural disguise. We're none the wiser. Do we have an address?'

'We will, boss, we will.'

Brian McMasters had assumed that his day had unravelled

completely. He was wrong. By mid-afternoon, in the unnatural silence of the empty gallery, he was summoned to the office of the director. He had spoken to her on the phone in the immediate aftermath of the alarm, and now she wanted to be briefed in full on the situation. He knocked and she called him in.

Miranda Goodheart's face was hidden by a newspaper.

'Come in, come in and sit down,' she instructed, as she continued to read. He waited and finally she closed the paper and looked at him.

'It's been quite a day for you,' she said, sympathetically.

'I have known better,' he said, wondering what to expect next.

'I'm afraid it's not going to get any better.' She tossed him the *Evening Standard* and watched as he took in the front cover. There was no colour left to drain from Brian McMasters' face but she could see the dismay in his eyes.

'It doesn't make pretty reading, does it, Brian?'

He shook his head for the umpteenth time that day.

'Is it true? I gather that all the pictures are intact and in place. But it's made rather a mockery of your position in regard to electronic security, hasn't it?'

Miranda Goodheart had been schooled in the art and politics of good manners and even when she was about to deliver bad news, she did it in such a way that the recipient felt that he was almost being praised.

'Some of this is guesswork,' he said, laying the offending piece face down on the desk. 'But it looks as though she has got it broadly right.'

'After all you've been through, it wouldn't be right to have a post-mortem now, but I have convened a meeting of the Board for tomorrow morning. I'm sure you will be around.'

He knew, of course, that his days were numbered and he couldn't imagine that life could get much worse.

He was wrong.

Chapter 8

She could not confront her worst fear. Not yet. Perhaps never.

She had been surprised to discover how early it was, the low sun dancing through the curtain on her east-facing window, which she had opened to air the room. The sound of the canal was louder now and it accompanied the tumult of thoughts that assailed her. It was six o'clock and already the traffic was beginning to thunder along the Mile End Road, a thick, low roar at odds with the sharper sounds of the water. Habiba felt like a different person, as if her identity had been removed from her, stolen and placed nearby, out of vision but tantalisingly close. She felt her necklace, running her fingers over the smooth round beads, hearing them bump together. She shook her bracelet down her slim wrist and remembered buying it in a shop in Oxford Circus. But why was she wearing this jewellery, items she normally saved for special occasions? It was as if she had found them on another woman. She needed an explanation, but her mind was like concrete, solid and without access. She moved over to the window and peered down on the canal basin. A pair of coots had built a nest out of sticks and plastic bags scavenged from the canal, but it had long since served its purpose and the chicks were now young adults. She watched them feeding, dipping into the water to reveal their over-large webbed feet. She raised her gaze upwards, towards the parkland which ran along the opposite bank and the fear began to grip her again. She held on to the frame of the window as she fought to remember what had brought her to this state. The truth lurked out there like a predator, waiting to pounce and destroy her, but she could give it no shape.

She felt dirty, unhappy in her skin, damaged.

She showered, the hot water beating against her brown skin, thrumming against her forehead and her closed lids. She knew she would have to face the moment soon. Her body was demanding it. She turned off the jet of water with a quick twist of her wrist and she heard the flow stop with a sudden clunk. Her eyes were still closed and she felt for a towel, placing it over her head for the comfort it afforded. She rubbed her hair vigorously before stepping carefully out of the shower on to the cold, tiled floor. Holding the towel by her side, she opened her eyes. The mirror in front of her was clouded in steam and for a moment she could not bring herself to wipe it clear. When she did, she revealed herself in parts, as if introducing herself to this different person. It was only when she surveyed her body that she saw the truth, even though it had already given her warning of what to expect. Her upper arms were blotched and blue and there was an ugly wheal across her right breast. Her hands were shaking and she steadied herself on the edge of the basin, knowing that worse was to come. Since she had woken, she had denied the dull ache from her groin, hoping that it was her imagination, that it was her period starting. But this was a different pain and it was not only physical. Her eyes dropped slowly down her body, her hands tentatively leading their progress to the edge of her pubic hair. She stared at that private part of herself and hesitated before sliding her hand further. She could feel the pain on the inside of her legs, which she now moved slightly apart. She adjusted her position so that she could see the inside of her thighs in the mirror. The bruising had spread, an ugly grey marbling on the tender skin, encased in vivid red. She dropped her head in despair, for even now the physical evidence that something dreadful had happened to her did not free her memory. A dark shadow hung over her, shapeless and menacing.

Even when she had dried herself and put on fresh clothes, she felt soiled and dirty. She jumped at the sound of her mobile phone.

'So where did you get to last night?' Sharifa asked slyly. 'We waited for you at the coffee bar but you didn't turn up.'

For a moment Habiba did not know what to say, for she couldn't say exactly what had happened to her. But it was as if Sharifa's question had thudded against her brain and shaken and dislodged some details.

'Hello, Habiba, are you there?'

'Sorry, Sharifa. I'm rather sleepy this morning. I had to see someone yesterday evening and I forgot to tell you.'

'That doesn't sound very convincing, my friend. In fact, you don't sound yourself at all this morning. Still, you can tell me all on the way to the gallery.'

When Sharifa rang off, Habiba wept quietly, her tears falling on to the back of her hand, which still held the phone. In the brief time her friend had spoken, several memories had come back to her. The picture was by no means complete, but it was enough for Habiba to guess what the other pieces might be to complete the jigsaw of last night's events. She had a vague memory of going into a pub with Sean Dunmore, but after that she had no recollection, except that which her imagination offered. That, and the physical evidence she had seen in the mirror. She felt ashamed and guilty, but she knew she could not hide away. She had to carry on as if nothing had happened, for the consequences of revelation were too awful to contemplate. She could barely look at herself in the mirror as she applied her make-up. She had, quite literally, to face the day ahead, but all the mystery and excitement which she had carried with her the day before had evaporated and been replaced by a dull and haunting apprehension.

For now, her worst fears were trapped inside her.

*   *   *

For the fourth morning, Sean Dunmore watched her arrival. He was feeling unduly pleased with himself, for the planning of last night's episode could not have gone any better and the arrival of the girl was the ultimate proof of this. If she had failed to show up she might have been called upon to account for her drunken behaviour and this he knew she would find almost impossible. In two days she would be gone, taking her secret with her, so all he had to do was keep out of her way. Seeing her again this morning, her tall body at the centre of the monitors, he recalled the shape of her breasts and her large, dark nipples and the firm narrowing of her stomach. His smiled at the memory. The position of her halls of residence could not have been better, for the ecological park that lay just opposite was accessed by two culs-de-sac, one of which contained a car park surrounded by trees. It had been empty when they arrived and the light had almost disappeared from the sky. The drug had worked its way through her body and she offered little resistance. It was the first time he had been with an Indian, or wherever it was she came from, and the sight of the unusual brown flesh had intensified his excitement. When he had tried to touch her down there, some primitive reaction in her kept her legs tightly closed and he had to force them apart. But this was all part of what he liked and he always got his way in the end. It was unfortunate the other car had arrived in the car park shortly afterwards, preventing him going all the way. Still, he got most of what he wanted and when he let her out by Mile End tube it was almost midnight. She'd be able to find her way back from there, the victim of one too many glasses of white wine in the wicked West End.

As he watched her, he enjoyed the sensation of having known her body, of having seen those intimate parts of her, of having been allowed access. For she wanted it, didn't she? Just the way she dressed gave him the clue, the backs of her legs, long, brown and beckoning. Those big eyes and lacquered curls were clearly signals. They were all the same, leading you on and then pretending they shouldn't. Yesterday, for example, when she stood in front of the picture of the naked sailor, wasn't it obvious what she was doing? He began to scan the rooms, his eyes searching for young girls willing to lead him on. Look at the blonde girl in front of the painting of a man standing by his bath. It was quite clear what she was so attracted to. He might have to go down and tell her about it but if the Indian was in the gallery, he would have to be careful. He continued his surveillance, his eyes tracking across the screens in the darkened room, his forefinger rubbing small circles against the flat of his thumb.

* * *

For Habiba to enter the National Gallery was an act of great bravery. She was too ashamed not to and she had to pretend that nothing had happened. Nevertheless, by the time she climbed the long stone stairs to the entrance, she more or less knew what had occurred. Stepping through the doors was like deliberately entering a zone marked 'danger'. But what could she do? When she saw again the picture of Christ, she almost wept as she fought a wave of revulsion which rose in her and made her look away. In the clear light of this summer morning, art seemed pointless, a mere indulgence, a way of distracting people from what was really happening in life. When Ruth Pitts waved her arms in front of a family portrait by Sir Joshua Reynolds, Habiba couldn't help but mock the faux gentility of the group, the fine clothes and careful poses. She knew that behind all this lay a dirtier and more vicious world, hidden by lace and silk. This was all pretence, a way of disguising what was really going on. She was doing it herself, the innocence of the day before lost somewhere in east London. She was staring at the picture but not looking, her mind not hearing the lecture but concentrating on the blurred image of Mile End Road tube station and the massive feelings of disorientation she had felt the night before. How had she got there? What had occurred and why had she found herself steadying her feeble body against an empty newspaper stand? It was instinct which had led her back along the busy road, the logical part of her mind barely functioning. Now, as she looked at the insipid and superior face of the squire in the painting, she remembered the uniformed porter at the halls of residence. He had shaken his head as she slowly entered the archway which led through to the interior courtyard. 'You should learn, you young people,' he had told her as she stared, blinking at him. 'Just look at your clothes.' His face was soured with displeasure and she looked down at her crumpled dress and undone buttons. 'I hope it wasn't drugs, miss, because we don't do any of that here.' She could neither agree nor shake her head and she had shuffled off to find her room.

Here in the gallery, the picture in front of her could not have been more repulsive. It mocked her condition and said to her, 'You have not got what we have got and you never will.' She hated it, just as she hated herself.

'Miss Popals. You have been unusually quiet this morning. What do you think of this wonderful picture?' Dr Ruth Pitts arched her eyebrows in readiness for a reply. Habiba frowned, forced out of herself and into the present.

'I think it is a picture of a group of people very pleased with themselves,' she said. 'And I'm not sure I like it.'

'But isn't that what he wanted you to think?' the expert persisted. 'Wasn't he capturing something of the arrogance of the ruling class?'

And it was only then, as the bruises on her body throbbed and her head ached, that Habiba Popals wondered who she was and what she was doing. And with this her fears came to the surface. What was worse, to be raped or to have to tell your family you had been raped? She knew the answer.

Chapter 9

The following morning, normal service had been resumed and the usual bustle of people thronged the entrance to the National Gallery, only today they spilled down the stairs in an untidy queue. During the night Habiba had been aware that the number of foot patrols around the perimeter had been increased and, amused, she watched them from her darkened room. They were a pointless exercise in public relations, a futile attempt by the gallery to show that security was important and that the nation's pictures were safe. And this morning, the bags of those entering the gallery were being checked and mothers were suffering the inconvenience of disturbing their babies so pushchairs and buggies could be examined. It was all an elaborate and stage-managed farce, a case of securing the gallery's doors after the picture had bolted. Well, not quite. Habiba, her long, black hair hidden behind her, her large eyes open to the fresh summer's day, waited in the queue on the stairs. A different-coloured hijab surrounded her face and hid her mouth. She was perfectly calm and looked out over the square towards Parliament, where the large Union Jack was waving defiantly in the gusting wind. She showed her artist's carry case to the security official. The large flat bag contained an A4 sketch pad, in which there were several drawings of pictures in the gallery and a small pouch of crayons and pencils. When Habiba's eyes smiled at the uniformed assistant, it was not in gratitude at her efficiency, but in mirth at the ridiculous solemnity of it all. Through the two glass doors to her right people leaving the gallery did so under the gaze of two uniformed security assistants, but they were not being searched. The National Gallery still thought yesterday's event had been a prank and did not want a repeat humiliation. They would soon change their tune.

Inside, she noted a new alertness amongst the uniformed security staff. She past the first of them, a middle-aged man whose stomach pushed against his buttoned-up blue jacket and he merely regarded her coldly from behind his wire-framed glasses. Her route this morning was direct. She was a woman with a purpose, her aim to copy an early Picasso of a young girl carrying a dove. Of the thousands of pictures she might have picked, she had chosen this one for two reasons. Firstly, she was attracted to the figure, a cropped-haired girl who might have been Algerian, or from further away still, perhaps even from the hills of her own ancestors. She sat and unzipped her bag, opening out her sketch pad and picking out a sharpened pencil. The second reason lay at the end of her line of vision, the entrance to the newly built wing of the museum, which was accessed by a wide, covered bridge over the alleyway which led to her flat. This was a rather elaborate structure with two semicircular seating areas opposite each other. These afforded views south down to Trafalgar Square and northwards to a small enclosed area of heavily pollarded plane trees. They were divided from one another by two walls between which visitors flowed to and fro. In her many surveys of the gallery, she had never seen this area permanently patrolled by the security teams. She continued sketching for more than an hour, slowly replicating Picasso's boldly outlined girl on the sheet in front of her. Throughout this time, she monitored the comings and goings through the portal ahead of her. Finally she lay down her pad and got up and stretched, bending down and touching her toes and raising and lowering her shoulders. Even as she did this last exercise, she wandered slowly over to the bridge and stood in one of the bays looking down on the alleyway. The box was still there, secured to the wall behind her, although she didn't look directly at it. She casually returned to her position in front of the painting and continued sketching. Around mid-morning, she repeated the routine, although this time she put the pad into the large carry case which she took with her to the bay window. Laying it across the wide seats, she quickly unzipped it and turned round to the box on the wall. Painted exactly the same deep grey colour, the shallow rectangular box looked perfectly natural on the wall. Placing one hand on the top and the other to support it underneath, she pulled it forward. The sticky tape securing the wooden box came away fairly easily, leaving a faint outline on the wall. The picture was face down, the back of the frame tucked neatly within its protective box. She quickly slid this into the carry case and zipped it shut.

She walked back through the gallery with the same purpose as when she arrived, not looking at the pictures, an art student, her project finished. A pair of uniformed security staff watched her go and she didn't give them a second glance, pushing open the glass doors and skipping down the stairs. It had been precisely as she had expected. The time was 11.52 am.

Moments later, as she passed under the bridge, she looked upwards and nodded at her own accomplishment, a gesture aimed beyond the new building and more to the grey skies. Perhaps her father had seen this and if so, he would have known that she had completed only the first part of her elaborate plan and that the next phase would give her, if not him, even greater pleasure. When she got home, she took the picture out of the wooden box and placed it above the fire. Christ's elegant and pained face hadn't changed at all, only this time the portrait had been painted in Italy, in the middle of the fifteenth century, and had not been copied onto canvas from a photograph three weeks ago in Snappy Snaps in Camden High Street. In the small, ill-lit room, the portrait took on even more power, filling the space in a way that it had been unable to do in the gallery. This was the sort of arena it had been created for, Habiba thought, a discreet space for individual devotion. She smiled, though, for in the gloom she found it difficult to tell the difference between the fake she had created, which now hung in the National Gallery, and the picture which was now propped in front of her. Only a faint residue of the force which had first attracted her to the picture remained with her but that early passion had been subsumed into a fierce and equally strong emotion. Revenge.

*   *   *

Brian McMasters had no option but to step up security on those entering the gallery, if only to allow himself a material defence when he saw the board later that morning. He had slept fitfully and entering the gallery at first light he'd been like a man on his way to the gallows, expecting the worst. In truth, he had no idea how bad things were to become and by the end of the day he might have concluded that hanging would have been preferable. An hour before opening, he gathered the security teams around him and spoke to them from the top of the steps leading up from the foyer. He told them what had happened the day before, but since all of the morning papers had made merry with the story of the smoke bombs, there was little he could add.

'We're worried about copycat incidents,' he told them, 'and so we will have bag searches for those entering for at least the rest of the week. As of now, we will be instituting a review of all our security proceedings.'

At the back of the group one of the listeners turned to her companion and muttered under her breath, 'Can you think of a phrase which includes the words stable door and bolted?' and giggled silently.

Later, arms folded, the head of security watched the first arrivals place their bags on the makeshift trestle tables that had hastily been assembled in the marble entrance, and tried to imagine what the place would look like with airport-style security. He would never get the opportunity to find out.

Shortly after eleven, about the time Habiba slipped jauntily out of the gallery, two further events coincided. Miranda Good-heart's PA called to say that the board would be obliged if he could join them now and Ruth Pitts, curious to see what all the fuss had been about the previous day, paid a visit to Rooms 4 and 5.

'Come in, Brian,' the director said in her warmest, welcoming tone. 'I think you know everyone here.' The eight faces in the room nodded towards him and it was not difficult to gauge their mood. 'As you might imagine, we have been discussing the events of yesterday and before we pass on the fruits of our discussions, we wondered if you would be good enough to bring us up to speed, as it were, on your thinking.' She gave him the brightest of her smiles and sat down.

'Can we legislate against what happened yesterday?' he began, somewhat ill-advisedly, since it was quite clear that everyone in the room knew that they could. 'If some crackpot decides to let off fireworks in a museum, can we stop them?' It wasn't getting much better and he felt the coldness of their stares boring into him.

'We have instituted bag searches this morning, which is certainly going to slow down entry . . . '

' . . . but which will surely discourage those who wish to tour the gallery with a collection of smoke bombs,' added one of the group.

'Precisely,' he replied

'And what has it led you to think overall, Brian?' added the same person. 'Are we going to have to change the way we do things?' The question was rhetorical and unfair, since the group had already decided this. There is often malice when people hunt in packs.

'Do you mean, have I changed my mind about full electronic surveillance? The portcullis system?'

'Precisely,' the man replied again, encouraging a reluctant student.

He couldn't really be seen to change his mind, so he replied as he had done at the security meetings a few months ago.

'Not really,' he said. 'I think such a system would fundamentally change the nature of the gallery.'

'Rather as the smoke bombs did yesterday,' the man offered again, with a look that was caught between a smile and a grimace.

Downstairs, in Room 5, Ruth Pitts was continuing her survey of the pictures in the two collections, slipping her reading glasses up and down her nose as she inspected the paintings. She was devoted to all the art contained within the walls of the gallery and she was thrilled that the experts had declared the smoke bombs non-toxic. She, herself, could see no evidence of discoloration. She felt like a sheepdog, rounding up the pictures after they had been suddenly dispersed by some predator, circling until she could be sure that all her charges were calm and intact. She came to Messina's picture of Christ, one of the smallest in the gallery, and stood back marvelling at its perfection. One of the smallest of her flock, she had not spoken of it very often and silently she resolved to change this. She moved forward and raised her head so that her glasses would help her close vision.

'Good heavens,' she said, involuntarily thrusting out her arm, as though she was about to turn right. 'Good heavens,' she repeated, slightly louder, as if she had become more convinced about something. She knew she couldn't get much closer to the picture, so she called over the nearest security attendant.

'Hello, Dr Pitts. How can I help you?'

'What do you make of that?' she asked him.

He looked over to the small picture of Christ. 'What do you mean?' he said, puzzled. Her frown told him to look again and he moved forward and peered more intently at the small masterpiece. She could see his body stiffen as he confirmed her fears.

When he turned to face her, she put his thoughts into words. 'It's a fucking photograph, isn't it?' Dr Ruth Pitts, world expert on Renaissance art, was not given to swearing.

Brian McMasters had just finished his case against the portcullis system, all too familiar with those in the room, when the director's PA knocked on the door, and without waiting, came into the room.

'Dr Pitts has some urgent news,' she said, as the art expert pushed by her.

'The little picture of Christ by Messina is a fake,' she said. 'In fact, it's more than a fake. It's a photograph.'

'Oh, Christ,' said Brian McMasters, and never had a word been better chosen. He walked over to the phone on the director's desk and called the main desk. 'I want searches on those leaving the gallery as well. One of the pictures in Room 5 has been switched. A small head of Christ.' Here he looked over to Dr Pitts.

'It's about the size of an A4 sheet,' she said.

'Did you get that?' he said. 'Right, I'll be down shortly.'

He was about to leave, when he stopped. 'Would you excuse me, Dr Pitts?' She looked at him and then, understanding the situation, left the room.

'I will, of course, be offering my resignation as of today.' He gave a small bow and left the room.

'Well,' Miranda Goodheart said, 'that's saved us a problem, even if it has given us another. Signor Baldini can't get here quickly enough for my liking.'

The board had set in motion replacing Brian McMasters some weeks ago and the current breach in security merely confirmed the wisdom of their decision, even if it was a high price to pay.

'He's due in tomorrow afternoon,' a voice told her, but she was already composing what she was going to say to the press about the missing picture.

Chapter 10

It is probable that Habiba Popals' resolve began to form itself in front of Gainsborough's painting, as Dr Ruth Pitts continued to extol its virtues. The depiction of the perfect family group poised before their grand house set within acres of parkland sweeping away into the distance confirmed her alienation from what she had appeared to accept not twenty-four hours before, unable to embrace the beauty of the art all around her. Unconsciously, she was calling on her considerable resources, about to embark upon a journey which would begin in a chemist's shop by Charing Cross station. She struggled through the last two days of the course, the colour of her wounds deepening even as her mind began to assemble its own defences.

Once upon a time, when life was more fixed, a doctor might know you all your life and would be able to present an intimate portrait of its triumphs and disasters, as reflected in your changing medical records. The modern world, more anonymous and unmanageable, demands a less personal service and for this Habiba Popals was grateful. Nevertheless, she chose not to reveal the extent of her injuries to anyone. The lesser of her two fears, though, had to be dealt with first, even if it meant enduring further moments of shame. The pregnancy testing kit was at the bottom of the basket, hidden by other items she had bought in the store, inadmissible evidence. By some ghastly chance, she found herself at a till with a girl, not much older than her, wearing a hijab. Habiba almost turned back, abandoning the wire basket with its incriminating contents, but forced herself forward. Did she detect the smallest of glances from the cashier, or was this part of her imagination? She wanted to test herself immediately, but she had to wait until the date of her next period, several days of mounting anxiety and distraction. Her father commented on this.

'You're not yourself, Habiba. I told you that going on that course would do you no good. You look tired and you're not talking to me. What *is* the matter, Habiba?'

You wouldn't want to know, thought Habiba, and tried her best to be light-hearted.

'It was a busy week, Father, and we had to concentrate hard.'

He looked at her suspiciously, which was his usual manner when speaking with his daughter.

'You have lost the sparkle in your eyes. Even when you were defying me, your eyes used to flash. But now they are dull.'

She could not doubt her father's observational skills but she recoiled at the idea she was transmitting so many signals about her state of mind. A few weeks ago she would have countered his constant querying with a dismissive toss of her head and it was this change that he had noted. It often takes others to tell us how we are and Habiba's anxiety was clear for all to see. Sharifa was as direct as Habiba's father.

'What's up, girl? You've changed. Do you want to talk about it?'

By now, just a week after the incident, Habiba had further tightened her defences and there was no chance that she was going to confide in her friend. 'It's my period,' she told her friend, which in some way alluded to the truth. 'I'm having a bad one.' It was a period, bad or good, that Habiba longed for but, according to her rough calculations, on the due date it had failed to arrive. She had hidden the pregnancy kit in two layers of plastic bag at the back of one of her drawers, an ominous presence in her bedroom. As the day of the start of her period came and went, she began to imagine that she was exhibiting other signs that she might be pregnant, feelings of nausea and tenderness in her breasts. But Habiba held herself together, putting the former down to her anxiety and the latter to the residual soreness from her wounds, less vivid now than before, but still apparent on her body, diminishing but unforgettable stains.

She waited until the early morning, although even then she could not be certain her father, notoriously nocturnal, would be asleep. Her curtains were drawn and she lowered the angled arm of the lamp on her desk and placed the container of her urine under the specific pool of light. The rest of the room had receded into gloom and as Habiba paused before applying the test, she felt part of a ghoulish ceremony, an experiment in genetics carried out in secrecy. Given the reasons that had led to this moment, she concluded that she wasn't far wrong and the beginnings of anger began to rise about her primitive fears. Why should she have to endure this indignity? How could anyone demean her to this extent? It was as if her whole life depended on this moment, the result of the test an indicator to the rest of her existence. She lowered the test strip into the golden liquid and closed her eyes. She did not hear the blackbird outside her window calling in the morning.

She opened her eyes and in that instant her anger intensified and her fear diminished. The verdict was negative and although she knew that she would have to test herself again, somehow she knew for certain that she was not pregnant. The small strip in her hand, though, was a pointer to more than just the immediate decision it had confirmed. It announced the next phase in her life, rising inside her in place of the child, ready to grow and emerge in a form that had yet to be revealed to her. If her tears expressed her relief, they were carried on a swell of anger which pushed itself through her and emerged between clenched teeth. These were not the tears of a woman who felt sorry for herself, but ones expressed in barely suppressed fury. The blackbird continued to sing unheard as the sun came up over Tooting Bec.

*　　*　　*

In a different room in the same house, the end of one life was being contemplated, just as the absence of life was being confirmed in the other.

Latif Popals coughed himself awake and reached for the handkerchief by his bed and wiped his mouth. He lay listening to the birds, the different sounds he had begun to identify over the years. Fighting for supremacy, the melodic and complicated rise and fall of the song thrush, first to announce the morning and then, in front of it, the wren, insistently hammering its staccato demands out of all proportion to its size. And now the blackbird, sound of the summer, effortlessly joining in with its familiar signature tune. Nature asserting itself, just as it had with him, revealing its unstoppable progress, guided by instincts that were beyond logical reasoning.

He felt quite calm, as he contemplated his truncated future. Since the death of his wife he had not feared a similar fate. Indeed, as he looked back over his life, he agreed with himself that there had never been a time when death frightened him. *Inshallah* had been his philosophy in all areas of his life, although he had found it difficult to apply it to his daughter. Was it Allah's will that sent Habiba spiralling away from him, out of his grasp? She was now the abiding frustration of his life, the one factor that worried him about his death, a loose end which demanded his attention before it unravelled completely. He coughed again, a rough, painful rasp which seemed to shake all the bones of his body. In recent days she had been so obsessed with herself, so distracted, that she had not noticed the deterioration in his health. He had been told that the cancer would kill him in weeks. Invasive surgery was not possible and chemotherapy might extend his life a little, but they held out little hope. He had accepted his fate and he wanted to approach the end with as much dignity as possible. Calm as he was, he had no idea how to tell his daughter the news that had been confirmed whilst she was away on her art course. He had phoned Badsha the previous afternoon and broken the news to him. Badsha had promised to see Habiba, for whom he had always had a soft spot. In a rapidly disintegrating world, where Latif's family was split between two continents, he was grateful for the continuity Badsha represented. He was handing on his daughter for his protection. *Inshallah.*

*　　*　　*

To Habiba, it seemed no accident that Uncle Baddy should phone at eleven o'clock that morning. She didn't suspect for one moment that he had been made to get in touch with her, but something in the tone of his voice, normally so warm and reassuring, chimed with her own mood. He appeared tentative, almost sad.

'My dear girl,' he said to her. 'I hear you've got lots to tell me. I can't wait to find out more.'

Habiba hesitated for just a fraction of a second, instinctively protective, before she realised he was referring to her course at the gallery, which her father must have told him about. At first, she didn't know quite how to respond and the pause prompted Uncle Baddy to speak again.

'Ah,' he said, 'it sounds like you might have even more to tell me than I thought. Whatever, I have something I want to talk about with you as well.'

Uncle Badsha, 'Baddy', had always been able to interpret her behaviour, deducing the real message behind what she was saying and correctly observing her body language. It was a relief to have someone with whom she neither had to explain herself, nor protect herself. But now, when he suggested that they meet at his restaurant in Bow, alarm ran through Habiba like a cold wind. It was less than a mile from where the assault had taken place, but Habiba could hardly have said no without having to explain.

She looked out of her window at the patchwork of small gardens which were trapped and compressed in the strip of land between the two parallel terraces. Some had been allowed to run to weed and bramble, others had been carefully manicured. Dotted here and there were lopsided wooden sheds and plastic furniture and remnants of washing drying in the windless day. She wondered how much she would be able to tell Badsha, if anything at all. She was surprised at her own reaction, for although part of her sought the relief of a protecting sympathy, another part of her scorned such a thought. Uncle Baddy never talked of the old country and seemed firmly rooted in the world of east London. The fierce authoritarianism of her father, informed by a culture that was both alien to her and with which she chose not to engage, was absent in Baddy, who seemed as modern as her father seemed old-fashioned.

Badsha's body reflected the fact that his daily life was surrounded by food. His round face was repeated in his equally round stomach and both exuded comfort and a degree of personal contentment. The fact that today his eyes betrayed other concerns was lost on Habiba who, as she had been with her father, was too absorbed with her own recent experiences. The restaurant was busy enough for their conversation to be disguised, but not loud enough for it to be swamped.

Habiba had rather expected to lead the conversation, to account for her week in the centre of London, and normally she would have looked forward to this, embellishing her stories and allowing herself to add colour in a way that she would never have been able with her father. At first, her concern that she might break down in front of Badsha prevented her from noticing what was happening. He took hold of the reins of their exchanges and it was only after a while that Habiba's senses were alerted and that she wondered if there was another purpose to this meeting.

'How are things with your father?' he enquired gently.

She shrugged, indicating that things were the same as normal. 'He wasn't keen that I go to the National Gallery,' she said. 'He wondered what I might get up to.'

Instead of picking up on this opening, which he would normally have done, Badsha continued to talk of her father. 'Have you noticed any change in him recently?'

And now she knew that there was an agenda beyond her own. 'How do you mean?' she said quietly.

He looked at her and she could see the kindness in his eyes, the tired concern. 'He's not well, Habiba. Not well at all.'

There was a moment of incomprehension in the young girl, a few seconds during which the dominance of her own needs was suddenly put into proportion. Badsha watched her and waited before continuing.

'He has cancer,' he said, stretching out his hand and placing it over hers. 'I'm sorry, Habiba.'

She recoiled. This was so unfair, for just as she was about to seek comfort for what had happened to her, so she was hit by another blow. Badsha watched the conflicting emotions caught in her face and decided that he should predict her next question.

'He hasn't got long, Habiba. A month or so. I'm sorry.'

Somehow, the two events instantly congealed within her and became inextricably entwined. It was as if there was a causal link between the assault in London and her father's illness; that one had led to the other and would destroy him.

'Habiba?'

She was shaking her head, the combined sadness for herself and her father too much for her to bear, a crushing weight for the young girl and one which rendered her speechless.

Badsha continued to watch her, monitoring the look on her face, unsure of what it was telling him.

'How terrible,' she said and if Badsha took this to refer to both father and daughter, he had no idea in what proportion. The fact is, at that very moment, Habiba felt more stranded than ever, a ship being towed in a storm only to be cut away and deliberately sacrificed.

'I'm sorry, Uncle Badsha, I have to go.'

She got up without looking at him and he knew, in the very aversion of her eyes, that there was something he didn't understand and which hung around him like distant thunder.

Chapter 11

The dust of a later summer's day in Florence still powdered his tan-coloured brogues as he stood in front of the gallery in London, square between the two towers, and regarded the building as if for the first time. He'd been through its doors several times, but always as a mercenary, a freelancer. Now he was to be part of its fabric and he was seeing it with new eyes. Giacomo Baldini was to become the new director of security, with a place on the board and the immediate responsibility of restoring a reputation which lay in tatters around its stone walls.

When he had left the Uffizi a few hours ago, he had paid a similar act of respect to the old building, although it had been harder to take in the whole of the famous museum, tucked, as it was, within the narrow streets of the city. He was leaving an elderly dowager duchess, who had seen better days, for a cavalry officer whose more uniform lines spread before him now. In terms of security, though, the old lady left the younger man standing for, within and around the sixteenth-century building, were twenty-first-century electronic defences to protect the priceless collections. He would introduce the two, he fancied, and to give his analogy a perfect ending, the younger man would certainly learn much from the older, more experienced woman. Taking a deep breath, he made his way across the wide pavement towards the main entrance.

For a man just thirty, Giacomo Baldini's close-cropped hair was surprisingly grey but, as he took the stone stairs up to the National Gallery two at a time, the litheness of his body was revealed and the smile he gave to Miranda Goodheart, when she came forward to greet him, had all the charm of a young Italian male.

'Signor Baldini,' she said, with an equally wide smile. 'Welcome to London and your new home. I fear we have little time to waste.'

By now, the gallery knew of his appointment and as the director led him through the collections towards her office, he could see the looks on the faces of the attendants, a mix of apprehension and excitement. He nodded at one or two as he followed his new boss, taking in the familiar hustle and bustle of a museum. This was the Uffizi in miniature, but for him it carried the same problem, the same intractable conundrum. It was the showpiece of the nation and had to be seen as such, attracting the world to its door to appreciate the excellence of the accumulated works of art. Each year the hundreds of thousands of visitors who flowed through the rooms, within touching distance of the priceless paintings, needed to feel that these belonged to them. Giacomo Baldini operated in that small gap between the painting and the viewer, making sure that the idea of possession remained illusory and that, at the start of the third millennium, these potent symbols were not used for other ends, personal or political. The safety of the National Gallery was maintained discretely, expensively and with meticulous care. At least it would be from now on, the Italian concluded, walking confidently into the director's office to be greeted by the same faces who, in the same room not twenty-four hours earlier, had sacked his predecessor.

Giacomo Baldini was fully briefed. Late the previous evening, he had been told of the missing picture and that morning, on the plane from Florence, he had read in the papers the details, such as they were, of the spectacular theft. Now he was impatient and did not want to be delayed by the glad-handing ahead of him.

'I would like to say that I am delighted to be here,' he said courteously in his perfect and only slightly accented English, 'but, of course, I wish the circumstances to be slightly different. You must excuse my haste, but I would like to begin my investigation.'

It was what they wanted, someone to lift them from the responsibility of failure.

A few moments later, in the control room, he met the immediate members of his team, still reverberating from the departure of Brian McMasters, whom they had liked and mocked in equal measure. With the two men was DI Colin Tyler, who had phoned with news of the picture's theft the evening before. Together the three had been scouring the CCTV footage from the day before, trying to pinpoint the moment the picture had left the building.

'To begin with,' the Italian said, 'you will have to help me and I will appreciate your support. Now, tell me, where is the picture?' He could see the surprised look on their faces and he laughed at himself. 'I'm sorry,' he added, 'the fake picture. We will find the other one, believe me.'

'Well, Jack,' Colin Tyler began. On the phone the night before, he had been encouraged by the Italian to use this easier form of his name. 'It's in your office. We've already dusted for prints but drawn a blank.'

The room was next door, long and windowless and painted, appropriately, Tuscan brown, to make it feel like a Renaissance library. Indeed, the end wall was covered in books, although the shelving along the wall on the right was empty, evidence of Brian McMasters' hasty removal of his personal possessions. On a large desk in the middle of the room, the picture was propped up on a small easel. Baldini approached it slowly, waiting for that moment when he could be sure that he recognised it as a copy.

'It's very good,' he said, when he got to within a metre of the picture. And then he qualified his statement.

'As a fake, I mean. May I?' As he turned to the DI for permission to pick up the picture, he was already pulling on a pair of white plastic gloves. Although he knew it was only a formality, Colin Tyler liked the way that the man was deferring to him. It was a politeness that took the tension out of the occasion.

'It's just a flat matt photograph, copied on to canvas,' he

offered, watching the Italian scrutinise the texture. 'It's the frame that's the clever bit. It's a very good copy.'

The frame was in four sections, each in wood. Directly around the photograph was a simple frame in polished wood, probably oak. Then came two further frames, also in wood, each lightly painted in gold leaf which had now faded and become translucent. These sandwiched a slightly wider and more dominant frame of elaborately carved leaves painted, or stained, green.

'Are there many places that could have made this copy? I assume it must have been done from a photograph?' Giacomo asked, still holding the picture.

'Probably a photograph from our website. There's a very clear representation of the picture there,' the policeman said.

The Italian chuckled. 'We want to help educate them, and look what they do to us in turn. We can't win.' He paused and carefully placed the fake back on its stand. He turned to face his police colleague.

'But we will.'

'To answer your question,' Colin Tyler continued, 'I'm afraid there are any number of framers about the place who would have been able to make a copy. We've begun to approach them now, e-mailing a photograph and details of the picture in the hope they'll recognise their own work. I think we can be certain that the frame was made independently of the painting, or, should I say, the photograph of the painting.'

'Sit down, sit down.' The Italian gestured to a group of chairs around a table in the far corner of the office. 'Now,' he said, placing the flat of his hands on the table in front of him, 'I want you to tell me what happened, from start to finish.'

And with that, he took from the pocket of his jacket a small leather notebook and a blue, marbled fountain pen, which he unscrewed as he waited for them to begin.

For the next hour, the pattern of events over the previous forty-eight hours was unfolded to him, the memories of the three men combining to present him with the facts as they remembered them. At the end, he lay down his pen and looked at his new colleagues.

'Can you be certain that the woman wearing the hijab did not manage to smuggle the picture out of the gallery under cover of the smoke bombs?' He held his hand up to stop them replying.

'Secondly, if not, where was it hidden and is it still here?' This time the group waited for more.

'And, thirdly, of all the pictures in the museum, why would she want to steal this one?' And with this, he gave a slight tilt of his head, a signal he was now ready for answers.

Understandably, it was Colin Tyler who spoke first. 'Put simply, the answers are no to the first and we don't know to the other two. We reckon there was about a five-minute gap between the alarms and the establishment of bag searches. She would have had to move very quickly to get out of the building in that time. But it would not have been impossible.'

'And,' Giacomo added, 'why would the fake have been put in its place? Were we *meant*,' he emphasised the word, 'to believe it was a prank so that the bag searches would be dropped? So, let's assume that the answer to question one is actually yes. So, to question two, where was it hidden? To this end, I want to address all staff this evening as soon as the gallery is shut. I'll do it in the central hall. We need to maintain bag searches until further notice.

'And that brings us to the final and most interesting question. Why this particular picture and for what purpose? Let us assume the most simple of motives. Money. Was it stolen to order? You will know,' and here he generously assumed that his listeners did, 'that throughout Europe and, sadly, particularly in Italy, pictures are stolen from galleries and museums on a fairly regular basis, more often than not, on commission. Most of them are never seen again.'

'It was a fairly elaborate, almost clumsy, way of going about it, though,' offered one of the security men.

'I agree,' said the Italian, 'but if it helped get the picture out of the gallery, you could hardly call it clumsy.' Feeling that he had been a little sharp, he added: 'But I take your point. Anyway, it is a small masterpiece that would grace the walls of any private collection from St Petersburg to Sao Paulo and we can only pray that it is not on its way to either of those places now.'

'What if it was a crank,' Colin Tyler suggested, 'someone who had a passion for that particular painting?'

'That's an interesting proposition, Colin, and one which we might be able to do something about. We keep the CCTV footage, don't we? So we can at least see if anyone has been taking extra interest in the picture during that time.'

Colin Tyler looked at the other two and they recognised that this would be an immediate task for them.

'Look, I'll catch up with you later,' the Italian said. 'I would like to wander around myself for a while. Would you mind?'

A few minutes later he stood looking at the space where the picture of Christ had once hung, the gap offending him and sharpening his concentration. He gazed across the large room to the next collection in the domed room and wandered slowly across. Just beyond was the narrow corridor where the buggy had been discovered. He looked back into the room and registered the new vigilance of the attendants at the far door, who had watched his entrance with some alarm. He saw also a woman accidentally drop her free guide to the gallery, which floated slowly beyond the green protective rope. She stepped forward to pick it up, her head only inches away from the picture she had been viewing. This went unnoticed and it merely confirmed what Giacomo Baldini had always known, that for most of the time the protection of these pictures was an unwritten pact which involved the goodwill of the visitors and the generosity of the gallery. He imagined the woman squirting acid at the picture and then calmly replacing the container in her handbag. She could easily have done this and escaped detection. He shook his head and walked on, past a young woman copying a portrait of Philip IV of Spain. Her pencil had caught the fleshy and rather weak dimensions of the man's face. A child went by demanding 'Can I go home now?' and a wheelchair was pushed across the room. It was as if the hustle of Trafalgar Square had been extended into the gallery.

Later, when the crowds had left and peace had once again descended on the gallery, he stood in front of his staff, fanned out in a semicircle in front of him. There was about Giacomo Baldini the air of the natural diplomat, although his easy manner disguised an uncompromising and often impatient character. He came from the south of Italy where the long, hot summers had taught him early the ways of conserving his energies. Given his perfect English and his sophisticated dress, it would have come as a surprise to the assembled group to learn that his parents were olive farmers, as had been generations of Baldinis before that.

Giacomo had recognised over the years that, although the job of a security attendant was dreary beyond words, these men and women were the last interface between the public and millions of pounds worth of art. Without their vigilance and support, much of the sophisticated machinery that he put into place would be rendered redundant. It was to this he alluded first.

'Ladies and gentlemen. I think, by now, you will know me, but those who don't, I am Giacomo Baldini and until very recently I was the deputy director of security at the Uffizi in Florence. And now I have taken over from Brian McMasters here and I wish him well in his retirement.' Here he paused. 'I cannot do my job without you.' He looked across their faces as they waited to see how he would continue.

'I will come straight to the point. There is a possibility that the small portrait of Christ, which was stolen the day before yesterday, was kept here overnight. Over the next hour or so, could I ask you to institute a search of the areas under your immediate control for any evidence that might help?' At this point, he brought a document out of his inside pocket and unfolded it.

'This is my contract here, setting out the terms of my employment.' He held it up for everyone to see. 'It is written on a series of A4 sheets, about the same size as the missing picture. You would make my life much easier if you could help me trace the picture, otherwise this,' he waved the contract in the air, 'might not be worth the paper it is written on. Thank you.'

With that the group dispersed, bleeding into the gallery, happy to stay beyond their normal time of departure for a man whose direct appeal to them seemed so genuine. Giacomo watched them go and continued his own reappraisal of the gallery. Each room, which had become familiar to him during several visits, now appeared completely different, more immediately his responsibility. The dome of one room, the arched canopy of another, the entrances and exits and the sheer accumulation of paintings so close together, he saw as a series of new challenges that demanded his attention. He continued his survey, lost in thought, until, looking up, he was confronted by one of Raphael's pictures of the Crucifixion. His immediate instinct was to cross himself, an automatic response which he barely registered.

'Mr Baldini.'

He hadn't heard the attendant come up behind him and he turned to find a bespectacled face defined by a short curling beard.

'I'm sorry to bother you, but I thought you might want to see this. Follow me.'

The man led him through several rooms to the bridge which linked across to the new extension. 'I found this,' he said, pointing at what appeared to be nothing more than a blank wall.

'It looks as though something might have been attached here,' the attendant said, the excitement showing in his voice.

Giacomo Baldini leant forward and looked at the vague outline on the grey wall. And then he felt in his jacket and produced his contract, which he held against the faint boundary. The fit was almost perfect. He looked at the man.

'Well done. What do you make of it?'

Delighted to be asked his opinion, the uniformed attendant could hardly wait to speak. 'Well, I think the real picture may have been hidden here after the fake was hung in its place.'

'How?' asked the director of security, who had already arrived at the answer.

'A shallow box, almost like those over there which contain some of the electrics needed for the audio-visual equipment. It would have just been a blank box, painted the same colour as the wall.'

'Easy to miss.'

'Easy to miss,' agreed the attendant, pleased that his theory appeared to have been accepted.

'And when do you think the picture was taken from here?'

The man shrugged. His thinking hadn't taken him that far yet.

'I would suggest,' Giacomo said, answering his own question, 'sometime the following morning, when whoever did it was sure that there were no bag searches leaving the gallery. We missed them by a whisker.'

'There is a problem, sir.'

'Another?'

'Well, I don't think this area is covered by CCTV. Perhaps the external camera might have picked up something, but I doubt it.'

'But we'll have footage of people coming in and out of here won't we?'

'We may have.'

'I don't like the word may,' he said, peeling away and making towards the control room.

As the two men passed the Raphael, the new director of security gave a small nod of thanks. He was going to need all the help he could get.

Chapter 12

Habiba stood by the edge of the road and the world that she could see confirmed the way she was feeling. In the gutter, a sturdy white gull picked at the remains of a hamburger, only to be scattered by the roar of a passing bus. In the breathless, gritty turbulence that followed, a Catherine wheel of rubbish whirled in the air and the dust stung her eyes and settled on her white shirt. On the opposite side of the road, two men were shouting death threats at each other for the sake of a parking place. The scribbled headline advertising the evening paper announced 'Child Abuse Horror.' And, somewhere, always, a siren. Her senses were open only to what was ugly and harsh. Beauty had departed her world and the noise of the day assailed her, the sheer unrelenting pressure of sound and with it the blurred images, the flashing traffic, the screaming birds, the descending jets, caught somewhere in her vision, unrelated images jumbled together, incomprehensible.

'You alright, love?' someone called to her and then laughed. 'Looks like you seen a ghost.'

The hot air from the tube blew into her face, carrying the familiar hot, fetid smell which caused her stomach to rebel. Sitting on the bus, she was drawn towards the heart of London, further into the whirlwind of sound and dirt. Thoughts bounced around her head like the balls on a roulette wheel clattering onwards, restless, unpredictable. Perhaps she didn't want them to settle, for then she would have to face what they were telling her. The bus swung around Old Street and there, in front of her, in letters four metres high, appeared the words 'AIDS AND YOU'. As quickly as she read them, they were gone, leaving her with another indelible fear. As her radar sought the worst that life could now offer her, Habiba realised that whatever god ruled her world had turned against her. The bile rose in her throat, her body indicating to her that it could not take any more direct hits. Could her life be any more miserable than this? She couldn't choose what to worry about first, because she was swept away by an apparently endless succession of bad news, coming at her like massive waves, each one knocking her underwater so that she barely had time to regain her breath before the next crashed over her. She was too stunned even to cry. She didn't know how to go home, could not imagine that moment of seeing her father again. She was frightened that her extreme emotions would collide in an unpredictable melt-down during which she might say, or do, things she would regret. She didn't notice the rest of her journey across London. In the slow walk along Tooting Bec she simply could not put together the words with which she would greet him.

Her father made it easy for her by reverting to type. He sat in his chair, imperious as ever, patriarch and ruler of his kingdom of one.

'You've been a long time,' he challenged when she was barely through the door. 'Did he tell you?'

She didn't trust herself to speak, so she merely nodded.

'They say I have only a short time to live, so there is a lot I have to put in order.'

She could see that he was fighting his cough, holding it back, breathing deeply between sentences, trying hard to settle the turbulence in his chest. She stood in the entrance to the living room, feeling once again like an eight-year-old girl about to be told off for being late.

'I'm sorry,' she said quietly and she could not have been specific about for what, or to whom, she was referring. The apology was offered for any number of the catastrophes that seemed to be falling around her.

'We all have to die sometime and Allah will decide my fate. But it is you that I worry about.'

He looked at her and for the first time she noticed how the whites of his eyes, once so clear, were now clouded and grey. Could she have seen the signs before and been more caring and understanding of her father's condition? But it was difficult to sympathise with this man and what he said next merely confirmed the familiar pattern of behaviour which had dogged her for as long as she could remember.

'How we conduct ourselves here is vital, Habiba. I worry about you, my child. I feel frightened to leave you here. When I am gone, who will warn you about yourself? You will be an orphan in this difficult world.'

It was the first time that Habiba had been confronted with the word and the reality of being without parents. She thought of the room in which she was standing without her father, fixed and familiar, in his chair by the fireplace and she was confused by her immediate reactions. To be alone in this house without his brooding presence was something she could imagine only too well. Should she be ashamed of this, as he sat there, in front of her, dying? And, then, a similar thought, the idea of being completely alone, the key touchstones to her life lost forever. Who would then know about her? She would become the guardian of her own history, the judge to her own behaviour, and she glimpsed at the strange and dangerous limbo into which she could fall and be lost.

'Who will be here to warn you of your behaviour, Habiba?' he continued, echoing her thoughts. His voice carried his disappointment directly to her and his words were followed by the inevitable cough which caused him to grip the arms of his chair.

'You mustn't worry, Father,' she said, wondering where these words came from. Perhaps, in this moment, she became father to the man, offering, for the first time, her comfort and understanding instead of demanding it. She registered this quite clearly, a realisation that her father was not only incapable of offering her support for her shocking assault, but for what she was as a person. In the sadness of this understanding, she stepped forward and touched him. His hand was cold and unyielding and at one and the same time she felt closer to her father and so very much more alone.

*   *   *

Latif Popals died four weeks later, in the front room of his own home. Although it was expected, it still appeared sudden and for Habiba it was as if the reins of a thoroughbred had been snatched from her as the horse bolted away, to be lost forever. The man, who had been born two thousand miles away in the shadow of the high mountains in another country, was buried in the flat lands of south London, on a plot that was once a market garden. Habiba had always been defined by her colour, a categorisation she despised but could do little to alter. She carried the legacy of her past with her, even if she chose to ignore it. Now, in a Victorian cemetery in a dreary London suburb, she was more aware than ever of the world that her father had come from and left behind. As his shrouded body was lowered into the grave, in a special part of the burial ground reserved for Muslims, the contrast became more real than at any time her father had been alive. For the first time in her life, Habiba Popals realised that her father was a long way from home. As the prayers were said and the body disappeared, she couldn't cry, her tears locked away somewhere deep inside her. Not even the comforting arm of Uncle Badsha would release them. She looked at the railings that surrounded the plot, thick and imposing and held in place by strong, stone columns, fine examples of Victorian gothic fantasy. Somehow it seemed so incongruous.

'He is at peace now,' Badsha told her afterwards. 'He was a good man and his heart was in the right place.'

'He wasn't happy when he died,' Habiba said, her head lowered, not looking at Badsha. 'He didn't know how to leave me. He had no faith in me.'

They sat together on a bench by the side of an ancient yew tree, its dark branches stretching above them.

'I sometimes wonder if he ever really saw me,' Habiba continued, 'understood me for what I am.'

Badsha nodded at her, encouraging her to talk, for he had been concerned about Habiba's recent behaviour. Something of her verve, her devil-may-care attitude to life had disappeared to be replaced by a dull wariness and he felt sure that it was not caused simply by her father's illness.

'And now he's gone, and I can't do anything about it. In the last few weeks, I felt I was closer to him but he didn't change. He brought me up as though he was still living in the old country.'

'He meant well, Habiba, and he loved you. In his way, he loved you.'

Somewhere behind them, a bird was singing, deep in the heart of the tree, a low mellifluous warble, repeating itself over and over again.

'There are things that happened in the past that your father carried with him, Habiba, which made him all the more protective of you. He was a proud man and whatever he did, it was for the honour of the family and you.'

The words flowed over the young woman, sentiments she had heard so many times, ways of speaking that were at odds with the life that she had to live. Badsha watched her ignore what he had said, registering the defiant set of her jaw and slight turn of her body away from him. On this of all days, he wondered how far he should go for, although he never doubted Habiba's spirit, he could see that it was fragile and might easily be smashed. Sadness and defiance had made her more beautiful than ever, her long and distinguished head raised towards the west, fighting the private battles within her.

Habiba was thinking that nothing had ended and nothing had started. The death of her father had not been a conclusion, had not released her in the way that she had expected. It was as if the shadow of her father still fell across her. Nor could she see the future, which seemed to stretch ahead in an endless horizon without paths or signs. For now, her energy had deserted her.

'Your father spoke to me a lot before he died,' Badsha said. 'He asked me to look after you and I gave him my word that I would. But, I know, Habiba, that you don't need looking after, you need understanding and I shall try to give you this. Remember, though, your father was a good man.'

Badsha could not be sure she had heard his words, for the young girl continued to look at the horizon.

Finally she spoke. 'Thank you, Uncle Baddy,' she said, adjusting her headscarf. 'I am glad you are here and I will be myself again soon,' she added without conviction.

'You know,' he said, in a voice that made her turn to face him, 'I have something I want to talk to you about, something your father told me about which I think you should hear. But this is not the place and today is not the time. I will call you and arrange a time.'

The old man and the young girl sat quietly on the bench, a few metres from the new grave, surrounded by thousands of London's dead, laid out in a sea of stone under a grey and shapeless sky. Higher still, the cemetery was merely a green segment in an uneven ribbon of streets and houses, a last reminder of the fields that not so long ago existed here but which were now lost in the burgeoning spread of London, swamped by its sheer enormity.

He led her along the gravel path, two tiny figures in between the graves, towards the ornate gates and the next part of her life.

Chapter 13

By the end of the day, he was known as Jack, although the director continued to call him Giacomo, taking great pleasure in elaborately emphasising all three syllables of his name. In his appraisal of what had gone on in the long day since he had arrived at the National Gallery seven hours earlier, he was careful not to blame anyone, particularly Brian McMasters. It would have been bad form on so many levels and his sensitivity was noted by the director.

'I'm afraid the picture has gone.' He wanted to be quite direct with the bad news, and there was more to come. 'We must have missed it by a whisker. It looks as though the picture was disguised, we think in a box, and kept here overnight and that it was probably removed just before we instituted bag searches on departure as well as on arrival.'

Miranda Goodheart marvelled at his English, until she remembered from his CV that he had spent a year at the Dulwich Picture Gallery in his early twenties. She couldn't imagine what 'by a whisker' might have been in Italian.

'But,' said the new director of security, 'we are working on several leads given to us by viewings of the CCTV recordings. I will report further tomorrow.'

'Ah, yes, tomorrow,' Miranda Goodheart said, with only half of one of her normal smiles. 'News of your appointment will be in the papers tomorrow and you may find some of the coverage, well, quite lurid. Our papers have a way, shall we say, of adjusting news for their own ends. Be prepared.'

Earlier that afternoon, they had viewed the CCTV footage of the comings and goings across the bridge from the old gallery to the new extension. There had been about three hours between the gallery's opening and the institution of the exit bag search and in that time a hundred or more visitors had passed backwards and forwards in front of the wide-angled camera showing the portal on the old side of the bridge. And of those, several could be seen moving to one side, towards the southward seating area, where it was assumed the picture had been kept.

Watching the people come and go was like viewing a documentary on a lost tribe of nomads. They filed through, singly and in groups, many of them, particularly those with children, looking bewildered and exhausted. It was quite clear that some of them did not know where they were going, that their presence on the bridge was accidental and that the new wing had been discovered by accident. There was a steady flow of backpackers, buggies, carrier bags and wheelchairs any one of which could have been used to store the stolen picture and remove it from the gallery.

'Mmm,' said Giacomo, 'I wonder whether we shouldn't look at this camera's coverage from yesterday, at the time of the incident.'

Colin Tyler didn't say anything, but he had his doubts, which were soon justified. The camera was high above the domed room and the red smoke belching out of the wide doorway had drifted upwards in the warm air and had fogged the output. It was possible to make out blurred shapes but nothing that could give them any real clues.

'Do you have a card game called *Memory* here?' He pronounced the word in what sounded like an exaggerated Italian accent. 'Where a pack of cards is laid face down and you have to try and pick up matching pairs? It's a game of geographical memory, really.'

'We call it Pellmanism,' said Colin Tyler.

'Pellmanism. Right, that's what we've got here. Lots of faces, from lots of monitors, at different times, and all we have to do is find the one that's in them all. And if we can't find a face, it might be a figure, a shape. We know where to start, don't we?'

'The woman in the hijab,' said Colin Tyler. 'But she doesn't have a face. Let's see if we can find her again.'

'Exactly.'

'It seems obvious,' the policeman said, 'but of all the people we were looking at, she was the only one whose face we couldn't see. She was face down, if you like.'

Giacomo smiled at the reference to the game. 'Maybe we dismissed her exactly because of that,' he suggested. 'As if we believed a woman wouldn't steal a picture, particularly a woman wearing a hijab.'

'Well, the truth is, we don't know she did. Look, this is the entrance cam about an hour before the incident. Here she is,' he animated the sequence, 'with the pram, looking just like any other mother. Except, of course, we can't see her face and we don't know if she had a baby. And now have a look at this.' He pointed at the third monitor. 'This is the footage of the bridge on the following day and, sure enough, she's here again, but without the pram, of course. She comes from below right, from the pre-Impressionist room. Let's hunt down the matching footage from the other camera in that room.' Again, he animated a different recording and there she was, sketching in front of a Picasso. He fast forwarded the sequence.

'Look,' the policeman was really in his stride now, 'She strolls over to the bridge after about an hour.' They watched the figure put down her pad, stretch and then walk over to the bridge and return, as in a super-fast silent film. 'Interesting, but she doesn't take her bag. Let's see what happens later.' He sped through the next section, covering about an hour, before pointing at the screen as the woman stood again. Colin began commentating on her movements, his voice rising in excitement.

'She's picking up her bag and taking it with her. Now she's gone out of vision.' They watched for almost thirty seconds before she reappeared and walked slowly out of vision.

'Go to the main exit camera,' instructed the Italian. 'Let's see if we can pick her up there.' They retrieved the recording and sped through to the matched time-code and there, about three minutes later, they saw her leave the gallery. The artist's bag was slung casually over her shoulder.

'And, assuming that she has the picture with her,' said Giacomo, 'she got out just in time.' He looked at the others. 'Well done. The day before, after the alarms, we reckon she didn't have time to leave the building before bag searches were put in place. So she must have left a name and address. I don't hold out much hope, but shall we see? Thank you for making this such a positive start for me. I think, gentlemen, we are going to get on very well.'

Never fail to look for the obvious, he thought, walking briskly through the gallery. We are deceived by our prejudices, seduced by our assumptions. Why shouldn't they have guessed immediately that a woman who deliberately shielded her face might have had an ulterior motive for so doing? Because we had already dismissed her, declared it impossible that she might be a criminal, he told himself. If, indeed, she had stolen the painting.

The list of names, as was the nature of these things, revealed a mix of the useful and the ridiculous and among the latter were two Joseph Turners, a William Gainsborough and a Brian Monet. There were almost four hundred names in all and the time of departure of each had been noted. The four men attempted to match these exit times against the security footage of their departure, which was coded to the time of day. Since the latter was dead accurate and the watches of those doing the searches were not, it was hard to relate one against the other.

They had found her departure on CCTV and watched the woman give her name as she was searched by the policewoman. Her face was still only visible in parts and she seemed unhurried, unconcerned at the procedure. They paused the footage to register the people directly in front of her and behind. By a process of elimination, they arrived at her name and address.

'How do you pronounce that?' asked Colin Tyler, looking at the name.

'Anmar Ma'ab Qadr,' said Giacomo, speaking each word slowly. 'Whether I have that exactly, I don't know. And there's the address. It couldn't be that simple, could it?'

Collectively they shook their heads. Nothing was ever that simple and later that morning they were proved right. Local police officers were sent to investigate and there was no one with that name registered at the address, nor anyone renting a room.

'So who is this woman?' the Italian asked, as much to himself as his companions.

'Could she be a terrorist?' ventured someone, but Giacomo Baldini shook his head. 'We would have heard something by now. And it would have been more violent in the first place. So we're left with the same question. Who is she and what did she want with that picture?'

'If, indeed, she is the one who stole the picture,' Colin said quietly, not wishing this to be the case. 'At no point do we actually see her do anything.'

He looked at the images of the woman on the monitors, the scarves masking her face and disguising her shape, and decided to take a risk. 'Find me the best still image you can. We'll release it to the papers. It might trigger a response, who knows? And whatever you do, don't make this a religious issue.'

'We won't have to, Jack. The papers will do it for themselves. They'll have a field day.'

Later he had a meeting with the director and he briefed her on the day's developments.

'Well done, Giacomo,' she said, clapping her hands.

In turn, he held out his right hand to slow down her enthusiasm. 'Two problems. We have no idea who she is and we haven't a clear view of her face. And the reason we haven't is that she was wearing a hijab.'

He saw the smile falter on Miranda Goodheart's face as she quickly absorbed the implications of both facts.

'We will have to tread very carefully,' he cautioned. 'My first instinct was to issue a picture of the girl to the press, but I think, until we are sure, this might make matters worse.'

'I couldn't agree more,' Miranda Goodheart chimed in, already imagining the repercussions if their hunch was incorrect. It was hard enough having to deal with the labyrinthine art world but the idea of Muslim fundamentalists as well caused her to shift uneasily in her chair.

'Until we know why the picture was stolen, we'll keep it to ourselves.' He paused, looking across to the windows and the tops of the plane trees before turning in her direction. 'One thing is certain. Having viewed hours of footage, we cannot allow such free access to buggies and bags into the gallery. It is virtually impossible to know who is hiding what. Now that the public has seen it happen once, they might want to do it again. I shall draw up a detailed plan of the changes I would like to suggest.'

She liked the way he put that to her, a demand dressed as a discussion point. He was just getting up to go when she asked him the question.

'And why do *you* think she stole the picture, Giacomo?'

'Maybe she fell in love with it,' he said, with a shrug of his shoulders. He paused as she watched him change his thinking.

'And instead of the girl's image, we'll release a photograph of the painting. Let's get all the bad news out of the way at once.' And with that, he gave her a small, polite nod and walked out of the room.

Later, he left the building and strolled up behind the gallery, making his way towards his hotel, just off Oxford Street, unaware that he had passed within metres of the missing picture, still propped on the mantelpiece in the small flat.

The day that began in Italy was now drawing to a close in England. How could he compare London with Florence? He crossed Shaftesbury Avenue and looked at the line of theatres staggered along one side, each announcing their production in an array of lights as far as his eye could see. That's one way, he thought, entering Wardour Street with some difficulty, since he was cutting across a relentless stream of people rushing to get to those theatres on time. Women weren't as pretty here, nor the men as handsome. They were somehow coarser and less sophisticated, at least to look at, and their type was much more varied. A true Florentine was easy to spot, but a true Londoner came in many guises. But perhaps Soho wasn't the best place to judge and compare. He had no time for the sex clubs, fetishwear shops and the relentless gay paradings along Old Compton Street. Even though he could not understand homosexuality, he had nothing against it except when it was thrust at him, as it was now, as he was brazenly stared at from the open-windowed bars along the street.

He was tired, the day catching up with him. He stopped for a coffee at the Bar Italia and for a moment, as he watched the world go by from his pavement table, it was like viewing the people in the gallery, some deciding to look at the rubber underwear in the windows, others marching quickly forward to a rendezvous and some shuffling aimlessly along, waiting to be taken by whatever came their way. Back at the hotel, he fell asleep quickly and in his dreams faceless people came and went, all tantalisingly familiar and yet totally unknown.

In the morning, the newspaper presented him with his day's work even before he had washed and shaved. The agonised face of Christ was on the front page of the broadsheet and then again on page three, printed actual size, with the headline 'Find this picture. That's the size of it.' The caption story was blunt and to the point. 'One of Europe's key experts on museum security has today been appointed director of security at the National Gallery, charged with recovering this Renaissance masterpiece. Giacomo – 'Jack' – Baldini, previously at the Uffizi in Florence, will also lead a complete review of the gallery's security measures and many of his ideas may meet stiff resistance. It is suggested that he will install airport-type scanning on entry, a measure that is sure to provoke alarm among the purists. In Italy it has resulted in frustrating queues outside the Uffizi and discontent amongst the tourists waiting under the scorching Italian sun to see some of the world's greatest art.'

And, you might add, since their introduction that the museum has not suffered one incident of theft or damage. But that wouldn't make a story, would it, Giacomo Baldini thought, as he left the newspaper open on the bed, Christ's eyes appearing to follow him into the bathroom. Still, in a way, the theft of the painting had made his job somewhat easier since the papers were in the process of preparing the public for the pain of what was to follow. Nevertheless, it was an abrupt welcome for him and, he imagined, he would always be branded a failure if he couldn't recover the painting. He smoothed his hair with the flat of his hand and slipped his soft leather jacket over his white shirt and looked at himself in the mirror.

'C'mon, then,' he said to himself, in a mockney accent, picking up the paper to retrace his steps to the gallery.

London, like Florence, is contained by low hills which form the rim of a saucer at the bottom of which is spread the city. The Florentine hills are more dramatic and more visible, and in summer help trap the hot and dirty air so that a view down over the Renaissance jewel is often seen through a filter of grey pollution. It surprised Giacomo Baldini that in London, so much bigger and so full of cars, the air seemed fresher. What else unexpected would he discover today? He wondered where the painting might be now, so small and easy to hide. Would they ever see it again? He quickly banished the negative thought and entered the gallery through the staff door.

Chapter 14

It was all too soon, all too close together and for several months Habiba lived in a world which, if she had chosen to describe it, would have been like a forest in the aftermath of a fire, bleak, ugly and desolate. She was without cover, unprotected. If it is possible to feel defeat and anger simultaneously, then this is what she did, furious at her father's death and yet often crushed by it to the point of lethargy. In life he had been unable to help and in death he was no different. And yet she railed at him, shouted at his empty chair, unleashing all that she had suppressed when she was forced to listen to his sermons on her behaviour. Sometimes, at night, she was convinced that his desperate coughing had woken her and she would cry out, uncertain whether it was his selfishness, or her own, that was making her angry. Sleep became a rationed commodity and a moist darkness appeared under her eyes. When her eighteenth birthday arrived, she could think of no reason to celebrate. She was now, according to his Muslim will, a free woman. She'd had just six weeks under the care of her appointed guardian, Badsha, but instead of any feelings of release she felt a woman in free fall, driven further into herself, detached and without reference points to help her establish the direction in which she was travelling. It was not the birthday she wanted.

'You look tired,' Sharifa told her.

'I am tired,' Habiba would agree, flatly, almost goading her friend to say more.

Sharifa was uncertain how to approach Habiba. She felt capable of consoling her about her father's death, for this was ground on which she felt safe. But to Sharifa, Habiba had begun to change even before Latif had died and it was this unknown element which confused her, the feeling that there was more going on than she could see. She decided to change tack.

'But you're going to St Martin's?'

'Yes, I'm starting the foundation year in October,' Habiba replied without enthusiasm.

In fact, there was part of Habiba that was grateful for the place at art college, for it gave her some structure for the next few years and it relieved her of any immediate decision-making. If she took any pleasure from it, which was little, it was that she did not have to fight her father about accepting the place. This would have been a battle which neither of them could have won and the consequences would have been bloody. As she thought about this, she became angry again, her fists balling on the kitchen table. Why shouldn't she have been able to tell her father about the assault? Why did she know that he would merely have blamed her for it. 'I told you,' she could hear him say. 'I told you that it would lead to no good. And now you have dishonoured the family. Who will want you now, girl? You are damaged.' His words, imaginary but only too real, thundered in her head.

'Are you OK, Habs?'

Habiba looked at her sharply, wondering what to say. 'No. I'm angry. I'm angry at lots of things and I don't really know why.'

'Don't you?' Sharifa asked, and watched her friend lay her head across her arms on the table.

'Anger is something you're meant to feel after the death of someone close to you,' she offered. 'I was just wondering if there was anything else that was troubling you?'

'I don't want to talk about it,' Habiba said, raising her head from the table. It was an admission of sorts, but Sharifa decided not to pursue it.

'I have brought you a present,' she said, taking a brightly wrapped parcel out of a carrier bag and putting it on the table. She looks much older than eighteen, Sharifa thought, and the death of her father had taken some of the softness out of her face, making it even more sculptured and striking than before.

From a white box, Habiba pulled out a wooden figure with articulated limbs, the sort that artists use as models.

'Thank you.' Habiba was just able to say the words before she broke down and cried.

This was a pattern that would repeat itself for Habiba over the coming months, the violent oscillation between anger and tears, as if she had no control over the extremes of her emotions.

There were two Habiba Popals that began to develop at St Martin's School of Art that autumn. There was the one she showed to the world and the other which limped along inside her. The contrast between the two could not have been greater. Gradually her clothing became brighter and more striking and she wore it like an animal, loudly, daringly, as a challenge to others. Her flamboyance and apparent confidence kept at bay anyone who might want to question her too deeply, a smoke-screen to disguise her uncertainties. In this way she carried herself through college, gradually building her defences higher, burying what had happened to her deeper and deeper. She thought things would get better, but they didn't. Sharifa, who could make a comparison between the Habiba she had known and the one who returned from college, registered the changes in her friend and it was she who first spoke to Badsha.

'I am worried about Habiba,' she told him on the phone. 'I can't really describe it, but it is as if she is not here, if you know what I mean.'

'I do know,' he said. 'I felt it some time ago, even before her poor father died. To tell you the truth, it is something I have been putting off addressing. The poor girl has had so much to cope with. Thank you for the support that you are giving her. I will see her myself and I will let you know how we get on.'

Badsha knew that this exchange could not have taken place between Sharifa and Latif for, however much his friend was fond of the girl, there were issues that he would never allow a woman to discuss with him. He wasn't sure himself how to bridge the gap and continued to procrastinate, putting off the moment to talk to Habiba.

In that first year at college, Habiba learned a great deal, as first-year students always do. But in one arena she remained adamant. Her friendships with men were rationed and controlled and not for an instant did she consider moving any one of them beyond the platonic. She surrounded herself with people remarkably like herself, loud and colourful, involved in their own talents and not given to introspection. She went around in this group, seeking safety in numbers, for they were all careful not to spoil the joint friendships by becoming couples. She went to parties, gigs, bars and trips down to Brighton but she always returned home alone. She told herself that she did not want to complicate her life. The truth was, she didn't know how to.

On the first anniversary of her father's death, she sat once again in the front room that had been her father's domain, attempting an audit of her life. Even now she felt her father's hand settle on her shoulder and guide her actions. Although she was the sole heir designated in his will, he had also decreed that a third of his estate should be given to Muslim charities, which meant the house would have to be sold. It never had been simple and straightforward with her father and his presence seemed to dominate her still. So, although a year had passed since she last saw him in this very room, coughing towards his death, she felt that nothing had moved forward.

The front doorbell rang. She was in the process of selling the house and the estate agent, not much older than her, smiled and introduced a young couple coming to view. They regarded her with some suspicion, which may have been the result of her clothing, a black-and-white striped jacket worn over a lime-green shirt and a calf-length layered white cotton skirt, topped by a French cap adorned with a red silk band. Or perhaps it was a different sort of colour that was making them look hesitant? The street was changing and many of the Asian and Afro-Caribbean families were now leaving, cashing in on rising values. She left the agent to show them round and she waited in the front room. She had never sat in her father's chair, she realised, for it would have been entirely inappropriate. The power of her father was still palpable.

She heard the clomp of their feet upstairs, as they walked between the rooms. She heard the words 'Well, you wouldn't expect it to be in our style' from the stairs, 'but we can really make something of this', before they were led into the living-room.

'Are your parents here?' asked the woman, smiling sweetly at Habiba.

'No, they're dead. I am selling the house,' she responded coolly, watching the couple absorb the information.

'Well, we're quite interested in the house,' the man said. 'What are the neighbours like?'

Habiba wondered if his question had been inadvert. Was it a way of finding out what couldn't be asked: 'Are the neighbours Asian, like you?'

'It depends what you mean,' Habiba replied. 'There's an out-and-out racist two doors down. It will be good to leave him behind.' The look on Habiba's face encouraged them to respond.

The couple looked at each other, not sure what to say.

'We'll be in touch,' the agent said, guiding them to the door, glancing back at Habiba, who remained in the room. She heard the door click shut and watched them stand outside and look at the front of the house, pointing up at the roof. A year ago she might have taken this exchange as nothing out of the ordinary, but now it grated on her. Perhaps she was looking for discord where there was none, seeking to justify the way she felt inside.

She looked around the room which, despite its familiarity, she had never liked and she knew that leaving the house would benefit her, further distancing her from her father. It was quite simply a matter of competing territories. This was his and no matter what she did, it always would be. The idea that she was carrying her father with her and that he was taking the blame for all that had happened to her, had yet to occur to Habiba.

Later that afternoon, the agent phoned with an offer from the couple. Habiba turned it down, partly out of spite, for she sensed that the couple thought she would be only too grateful at their interest. Eventually, they offered the asking price and even then Habiba kept them waiting for an answer. And so her life moved on. She would use the money to buy a small flat nearer the centre of town, another gesture of defiance towards her father. She imagined his booming voice issuing instructions of what she should do. But she was beyond all that now.

Soon, she hoped, the sense of desolation would leave her, that time would somehow heal her, as she'd been told so often it would. Regularly, disappointment would grab her so firmly that she felt exhausted, unable to do the simplest of tasks, taking to her bed in the middle of the afternoon, staring, wide awake, at the ceiling. Afterwards would come the guilt, the idea that she was here because of her own failures. Sometimes, when she was out with her friends, her laughter rising above the music and their shouted conversations, she would freeze and ask herself what she was doing. For the moment, she didn't have the answer.

Chapter 15

The newspaper lay open over the remains of Sean Dunmore's breakfast. His flat was in a new block in the middle of Glasgow, a steel and glass box with views over the river. The living room was dominated by a large flat-screen television mounted on a wall opposite a leather sofa. The kitchen was part of the living space, divided from it by a worktop which doubled as a table. Sean Dunmore sat staring at the picture, a slice of toast halfway to his mouth. There were several stages of reaction which had brought him to this frozen position. First, the front-page story of the theft of a picture from the National Gallery had caused him to pause the moment he had picked up the paper from his front doormat. Second, when he had opened the paper and seen the full-scale photograph of the painting, he had again stopped in mid-action. Why did he know this picture so well? And then, when the process of remembering was complete and Sean Dunmore had organised the fragments of recollection into an understandable whole, he remained motionless because, frankly, he didn't know which way to turn.

Some other sense was alerted in Sean Dunmore, a distant instinctive alarm. He was taken back several years to his time at the National Gallery and his quick assimilation of facts created contradictory responses.

'Well, would you believe it?' he said out loud to himself.

This was the painting that the Indian girl had liked, for whatever reason, the one she had stood in front of on many occasions and had appeared to be transfixed by. He recalled her obsession with the tiny picture, how she would stand in front of it for ages, sometimes leaning forward towards it, once even appearing to talk to it as if expecting an answer.

He stood and held the newspaper picture out in front of him. Surely she couldn't have had anything to do with its theft? He was making too much of the coincidence, and yet a worm of doubt was active inside him. Sean Dunmore did not entertain guilt, but he had an instinct for self-preservation and it was this that was now alerted. He had no difficulty in remembering the girl, tall and sexy, but the memory did not bring a smile to his face. The ambitious part of him wanted to phone the National Gallery, to say that he knew of a connection with the painting which might help their enquiries. He knew that any titbit of information would be useful and if it led to the recovery of the picture then it would do him no harm. He would like to impress this Giacomo Baldini, but then he realised that this might put him on a dangerous path and this conflict again immobilised him.

Sean Dunmore had been lured back to Scotland by a mix of ambition and caution in equal measure. After two years at the National Gallery in London, the Gallery of Modern Art in Glasgow wondered if he would return in a senior position on the security team. By this time, he knew that he would never succeed Brian McMasters when he retired and, although London offered him an exciting playground, he rather missed the familiarity of his home town. And then there were the women. There had been several after the Indian girl, all tracked down in the same fashion. But his technique was becoming familiar and when one day Brian McMasters had caught him in the control room focusing on a particularly striking blonde girl, he realised he would have to be more cautious. And then there were the scratches on his face, which the American girl had given him. He'd managed to get her into the car park, but she had reacted furiously and attacked him. Maybe he had failed to give her the right dosage of the drug, or perhaps she was more resistant than the others. Whatever, she had created a real fuss, lashing out at him, tearing his face with her nails, before threatening to go to the police. 'It's my word against yours,' he threatened her. 'You came out for a drink with me and then wanted to mess about in my car. Think what it would look like in the cold light of day.' She had backed off, but it had alarmed him and the next day Brian McMasters looked less than convinced when he explained away the lacerations as an accident with a tree after too much to drink. Perhaps he should think of moving on and when the Glasgow job came up a few weeks later, the timing seemed perfect.

He walked over to the window and looked down on to the waterfront. Sean Dunmore was angry at the idea that women should get the better of him. He could barely acknowledge that the American had caused him to leave London and now his thinking was confused by the Indian girl. Surely she couldn't have had anything to do with the theft of the picture, could she? And, yet, she had seemed obsessed by it. The ambitious part of Sean Dunmore, which was considerable, forced him to think about the benefits of helping find the painting and this was a lead, however slender, that might be useful. It would involve looking at the CCTV footage and if, by chance, he saw her, then his hunch would be proved correct. But, then, it might involve him coming face to face with her again, which might prove embarrassing. He looked at his watch and realised that he would be late for work unless he hurried. Any decision would have to wait, he thought, and it was only as he hurried between the massive columns in front of the gallery, that the answer came to him. It was a solution which offered very little risk and the chance of considerable reward, one way and the other. He rubbed his hands together at the prospect, now remembering the image of the girl's half-naked body in the back of his car. What a wonderful way to start the day.

*   *   *

Habiba thought of the three images of the painting, the two that she could see in her room and the one she had left in the gallery.

The real picture looked down from the mantelpiece and the newspaper photograph lay on her lap, one reflecting the other. What is value, she asked herself? Why is one worth millions and why are the other two worthless? How many visitors to the gallery yesterday morning had seen the fake before it was discovered? Ten, twenty, a hundred, all believing the picture was real. And to them it was, as real as the one above the fireplace and no less real than the one in the newspaper. She cut out the picture and pinned it next to the original and, apart from the depth and the definition of the frame, they were remarkably similar. It had been the same when she first mounted the photograph on canvas. She had just come back from Paris with the frame, which had been copied in an old workshop in Montmartre, and when she united the two she had been astounded at the combination, knowing then that if it was assumed to be real, it could be. Would it matter if all the pictures in the gallery were fakes, if the visitors believed they were real? How different would the value be to the beholder?

What was real to her now was Sean Dunmore. A few weeks earlier she had visited a private detective in Hatton Garden, whose tiny office was tacked on to the roof of a late Georgian house. It was more of a Nissen hut than a room and had clearly been put there just after the war, before the days of strict planning regulation. She wore a hijab, her scarf covering the lower part of her face. She could see that he was intrigued. He, in turn, was an extraordinary-looking young man whose dark brown hair was brushed up from his brow in a permanent standing wave. His eyes were wide-set, as was his jaw, so that he took on the appearance of a cartoon character caught with an inane grin. She had seen his business advertised on a website.

'My bread and butter work I get from across the way,' he told her, gesturing behind him with his head. 'I work for lawyers in the chambers. You'd be surprised how many people lie and cheat. I had a case the other day of a woman who had forged her husband's signature on his will, in order that he left everything to her.'

Habiba wondered why he had chosen to tell her about a female criminal when she was sure that most of his miscreants were undoubtedly men. Perhaps he was intrigued by her partly covered face, that this lent the occasion an air of mystery. She explained what she wanted and this gave him another opportunity to show off.

'No problem. I can't of course tell you how I do it, but he'll be easy to trace. I should have an answer for you by later this afternoon.'

And that's how Habiba Popals discovered that Sean Dunmore, the man who had raped her, was living in Flat 23, Dockside Apartments, Glasgow, and worked at the Gallery of Modern Art. For such an easy piece of work, she still had to pay £150, but for her it was worth it. It gave her a goal, even if she couldn't quite imagine the ending.

She sat in the carriage of a Virgin Express train watching the fields gallop by and felt her larger journey unfold. The painting, secure in its wooden box, rested on the seat by her side and she began to doze. Sometimes, when she slept, she would remember what happened that night, re-live it in lurid detail, only to wake and find it a dream. No matter how hard she tried, she could not be sure of the sequence of events and now she doubted even those fragments about which she had once been certain. It had happened over four years ago but if her memory of the rape was vague, her recall of its consequences was vivid. It had led her to be here, in a train speeding northwards and it had dominated her life in ways that she could never have guessed and, even now, could barely acknowledge.

Chapter 16

The party was held in a warehouse on an abandoned industrial estate out towards Heathrow, a 1930s building with a curved, stuccoed frontage and metal windows, many of which were smashed. Imitation flambeaux flanked the entrance and lines of candles snaked up the stairs and guided her progress to the top floor. Habiba was wearing an orange jumpsuit with a wide zebra-skin belt and a mauve chiffon scarf, the heels of her leather boots making her taller than ever. Upstairs, the large room was lit by three enormous film lamps supported on sturdy tripods, their lights directed at the ceiling and reflected against walls of silver foil which covered three sides of the room. A line of windows made up the open side, with views over the ruined estate towards Heathrow where a succession of planes landed at regular intervals, their lights flickering in the dusk. The music was loud and sixty or so equally exotically dressed people danced and talked in groups in front of her. As she always did these days, Habiba felt both part of the group and entirely alien to it and from time to time she glanced out of the windows and wished she could have been on one of the planes flying away. Anywhere.

She was well into her second year at St Martin's and the intensity of her life, both in work and play, continued unabated. She had thrown up a wall of activity to prevent any moments of introspection so that, at the end of the day, there was no gap between exhaustion and sleep in which to meet her demons. The night unfolded and she danced and chatted, the noise in the room rising all the time, the throng of people thickening, the laughter more shrill, the lights of the planes more vivid as they landed. Sometime after midnight, she came across a friend of hers with his back to the party, staring out of the window. She tapped him on the shoulder and he turned.

'Oh, hello darling,' he said, 'you caught me in a moment of, shall we say, introspection, ruminating on my fate.'

He had a small, delicate face and close-cropped hair and his cheeks were touched with rouge.

'What do you mean, Charlie?'

'Oh, you haven't heard the news, my dear?'

She shook her head.

'Well, it seems, my adventures have given me a positive outcome. Positive as in you know what. It's a bummer in every sense of the word, darling.'

Even as she said that she was sorry, Habiba could feel the familiar and ghastly emergence of her own story rising to claim her and she dropped her head.

'Oh, don't worry Habs, there's all those drugs now. And I've got lots of chums to go through this hell with.'

She looked at him and kissed his cheek, feeling the sweat cold on his face. He turned back to face the night sky and she was left with the hollowness of her thoughts.

She had pretended that she didn't need to have an Aids' test and it had taken her many months to pluck up the courage to have one. During this time her fears had grown to the point where she was imagining all the symptoms of HIV that she had read about on the Internet. When she was alone in the house, after her father had died, she would shout, 'Aids has nothing to do with the old country! It is about now, today, here.' She had never been promiscuous and always careful and now here she was wondering if she had Aids. The unfairness of it weighed down on her and she knew that there was no one she could talk to. She had to carry this burden alone and at night she stared for hours into a dense blackness, trapped and hounded by her own fears.

She did not send away for the testing kit, not trusting a marked package being delivered to her door. She imagined that the special clinic in Moorgate would be more anonymous but as she walked into the marble entrance she felt that a spotlight was following her. It was a day that she would never forget and a residue of the humiliation remained now and was lodged deep inside her only to be triggered and released yet again by Charlie's story. She looked hard at her own faint reflection in the broken window and recalled the prickly sensation of everyone staring at her in the clinic, knowing that there was only one reason for her to be there: sex. Waiting for the result was a misery she never wished to go through again. Her life, it seemed, rested in the hands of the nurse who now approached, the clip of her shoes on the shiny floor. Was her future about to be consigned to a slow death? She was negative, the nurse in her trim white uniform told her in a voice of controlled neutrality. Her heart sank when she added that she should have another test in a few months, just to be certain. So she endured it all over again, asking herself whether the fear of meeting someone she knew in the clinic was greater than the fear of having the test come back positive. The shame would have been intolerable and she pushed back the thought, physically repressing it, unaware that it was to fuel so much of what was to happen next, that it would be joining the other unaccepted memories that Habiba fought so hard to deny. So much had happened to the simple girl who had tripped into the National Gallery that summer's morning. And the story had not ended yet.

Chapter 17

Giacomo Baldini spread the information on the table in front of him, smoothing down the crumpled edges. In the rush of the evacuation, certain niceties had been abandoned and the papers had been crushed into files once the details had been taken. The writing was in capitals and the name was as clear as it was unusual: Anmar Ma'ab Qadr, with an address in south London. If the address had proved to be false, then he assumed the same of the name. Anmar Ma'ab Qadr. It looked real enough, but then what did he know about foreign names? He thought of an Italian equivalent, pushing two unusual Christian names together: Abrianna Talita. He imagined that combination would sound real enough to any of the security team at the gallery. They were, in fact, the Christian names of his mother.

He Googled the complete name, just in case, but he was directed to each of the names in turn and discovered that they, too, were a series of first names, Arab in origin. He made a note of their translated meanings: 'leopard', 'place to which one returns', 'fate or destiny'. He got up and walked around his office, an environment he was already beginning to hate. Window-less, except for a heavily frosted skylight, it was claustrophobic and gave no clue about the weather in the street. He wanted to look out, to be distracted, so he could think. He had been brought up on a farm that had once been a communal fortress, a series of buildings and courtyards within a curtain of higher walls. There were views in all directions, hence its location and the slopes which led up to the farmstead were dotted evenly with olive trees. Real winter barely touched this part of the world sand-wiched as it was between a long hot summer and a benign spring and autumn. Trapped now in his terracotta office, he suddenly longed for the views of his childhood and to walk amongst the olive groves. Instead, he paced around in the artificial light and spoke the Arabic names out loud. Were these random, or did they carry some deliberate meaning?

His thoughts were broken by an incoming call on his mobile. He could see that it was from Ruth Pitts, with whom he had left a message late the night before. She came straight to the point.

'Da Messina. Lucky to have a Christian name in those days. Antonello. Came from your part of the world. Sicily. But you probably know all that.'

He didn't, in fact, and he was rather ashamed that he was unaware of a fellow Sicilian, even if more than half a millennium did separate them. He kept this to himself.

'But, to the meat of your question. He is of particular interest to some current Dutch collectors. He was very much influenced by the Flemish school. Portraits in great detail. Almost like photo-realism, really.'

She was speaking in short, staccato sentences, as though she was reading from notes.

'Could you imagine any of them employing a Muslim woman – well, we assume she is a Muslim since she wears a hijab – to steal pictures for them?'

'I'm not quite following, Jack,' she said.

'We have a suspect who appears to be Asian, tall, who was in the gallery on both days but whose face was masked by her headscarf.'

'Well, "no" is the answer to your question. Both men I have in mind have the most impeccable credentials. I do know that one or two pictures contemporaneous to the Messina have found their way to the southern hemisphere but they would certainly have nothing to do with that.'

'What about collectors in India? Are there any?'

'I'm not sure about in India, but there are one or two Indian collectors here in England. But, again, no, I cannot imagine their interest being *that* extreme. Curiously, though,' she continued, 'the painting is exactly the sort that ought to be in a private collection. It really needs to be viewed in miniature, if you like, rather than in a large gallery like our own. But I don't suppose that is very helpful, is it?'

'It's all been helpful,' he told her politely.

Earlier that morning he had called Ruth Pitts' equivalent in Florence and had a similar conversation. Usually, somewhere, there is a logic to the theft of an object as particular as a Renaissance painting. His job was to find it. He recalled what Colin Tyler had said about it perhaps being the work of a crank and his heart sank at the prospect of unpicking the motives of such a person. He sat at his desk and wrote a brief e-mail to Miranda Goodheart saying that he would be out of the office for the morning but that he was available on his mobile.

Giacomo Baldini's idea of what Tooting Bec might be like was influenced in the main by his knowledge of another south London borough, Dulwich, where he had spent a year when he was twenty-two. He also thought the name was quite appealing and imagined a leafy suburb built around a winding high street dominated by an ancient church by the side of which would be a large pond. The scene that greeted Giacomo Baldini when he emerged from the tube could not have been further removed, an ugly junction of four main roads. It took him a few moments to orientate himself, for each of the roads seemed identical, ugly ribbons of run-down shops and parked cars. There seemed no focus, no centre, other than the tube station behind him. No spire graced the low horizons and the trees had long since gone. Dulwich this was not. Having established his bearings, he turned southwards, making his way to the address on the sheet, the one they had discovered to be false. He was working on a simple hunch. Why had the girl given a real address, even if it wasn't her own? Did she expect to be searched and questioned on leaving the gallery? If not, then she might have had to make up something quite quickly. He was trying to ascribe logic to her decisions, even if she had not been fully aware of them herself.

Tooting Bec did not improve, the further he walked. It seemed unremittingly bleak, a road without redemption. He passed a shop displaying vegetables propped on boxes on the pavement which announced that it was open 24/24. A bus was waiting at a stop close by and when it pulled away a grey cloud of diesel smoke remained in its place. A little way further on, a direct-mail fetish shop displayed some of its wares in the window, a maid's outfit in shades of claret and grey rubber, a latex balaclava. Somewhere, down around the long bend ahead of him, a signpost told him that Tooting Bec Common existed, but he was never to reach this nirvana. He found the road he wanted and the house a few doors up from the turning. The terrace of small, bay-windowed houses was probably a hundred years old and in that time some had fared better than others. The house that Giacomo wanted had varnished brickwork with the pointing picked out in black. The old wooden windows had been replaced by steel double-glazed units, as had the front door. A cross of St George was stuck on the inside of the downstairs window and when he rang the bell a dog barked and he could see its outline the other side of the glass door.

'Shaddup Caine. Will you getaway from that door. Now.'

Giacomo heard the latch slide into place and through the narrow crack in the door he saw the face looking at him. Below, a wet nose poked through with a low growl.

'Yes?'

'I'm from the National Gallery in London and I wonder if I could talk to you? My name is Jack Baldini.'

'What's it about?'

'I am investigating a crime.'

'Not the fuckin' police again. We had your lot round yesterday. I told them nobody with that name lived here.' The man made to shut the door.

'Please,' Giacomo said. 'It's important. We think you might be able to help us. We have a suspect, an Asian suspect.'

He could see the man stoop down and clip a lead on the dog, before opening the door. He had cropped hair and looked not unlike his dog, who was eyeing Giacomo threateningly. Although he didn't like to admit it, he was pleased to see the type of man who was standing in front of him, equally as suspicious and unwelcoming as the dog. He took a photocopy out of his pocket and handed it to the man. It was the best freeze-frame image of the girl they could find, most of her face disguised by her scarf.

'This is the woman we're interested in.'

'Paki, is she?' the man said.

'Perhaps,' Giacomo replied. 'Do you know any?'

'Place is bloody crawling with them, isn't it?' He looked at the picture and pointed at the woman's head. 'Bloody useful those things, eh, if you don't want to be recognised.'

'Hijabs,' he said, encouragingly.

'Whatever. Plenty of them round here, mate, let me tell you. There used to be a woman up the road who wore the whole tent-like thing. Y'know? Bloody sinister, if you ask me. Shouldn't be allowed in this country. They should do things our way. Or go back home.'

'A burka. Does she still live here? The woman who wore the burka?'

'She died. So did the bloke. The rest of the family moved away not so long ago.'

'Was there any family?' Giacomo leant forward and tapped the picture.

'Never knew them myself. Anyway, they keep themselves to themselves, don't they? Integration my arse.'

There was an all-pervading menace to the man and his home, with the dog straining on its studded lead and the smell of fried food heavy in the air.

'Where did you say they live, this family?'

'First house up from the high street. Just here. But they're not there now, like I said. Moved away, thank goodness.'

Giacomo was relieved to step back into the fresh air, even that of Tooting Bec. In Italy, particularly in the south, the hatred of outsiders, Africans in particular, was just as intense as the prejudice he had just heard. He supposed that a fear of the unknown was understandable, but it was the graceless dismissal of anyone who was different, the instinctive hatred he found troubling. And here he was, Giacomo Baldini, a Sicilian whose roots ran back at least six generations, deep into the very soil of his country, living and working in another country. What had propelled him away from the traditions he had been brought up in and had been expected to follow? Why was he in an ugly London suburb talking to racist Englishmen in the quest to find an Asian woman of unknown origins? He pushed the thought to one side as he opened the gate to the house that had been pointed out to him. Small paving stones and pale gravel made up the front garden and the house, with its white-painted windows and pale blue door, was charming in comparison to the one he had just visited. A young woman opened the door and he explained who he was. He was shown into a neat and tidy living room that smelled of polish.

'I wonder if you could tell me anything about the family you bought the house from?' he asked. 'It might help us with our investigation.'

'Well, it wasn't really a family. I understand the father had died and for some reason the daughter was selling the house.'

'Daughter?' His instincts were alerted now and he showed her the photocopy.

'It's impossible to tell, isn't it? They all look the same.' She immediately corrected herself. 'What I mean is, it's hard to tell from this picture, since her face is obscured.'

'Can you tell me anything more about her? Age, height, hair?'

'Hair? They all have black hair, don't they? Anyway, she did. Cut short, with two big curls here.' She described the shape with her fingers. 'They were flattened against her face. Looked a bit ridiculous to me. I must say, I didn't find her very pleasant. I suppose she would have been twenty, early twenties, something like that. She was tall, I do remember that.'

'And her name, do you remember that?' he asked quietly.

She got up and left the room, returning with a yellow box file. She clicked it open and removed a piece of paper.

'Here it is,' she said, turning the paper the right way as she handed it to him. 'Habiba Popals. Strange name. But then, who are we to say?'

'And a forwarding address, perhaps?'

'No, we don't know where she went and we've had no need to get in touch with her. We changed everything, anyway. It wasn't, you know, our style.'

Was it that easy, he asked himself again afterwards, standing on the corner of Tooting Bec, watching the traffic flow by? He flicked open his phone and called Colin Tyler.

'Habiba Popals.' He spelled out the name. 'Early twenties, tall, dark hair, probably short. See if you can get an address for her. I'll be back in about an hour.'

Even as he gave out her details, he could feel the questions rising in him. There were pieces of information missing, for if it turned out to be true that she had taken the picture, he was left with merely a conclusion. The why and the wherefore were absent and without these he felt incomplete. There was, though, something that was beginning to intrigue him about this case and although he couldn't be certain what it was, he felt curiously excited, as though he was beginning an unknown journey and not even Tooting Bec's dishevelled high street could dispel this.

Chapter 18

It was late in the second summer after the death of Latif that Badsha decided to talk to Habiba. Already the leaves were beginning to turn and the grass in Victoria Park had the tired and worn look that comes with the end of a long, dry summer. Habiba was about to go back to college and he had invited her to lunch. Of course, he had seen her many times in between, but, for one reason and another, he had kept his counsel on the story that he planned to begin to tell her today. There were two reasons he had waited so long. He had watched her emerge from the loss of her father and shrug off the pain that had seemed almost to crush her in the early days. She was now the multicoloured bird that her father had always feared, bright, elusive and out of his grasp. Badsha saw it all from a distance and attempted to keep it in perspective, something her father had never been able to do. But, at the same time, he could see the brittleness of her condition, the sometime vacant look in her eyes and the loss of what had always been a knowing easiness in her manner, a natural confidence. It was for this reason that he had delayed this moment, for he was uncertain what impact it might have on the young girl, for young she was, despite the sophistication of her dress and the independence of her ways.

Every family carries its secrets in silence but, in one way or the other, the pressure of disguise and deceit, of deliberate and practised ignorance creates pressure elsewhere. Somewhere the petticoat shows and for those who care to look, the clues exist. Habiba could never really understand the severity of her father but to Badsha it was obvious. He could see in his daughter an echo of a past which haunted him. He wanted to warn her away from it, as if, from a distance, it somehow existed to taint her indelibly. Even as he waited for her, Badsha was troubled about what he should do. He had given his word to Latif that he would tell the story of her past, but he had his responsibilities to Habiba as well. He paced his restaurant, straightening pictures and table settings until the first customers gave him something to occupy him properly. When Habiba arrived, he was sitting at a corner table and at first she didn't see him. She looked as exotic as ever, her dark hair, today worn in what he could only describe as a high ponytail erupting behind her, a black-and-purple striped polo neck, a black skirt and pale grey jacket, the perfect embodiment of a young woman, beautiful and self-possessed. The image would have driven her father wild with anger. 'You should not draw attention to yourself in this way,' he could hear him shouting now.

'You look a picture,' he said to Habiba, as she joined him at the corner table. 'Tell me about what you have been doing.' For the next ten minutes, as they ordered the food, Habiba described, with considerable editing, some of the projects she was involved with and what she got up to with her contemporaries. Then, in a pause to allow the dishes to be put on the table, he changed from attentive listener to concerned speaker.

'I mentioned some time ago that I wanted to talk to you, in fact, had been asked to talk to you by your father.'

Habiba continued to look at him and he found her dark eyes, almost without pupils, quite disconcerting. He would have preferred it if she had thrown her head back and groaned.

'I don't know whether to start at the end and work backwards, or at the beginning, if, indeed, there is a moment that could be called a beginning.'

She answered his conundrum for him. 'Wherever you choose the beginning to be, start at the beginning.'

And so he did. Almost.

'This is a story about you,' he began, 'but for some time you may not think so. I ask you to be patient.' With his fork, he reorganised the chicken on the plate in front of him.

'I think you would regard yourself as English, wouldn't you?'

Again, the unmoving face. 'I think I would be more specific than that, Baddy. I am a Londoner.'

He wondered whether she was going to make this easy for him. 'Well, you know, your father never stopped seeing you as a Pashtun. He found it impossible to believe you were anything but.'

'Tell me about it,' she said flatly.

'I know that he made life quite difficult for you in this respect, but he wanted me to, well, try and explain why.'

Again, the expressionless stare.

'Your father loved to quote Winston Churchill, who, you know, was once a reporter in the hills where our families come from. He said that every rock, every hill, had its own story to tell and this is certainly true.' He waited, but her face didn't change. 'This is another one.'

Although listening to Badsha talk about the family history was quite different from when her father embarked on one of his long stories, Habiba could feel a resistance building in her already.

'Your father loved to say that we don't come from a country, we come from land which is ours despite the boundaries that other people have drawn over it and around it. He used to say that we have never been beaten, particularly by the British.' This wasn't the way he meant to start, but it helped him order his thoughts for what was to come next.

'It meant, of course, we were always fighting and if we weren't fighting an enemy we were fighting among ourselves. Latif had this in him. He was instinctively combative.'

All this was only too familiar to Habiba and she perhaps showed this on her face for Badsha immediately changed tack.

'It is hard for me to believe that the story I am about to tell you began just a hundred years ago. In some ways, things have changed completely and, in others, not at all. The British are fighting in Afghanistan, on our borders, today just as they were back then. I suppose their attitude was the same. They believed they somehow knew better than us and had the right to be part of what had always been ours. But, again, I am not getting to the point.'

And, again, the way she was regarding him was anything but encouraging. He met her eyes and held her look for a moment.

'There was a big uprising against the British back then. The Afridi, our people, stormed all the forts and this drove the British mad. Typical mountain stuff, the sort that had been going on for ages. Except,' and here he looked at Habiba again, 'except there was a complication. A young woman had a relationship with a British soldier. Your great-great-grandmother. Her name, we are told, was Anam. She had been married to an Afridi who had been killed in the fighting. At first, no one was sure if the child had been conceived before his death and for a while after the birth, the little girl was brought up as his child. Even though, as a tribe, we are paler than most, it was clear after a while that Noreen, for that was the name she was given, was not her father's child. No one was completely sure what had happened, and it was perhaps this that saved Anam. Some say she might have been raped but, whatever, the shame on the family was enormous. It was a miracle that Anam survived. You could be stoned to death for just looking at another man, let alone a British soldier. Nevertheless, Anam's life was a misery and she died young and Noreen was raised by other members of her family.'

Habiba listened to this story dispassionately. It came as no surprise to her that, somewhere in her past, there were events which were deemed shocking. Which family could claim that they were free of such skeletons? The fact that it had happened so far away, in a place that she had never seen, merely emphasised its remoteness from her. Badsha could see that she had received this information without curiosity and so he continued.

'Noreen was different, as you might imagine, and her life must have been difficult.'

He could see that Habiba had still not engaged with the history of her own family and she continued to look at him as though he was telling her about a recipe she ought to try.

'In so many ways, we are a ridiculous people,' he offered, to see if this might change her demeanour. 'Customs run deep in our society and, usually, it is women who come off worst. Noreen, you see, was bartered in a deal between two families. By this time she was living with an uncle, her mother's oldest brother, and it was his son who was involved in a dispute about land with a neighbour. In an ensuing fight, the neighbour's son was badly injured. As compensation, Noreen was offered in marriage. This was how it was, this is how it still is.'

'An arranged marriage?' said Habiba.

'Well, not exactly, more of a bad marriage, as they are known. One that came around negatively.'

'Bad marriage?' Habiba frowned, as much with the concept as with Badsha's casual acceptance that this was a normal and accepted practice.

'Yes,' he continued. 'It was the way things were done and, some say, still are done. The local councils decide. Anyway, this marriage produced your grandmother, Kiran.' He paused, still not sure yet whether he had the full attention of the young woman sitting opposite, who was picking away at her food as he spoke, occasionally glancing up at him.

'Kiran, by all accounts, was an exceptional woman, but, then, it seems the same of all the women in your family. In fact, as I sit here now, it is strange for me to tell the story of a Pashtun family from the point of view of the women. But I hope you are beginning to see why?'

Habiba did not respond. Her mother had rarely referred to Kiran and it was odd to hear about her now.

'It would appear,' Badsha continued, 'that your grandmother was the most, how shall I put this, the most normal of the women I am describing.' He waited and looked up at Habiba. At first she didn't grasp the implication of what he had just said. It was only the silence that alerted her to its significance and at that moment she felt her resistance grow even stronger, a familiar gathering of her defences. From the grave, her father was still attempting to define her by reference to a background that bore no resemblance to the life she was leading.

Badsha could see the defiance in Habiba's eyes, their slight narrowing creating the faint lines on her brow and the set of her mouth. He continued, nevertheless.

'She had an arranged marriage, but your grandfather and Kiran seemed to have been very compatible. There were two children, your mother Jamila and her brother Salman, who was killed by an explosion when he was quite young.'

This was the first time that Habiba had been aware of Salman and within a sentence he was dead. She assumed there was more, and worse, to come and her barricades continued to assemble around her.

'I don't suppose you know why Jamila came to this country, do you, Habiba?'

It was strange to hear her mother described by her first name and it had the contradictory effect of making her more real and yet more of a stranger at the same time. She waited for Badsha to continue.

'The truth is, she came alone, a young girl, barely twenty years old. Your father always said there was something distant about her, not of this world. I found her fascinating, although this was some time later. She was sent to be with Latif, who had been living in London for about fifteen years and was considerably older than your mother.'

Even though Habiba had begun to wonder where this narrative was going, she was already in the process of filing the information away, of storing it in a vault and sealing it off somewhere in her mind. She was determined that it would not be more important than the life she was living now. In fact, she resented its intrusion, the very assumption that it could dominate her own concerns.

'Your grandmother was a resourceful mother, and wise. She brokered the marriage of her daughter to your father from a distance of two thousand miles. She knew your father's family and had watched Latif grow up. She knew him as an intelligent man who had come to Britain to try and better himself. It did not matter to her that he was almost twenty years older than her daughter. In some ways, it suited her purpose, for purpose she had.'

The restaurant had filled now and the chatter from the other tables acted to seal his story into the corner of the room where they were sitting. Every so often, Habiba heard a particularly loud laugh or the clatter of a plate but these merely acted as a focus for her mood, further isolating her, just as Badsha's story was in the process of doing. It had always been a source of embarrassment to her that her father was so much older than her mother, one of a cascade of anomalies which divided her off from many of her friends, or from other girls with whom she would have liked to be friendly. Badsha was now in the process of making it difficult all over again.

As the story had gone on, so the impassiveness left Habiba's face and Badsha watched her eyes betray the arrows of doubt that were attacking her from within. She had stopped listening and it was only the voices inside her that she could hear and they, he guessed, were warning her to beware. They had good reason and he hesitated before continuing, slowly sipping at his glass of water and wondering whether he should go on. At some stage he would have to, of course, but a growing uneasiness warned him that this might not be the moment. And she sensed it as well, like an animal on a mountain detects danger, a distant clatter of rocks, the faintest whiff of an unusual smell, a sudden stillness in the wind.

'It's a little obvious, isn't it?' she said to him. 'Three generations of Pashtun women, and now me. Is this what my father was frightened of? That I had been handed the defective gene that runs like an igneous intrusion through us all? Uncle Badsha, I thought you would have seen through all of this, would have put a stop to his obsessions. What was wrong with my father? It was as if he was blind to what was happening under his nose for what took place a hundred years ago.'

The indignation rose in her, controlled at first, but now rolling into anger and the eyes, which had been so still at the outset, were now flashing left and right as they reflected what was going on inside her.

'I cannot take any more of the Popals. My father felt he had a direct line to understanding, to pain, but he didn't know where to begin. I'm sorry, Badsha, but I must go. What you have told me is not merely the history of the women in my family, it is yet another admonishment. Do not be like them, he is saying, be warned. I am only doing this for your own good. Ha, he wouldn't have known my own good if it came packaged by Allah himself.'

She stood up, gave him the curtest of nods and left the restaurant.

Badsha smiled and raised his eyebrows, not in surprise but at the voice that said I told you so. He couldn't help but admire Habiba and her fierce reaction to the history she had been told and yet, he thought sadly, there was more to come. He feared for the beautiful young woman, and whilst once upon a time he might have expected her intelligent and questing mind to have been open to the true story of her past, he now wasn't so sure. His ability to steer his way through her natural defences appeared to have deserted him and he wondered why. Was it the vestiges of grief that were still upsetting Habiba, or was there something else? Just as her father had lived with a secret for so long, was Habiba?

He sat there in the corner for a long time, until the restaurant had emptied and the sign on the door had been turned so that 'Open' faced inwards.

Chapter 19

Habiba slept on the train to the continuous hum of the track and the gentle sway of the carriage and for a moment when she woke she was lost, not quite sure where she was, neither in sleep nor out of it. She sat there, gently rocking to the motion of the express, and thought about this state which so accurately defined the limbo in which she found herself. What she had embarked on was a parenthesis in her life, a bubble that floated above normal existence and, for now, was more real. It didn't seem strange that she was speeding northwards to an unknown city and a conclusion she couldn't define. She had carefully planned the theft of the painting but her path became less clear the closer she got to Sean Dunmore. All she knew was that he had taken something from her, at best, four years of her life, at worst, her innocence. Until the assault she had been an optimist, believing in the essential goodness of people, but he had shattered that state and for this he would pay the consequences. From the window she looked out at a lone tower on a bare hilltop slip slowly by, a crenellated folly, placed there for no other reason than to catch the eye, a whim of its creator. For Habiba, this venture was a folly, too, existing only for itself, devoid of any proper logic and sustained solely by the power of her own wishes.

In Glasgow, she checked into a run-of-the mill hotel not far from the station. She slipped the artist's case with the painting behind the cheap wardrobe and left the room to orientate herself to the world of Sean Dunmore. There was no sense of passionate revenge in Habiba, more an even-headed coldness which allowed her to approach this stage of her journey with calculated detachment. She found her way to where he lived and stood opposite, looking up at the low-rise modern block of big windows and small balconies. She crossed the road to peer at the rectangular plate of bells by the front door. She found his name, Dunmore, neatly framed behind plastic and she assumed from its position that he had a top-floor flat. It was easy for her to recall his easy, cock-o'-the-north manner but the smile that came to her now and the watchful eyes that accompanied it, were laden with malice. She held the image for a second or two, unafraid of it and knowing that when she came face to face with him again, it would be just the same.

She waited in a doorway opposite the flats. It was after five and a grey dusk was quickly overtaking the city. From the little she knew of him, she doubted that he would come back to his flat immediately after work and she decided that she would return early the following morning. Although the evening was still, without a breath of wind, she could feel the cold rise up from the Clyde and hover over the cobbles and parked BMWs. She shivered and began to wander back to the hotel, taking a longer route through the unfamiliar streets. After four years, she could wait until the morning for what she had to do.

*   *   *

Less than half a mile away Sean Dunmore finished work for the day and took the steps in front of the gallery two at a time and made for the wine bar a few streets away. This was part of the regular pattern of his day and he was joining a throng of young people for whom a drink after work was part of the routine of going home. He came to see the girls who spilled out of the offices and talked noisily to one another, their volume increasing with every drink. There was one girl he had been watching for some weeks, a woman he would call a natural flirt, the sort who knew the power of her own body and used it to her advantage. She had the habit of slightly dropping her head and looking up with her pale eyes in a gesture that to him meant only one thing. She was up for it. He had managed to strike up a conversation with her a few days ago and she had agreed to meet him for a drink this evening. He arrived early and watched the elaborate rituals being played out in front of him, pursuer and pursued, eyes meeting, eyes averted, signals given, signals received all for one purpose. He watched a man place the flat of his hand against the bottom of a woman wearing dark trousers who, not looking at him, turned her body and pushed his arm away while continuing her conversation with a friend. No different from animals in a zoo, he thought, except for the clothes.

'Hello there.' The woman stood over him, hands on her hips, with a look on her face that said, 'I have been standing here a while now and you haven't noticed.' When he was at the bar buying her a drink, he thought that this was going to be easy. Women were all the same, but this one was a bit more obvious than some of the others. He looked over to her now, her legs crossed and seemingly unaware of the acres of thigh she was showing. Sean Dunmore was careful not to use the drug on women like this, regulars at the bar. He preferred the anonymity that the gallery gave him, the tourists and visitors who had no fixed pattern to their days.

He handed the woman her glass of wine and the conversation took up the expected pattern.

'I work in the world of art and security,' he said, as he had, word for word, many times before. 'My job is to protect priceless works of art in such a way that no one notices.' He pretended he didn't care how they responded and he had now perfected his throwaway style. 'Best if they don't know I exist, if you know what I mean.' And then he would explain about some of the electronic detection equipment he worked with and the subtle ways they had to stop the paintings being damaged. He failed to mention that he disliked many of the works, especially the modern installations, which he would gladly have destroyed himself.

The girl leant forward. 'And what do I do?' she said.

'Tell me,' he replied, although he wasn't that interested.

'I work at the hospital,' she said.

'A nurse,' he responded, enthusiastically.

'Not really,' she said. 'I'm a psychotherapist. I work with children.'

Sean Dunmore's deductive logic about women was limited and on his radar a woman who worked in a hospital was automatically a nurse. He didn't know how to respond to this woman, who suddenly moved from being an object of desire to something altogether more threatening.

'Mmm, I usually have that effect on men,' she said and smiled.

He was about to say something dismissive about shrinks, when his eye was taken by someone walking along the pedestrianised lane outside. As soon as the face was there, it was gone and he was left with a glimpse of a profile and a sudden jerk of recognition.

'See what I mean,' the therapist said.

He looked blankly at the woman sitting opposite him, not quite understanding what she had said. Some unacknowledged part of him had realised that her way of looking at him was not the 'come on' he had first imagined, but more a critical appraisal. This was a challenge he wasn't prepared to take on.

'Excuse me,' he said abruptly, as he got up and walked to the open door of the bar. He looked up the road in the direction the woman had walked but there was no sign of her. He went up to the next junction, but again he could not see her. There was an uneasy sensation in his chest, an odd mix of excitement and apprehension. Could it really have been the Indian girl and if it had been her, what did it mean? Surely this was too big a coincidence? But, then again, maybe he was mistaken. He returned to his chair to find, much to his relief, that the woman had gone. Too clever for her own good, he thought, as his eyes scanned the room again.

*   *   *

'We have a name,' he told Miranda Goodheart. 'Habiba Popals. But we don't have a motive. And, for the time being at least, we don't have an address.'

'But this is spectacularly quick,' enthused the director. Giacomo was less sure and expressed it by shrugging his shoulders.

'Up to a point. We have no absolute proof that this is the same woman who took the painting. And, if it is, we have no idea why a woman, a Muslim woman at that, should have stolen it.'

'Do you mean that it is a surprise that a woman might have committed the crime, or that a Muslim should have committed the crime, or that a Muslim woman should have committed the crime?' Miranda Goodheart asked mischievously.

'Well,' he said, acknowledging the blind alley he had led himself into, 'I suppose I mean all three. I have never known a woman steal a picture before, at least not from a gallery. Secondly, why would a Muslim steal a picture of Christ?'

'To destroy it?'

'She could have done that without going to all this fuss and got away without being detected,' he added quickly. 'But a Muslim woman comes to the National Gallery and plans the removal of a very specific picture from under our noses and gets away with it. I have to say, for the moment, I am flummoxed.'

And there's another one of those words, thought the director. Where on earth did this Italian get flummoxed from?

'I'll let you know,' he told her, 'as soon as we have an address for this Habiba Popals.'

Gaicomo Baldini spent the rest of the morning in the terracotta tomb, as he now described his office, preparing an outline submission for a complete review of security at the National Gallery. From time to time his mind wandered back to the tall Asian girl and her motives. Was she acting by herself or were there others involved in the elaborate abduction of the painting? If she wasn't doing it for money, what other motive would there be for the theft? He was distracted, and when he looked back at his computer, he saw that he had written the previous sentence in Italian. The room was pressing in on him and he needed space to think, so he pushed the laptop away and went for a walk around the collections. Each day the pictures became more familiar to him and he now saw them as his own, part of his charge, as if he was a nursery assistant left with other people's children for the day. He paused and sat down in one of the larger rooms and scanned the pictures around him. What a different world he had created for himself, he thought. There weren't many, if any, of his contemporaries who had achieved his level of success. You might have been an olive farmer, he told himself, but instead you are sitting in front of a Rembrandt worth, shall we say conservatively, one hundred million pounds, and it is yours to protect on behalf of the world. He walked on and only a tiny part of him felt uneasy about the casual dismissal of his past.

By the time he had completed his tour, an idea had arisen in him which caused him to speed up his return to the terracotta tomb. As soon as he got there he called the control room.

'Listen,' he said to the duty officer. 'I know we keep the CCTV recordings for a certain length of time. But what happens to them then?'

'I'm not completely sure, but I think they go to secure storage somewhere.'

'Well, can you be sure for me, please. And if we have them in storage, could you let me know how far back they go? Let me know one way or the other as soon as you can.'

It was a hunch, but an important part of him believed that if the picture of the anguished Christ had been stolen by the girl in the hijab, she would have been in before. When, and how, might give him the clues he was seeking. It would be a mammoth task, and maybe a complete waste of time. In fact, he would be asking for time to be compressed, fast forwarded, so that he could see everyone who had viewed the small painting by Antonello da Messina.

Half an hour later it was confirmed that the recordings were kept in secure storage off the Tottenham Court Road. He called Colin Tyler and outlined his plan.

'I'm only interested in the output of Room 5 and I want it split into years. So we'll go backwards, year by year from now and see what it reveals. Split the task between the team. You know who we're looking for. It may be a wild goose chase, but . . . '

' . . . but you never know.'

And there it was again, the strange feeling of excitement, the sense that there was more to this investigation than he could see and that it would lead him down paths that he couldn't now imagine.

Chapter 20

At times she became so low that she shut the door on the world and so it was that cold morning at the beginning of her third year at St Martin's. She didn't want to see anyone and inside the four walls of her living room in Shepherd's Bush she felt, if not safe, then able to limit the times when she might have to expose herself. The day before she had been driven back from a party somewhere on the south coast, a weekend of noise and shrieking company where, with her other outrageously dressed friends, she had given the impression that the world was at her feet and that she was in her pomp. On the way back in the open-topped sports car, they had been snapping pictures of themselves, their heads thrown back as the wind tugged their hair and clothing. Now, holding one of the photographs in her hand, she felt the desolation surround her, not so much the corollary of joy that appeared to be in the picture, but its necessary conclusion. It was always like this, the desperate need to block out followed by the misery of failure. She pinned the picture to a board next to her easel and for the rest of the morning made small steps to various piles of papers in her small room, returning to the board to pin them up. From her chest of drawers she took some items of clothing and cut them into pieces, attaching patterned sections to the accumulation of items in front of her. She worked in silence, the hours floating past her unnoticed, the days coming and going. During the course of almost a week, six days, many hours, thousands of minutes and countless seconds, she was after defining just a moment. She looked at the photograph of herself, her head thrown back and her long scarf blowing behind her. She looked at her teeth between her parted lips and her wide eyes staring upwards. She registered her gaunt face and her hands gripping the back of the seat in front of her. Speed had blurred the background and the road to her right. She was travelling at speed, oblivious to her surroundings, her eyes fixed somewhere distant.

She began with the photograph, recreating its outlines on the canvas in front of her, accentuating the lines of her face as if somehow the wind had elongated and distorted her. Part of the scarf which billowed behind her she painted, another part became a fragment of the scarf itself, one blending with the other. Day by day the collage grew, sections from letters, corners of discarded artwork, pieces from old newspapers and photographs, slowly producing a whole. As the week disappeared around her, so her body began to ache and her eyes narrow, but she remained oblivious of the pain. She did not stop to admire her work, to stand back and take in its development. She continued relentlessly, building up the whole rather as a house martin would build its nest under the eaves of a house, instinctively adding tiny pieces until it was complete. By the sixth day she was exhausted and she sank back into the sofa and fell into a deep sleep. When she woke it was dark and she lay there, her body throbbing, trying to recall a time when she was free of pain, free of the demons that seemed to march towards her in solid ranks to jab and torment her. She was afraid to turn on the light, to look at the work she had created. It stood there in the dark, beyond her vision but tumbling around in her imagination, the fragments free floating in a wild jumble of disconnected images.

She sat up and felt for the light. She stood and looked at the painting for what appeared to her the first time. She stared hard at the wild aggregation of paint and material, her eyes taking in the dramatic representation of a moment in her life. She remained motionless, transfixed by what she had done, pierced by its accuracy, its unflinching portrait of what she had become. She suddenly sat down, as if her legs had been cut from underneath her and continued to look at the picture. She saw only too clearly that it was Habiba Popals, but she didn't recognise herself.

She went into the kitchen and made herself a cup of coffee, returning to her seat on the sofa in front of the collage. She held the warm cup in her hands, turning it slowly round and round. Only much later, when it was cold, did she drink it.

Chapter 21

She remembered that moment now as she sat on a low wall in the cold morning air, warming her hands around a polystyrene cup of coffee, watching Sean Dunmore's day begin. She wore a black ski jacket, with the hood up and the position she had taken was slightly further back from the doorway she had stood in the day before. From her vantage point, she could see him wander around his flat, occasionally coming to the big window and looking out, first in a dressing gown, then in a suit, then with a mug in his hand. Finally, he emerged from the main entrance to the flats, not looking behind him as the door slowly closed and locked. He had the purposeful walk of someone going to work and it was easy to track him at a distance as he followed what she assumed was his familiar route. He joined the bustle of the main street, threading his way with confidence through the steady stream of people all walking quickly and silently to their destinations. She was aware of being in a street of unremittingly bleak buildings, their stone façades stained by the passage of time. The front of the Gallery of Modern Art had the same forbidding appearance, muscular columns supporting a giant pediment almost threatening in its scale. She followed him up the stairs, but hesitated halfway up, realising the museum was not yet open and that she would be exposing herself if she continued to the top. It dawned on her that he had swapped a big gallery in London for a smaller one in Glasgow. In the instant she wondered why, she knew the answer and for the first time she realised that she probably wasn't the first or only woman that Sean Dunmore had assaulted. The smart young man who had just disappeared between the giant columns was an animal whose spoors had perhaps been discovered, driving him to new hunting grounds. She knew that she should not enter the museum for, in the process of trying to remember everything about those few days four years earlier, she had concluded that Sean Dunmore had been watching her in the gallery. He knew which paintings she had looked at and, although she couldn't be certain, she imagined him tracking her on the CCTV screens, playing with her image, zooming in, taking advantage of her. The thought made her feel vulnerable all over again and although the day was warming up, she shrugged herself deeper into her jacket.

Once again she was waiting, as she had been, she decided, ever since it happened. It had taken her a long time to understand, though, that the unfinished business inside her could not be ignored indefinitely and that, sooner or later, it demanded action. It never really crossed her mind to question the way she had chosen to do it, for in the beginning her course of action had been driven by instinct and a bizarre logic that she only half-understood. She sat in a café opposite the gallery, happy to continue the process of waiting, almost enjoying not being able to define exactly what was going to happen next. Now that she was so close to him, the anger, which she had expected to bubble up and explode uncontrollably, was converted into something much colder and more potent. It was three hours before he emerged again and she watched him pause at the top of the steps, raising his head to the sky and the weak sun which had just broken free of the clouds. He slung his jacket over his shoulder and crossed the road towards her. Alarmed, she thought he might be coming to the café, but he turned away and she followed him for a few minutes until he entered a pub on the corner of a nearby side street. From outside, she watched him go to the bar and, a moment later, take his drink further into the pub and out of her vision. For a second she was caught, for she had only half-thought through the next part of her strategy and whichever option she took involved a risk. Keeping away from the windows of the pub, she made sure that there was a second entrance to the pub around the corner. Having done so, she took the smoke canister from the inside pocket of her ski jacket, one of the batch she had bought on the Internet a month ago. Doubling back on the other side of the road, she approached the entrance that Sean Dunmore had used a few minutes earlier. She waited until she could follow a couple of other pedestrians and as she passed the doorway she pulled the pin from the canister and dropped it in the entrance, red smoke instantly gushing into the space. Casually, she continued on to the other entrance and walked in to find everyone was staring at the billowing cloud of red smoke. Sean Dunmore, his back to her, was standing, his jacket hung across the back of the chair by his side. Her decision was immediate and unpremeditated as, using both hands at the same time, she felt in his pockets for his keys. In just seconds she was walking away and, once around the next corner, running towards her hotel, the adrenalin lifting her feet from the ground, her heart pumping. She retrieved the carry case from behind the wardrobe and made her way to the apartment. Even if Sean Dunmore had discovered immediately that he had lost his keys, she doubted he would have returned to his flat, so she reckoned she had perhaps two, maybe three, hours to accomplish what she had to do. Plenty of time.

There were several keys on the ring and Habiba fumbled her way through them, her task made more difficult by the fine leather gloves she was wearing, until she found the correct one for the outside door. Habiba felt vulnerable standing alone outside the flats and suddenly the possibility of having come this far only to fail began to dawn on her. Even when she was inside, in front of the door to his apartment, the apprehension lingered. She took a deep breath and turned the key and stepped inside. The very smell that greeted her was an affront, a mix of male aromas that she fought hard not to identify. Sean Dunmore's presence was palpable, an animal who had left his lair but whose smell lingered as a warning.

The entrance opened on to a small lobby, with a bathroom to her left, a series of cupboards to her right and, directly ahead, the opening through to the living space and kitchen. The mug was on a glass table by the window, standing on a plate with a half-eaten piece of toast. A stained wine glass lay on its side by the leather sofa. A framed film poster hung alongside the wide-screen television; otherwise the walls were bare. There were no books, or flowers and in the bedroom the bed was unmade. Sean Dunmore may have been fastidious about his appearance, but not about that of his home. She sat on the sofa and looked around, acclimatising herself to this anodyne environment. She saw the men's magazines on a shelf under the glass coffee table, the top one showing a model dressed as a scuba diver, her wet-suit unzipped and the three-pronged harpoon held upright by her side. She placed the artist's case on top of the table, blocking the image, and removed the wooden box before carefully lifting out the painting. What sacrilege, she thought, that it should end up here in a room so devoid of spirituality. But the sacrifice was as deliberate as it was temporary.

Taking the picture by its frame, Habiba walked around the room, here and there holding it against the white walls. Then she took down the film poster, keeping the stare of Uma Thurman at arm's length, before resting it against the kitchen units. In its place she hung the painting, Christ's face looking away from the dark void of the television screen. From the artist's carry case she fished out a small digital camera, before moving the case and placing it against the film poster behind the kitchen counter. Standing in the entrance to the room, she set the camera on 'movie'. Holding it steady in front of her, she began recording a slow panning shot of the room, the painting of Christ slowly entering frame and then departing a few seconds later, before the camera came to rest. She replayed the footage and then repeated the process the other way. She then took down the painting and stored it once again in the shallow wooden box, putting the poster back in its original position. Flexing her fingers in the gloves, she then returned to the lobby and began looking in the cupboards. It was perhaps not surprising that Sean Dunmore's untidiness had spread to his storage spaces: a chaos of odds and ends, a broken iron, old telephone directories, empty paint tins, muddy trainers, a rowing machine tipped on its nose. She chose the bottom left-hand corner of the upright cupboard, almost as tall as she was. The tape which had held the box to the wall in London was still sticky and bending down she removed several items from the cupboard before carefully fixing the box on to the wall. She piled the removed items in front of it and shut the door. She lifted out the final object in the artist's case and held it in her hand. Opening one of the overhead cupboards, she tossed it in. Before leaving, she caught a reflection of herself in the cabinet above the lavatory and some impulse made her step forward and open the mirrored door. Inside, there were two shelves. The lower one was lined with a jumble of men's toiletries, aftershave lotions, shaving creams and deodorants. On the upper shelf was a neat line of small white boxes marked Rohypnol. Although Habiba had never seen the name before, she knew what they contained and the eyes that stared back at her when she shut the door were cold and focused. She let herself out of the flat, pushing the keys through the letterbox after her and heard them land softly on the doormat.

*   *   *

It took a surprisingly long time for the penny to drop.

The billowing red smoke brought the fire brigade, several police cars and the obligatory evacuation, but the incident was over almost before it had begun. An act of gratuitous vandalism, they were told, and the episode united those who had been drinking in the pub. The manager offered them a drink on the house and they stayed on, bemoaning the youth of today. Back at the gallery, it was almost five o'clock before Sean Dunmore realised that the keys were not in his pocket and his first thought was that he had somehow lost them in all the excitement at the pub. He popped back in on his way home, but nothing had been handed in. He groaned as he calculated what a call-out locksmith would cost, but he realised that he had no option. At half-past six, instead of sitting in the wine bar enjoying the throng of young women on a Friday night, he was standing watching a locksmith break into his flat with remarkable ease.

As he stepped into the flat, he kicked the keys on the doormat.

'You lucky bastard,' the locksmith said to him. 'You must have left them in the lock or dropped them just outside. Kind neighbours you have.'

Sean Dunmore stood above his keys, looking down at the bundle at his feet. He was desperately trying to repeat in his head the physical act of leaving his home that morning. Could he be certain that he had put the keys back in his pocket? What exactly had he done? It was an action he had repeated so often that he did it without thinking.

'Saved you a lot, anyway, mate. It's just the call-out charge. Maybe you had a bit of a night the day before. The number of times I've seen hangovers cause this sort of thing.'

Sean Dunmore was glad to see the back of the chatty locksmith and he lay down on the sofa, kicking off his shoes and putting his stockinged feet on the glass table. He thought of the red smoke rolling towards him in the pub and as he did another thought began to drift and form in his mind. He tried to fix it, but like catching smoke, it eluded him. He got up and poured himself a drink and resumed his slouched position on the sofa, the glass resting on his stomach.

'It couldn't be,' he said quietly to himself.

Whatever process the mind uses to sift connections, whatever mix of chemicals and electrical impulses and stimuli it takes to draw the correct conclusions, now offered Sean Dunmore the answer. It came to him as if through a red mist and although the three items of memory were presented to him separately, they all made one conclusion. The smoke grenades, he recalled, were used in the National Gallery theft; the image of the girl he had seen in the street yesterday was probably the Indian who had loved the stolen painting; and the loss of his keys: surely they were all linked. He couldn't see them in isolation any longer. They were combining to tell him something and what he was hearing he didn't like.

Chapter 22

Habiba Popals, child of Tooting Bec, in the Borough of Wandsworth, in the noisy, dirty suburbs of south London, excelled at what she did. Even before she graduated from St Martin's she had been headhunted and several companies were tracking her progress, offering her incentives to join them after she left. The excellence of her work was clear for all to see, easily surpassing that of most of her contemporaries who, instead of feeling competitive or jealous, merely accepted the comfort of knowing they couldn't match her pre-eminence. Habiba's skills bridged several traditions and in each she showed uncanny ability, whether it was fine art, or computer-aided design, or sculpture, and she produced a line of work which was astonishing in its quality and diversity. Habiba knew that her parents would not have exulted in her success, so their absence was not so much a loss as a relief, for she was freed from having to explain the direction her life had taken. Habiba wrapped her autonomy around her like a steel cloak, answerable to herself and no one else. In artistic terms, she was not influenced by current fashion, or by the work of her fellow students, but the private dialogues she had with herself were vigorous and critical. She created a fortress of excellence and her work was there for all to see, shining, brilliant, beguiling. Habiba was wanted and she could choose where to share her skills. This part was easy, but the steel shroud worked in other ways as well. Her success isolated her, as success often does, and, in the beginning, this suited and complemented her state of mind, allowing it to remain unchallenged. The closer she came to leaving St Martin's, though, the more she began to realise that her very success was allowing her to ignore other messages that her body was occasionally sending her, shapeless doubts rolling in like cold mists and depressing her brittle good humour. She would try and swat these away, delve more deeply into her work, feign indifference and soldier on. She had no need to use this strategy after she had seen Uncle Badsha, for her anger and dismissal of what he had told her merely served to send her scuttling back to her fortress of indignation.

This situation remained the same until the midwinter of her final year at St Martin's, when events conspired to unsettle Habiba and bring her face to face with many of the demons she had so fastidiously stored away and ignored. In the September of that year, Sharifa had called to tell her she was pregnant. The news had reverberated with Habiba and initially blurred her responses.

'Aren't you pleased for me?' Sharifa had asked, detecting the hesitation in her friend's response to the news.

'Of course I am, Sharifa. I was just wondering what was going to happen to your career as a lawyer.'

'On, you're so old-fashioned, Habs. What makes you think I can't be a mother and a brilliant advocate?'

At this moment Habiba did not trust her response, for she realised in a rush that if she couldn't be certain of her feelings towards her own emotions, how could she answer her friend honestly. There were too many sedimentary layers on top of her base feelings, disguising what she really felt and until these had been cleared away her reactions would be unreliable.

'I'm thrilled for you, Sharifa, of course I am. It's just that, from where I am at the moment, it's a position I can't imagine.' And, in this statement, Habiba was being perfectly honest, for her imagination could not embrace what it would be like to have the responsibility of a child and a new life.

When, five months later she saw the newborn child for the first time, it was worse. Sharifa had given birth to a boy and she had invited Habiba to her home to see the new arrival. Habiba had been excited at the prospect and had chosen to ignore the faint shadow of apprehension that accompanied her to the house of her friend. It was a cold day at the end of January, the sort of day when it is hard to even imagine sitting in the warm sun again. The icy wind had found its way into her gloves and under her ski jacket and when she first saw the tiny child in her friend's arms she was overwhelmed by its vulnerability.

'Meet Rafi,' Sharifa said, offering the tiny bundle to her friend. Habiba hesitated before accepting the precious cargo.

'Hello, Rafi,' she said, looking down into the tiny face and the two eyes which seemed to be looking up directly into hers. She tried to say more, but the swell of emotion which rose unexpectedly within her, prevented further speech. She turned her body so that Sharifa was unable to see her face. A tear splashed onto the forehead of the baby and trickled into the wisps of dark hair which erupted in surprising profusion from his head. Habiba was doing all she could to contain her emotions, trying to breathe deeply through her nose and pushing her head back in an attempt to stop further tears from falling. She was failing and her silence and the fixed set of her shoulders were observed by Sharifa.

'Are you OK, Habiba?'

It was a simple question, but the care it conveyed, the gentle way it was spoken, broke Habiba's resolve and she began to cry, her body shaking around the cradled child. It is not unusual for new-born babies to engender tears, but Habiba's reaction was the release of so much more than the expression of tears of joy. Somehow, the baby was allowing her to cry for a different agenda and although Habiba didn't recognise this at first, on her journey home the truth began to dawn on her. This was the first time she had cried in a long time and the exhaustion she was ex-periencing was disproportionate to the happy event she had just experienced. The vulnerable child had triggered a visceral response in her and she hugged her bruised body and slumped lower down in the seat of the bus. This was not the Habiba that had won all the prizes, the Habiba that was being courted by design firms, the Habiba admired by her contemporaries, but a damaged and limping Habiba, seeking the refuge of home to lick her wounds and regroup. She was living in a flat in Shepherd's Bush and in the small ground-floor flat of a terraced house, within earshot of the tube, she lay on her bed and curled up, attempting to shut out the world. Her mind, though, had been freed by the emotion and began to play over the topography of her current life. She was wise enough to know that her emotional reaction to the baby was disproportionate and that it had offered her a chance to express herself about other, unacknowledged anxieties. In amongst the tumble of thoughts which came and went, were the stories that Badsha had told her. When she had heard about Anam, Noreen, Kiran and Jamila she hadn't recognised them as real people, but as dry-as-dust remnants of history. Now, having seen the baby, it was as if the new life had given her a path to those other lives, so that they became new as well. Tiny Rafi had made her realise that her line of relatives had, too, been like him, vulnerable and at the mercy of the world. She wept again and her sobbing mixed with the clatter of the tube heading westwards as the day drew to a close.

Later, when it was dark and her room was lit by night lights, Habiba sat cross-legged on the bed, calmer and clearer. The room was a perfect reflection of herself, neat and ordered and beautiful. Looking back at her, on the wall directly in front, was the portrait she had painted of herself, the wind blowing her hair back from her head, the grey silk scarf flowing in the same direction. It mocked her. It was an illusion, a lie, a mere pretence of reality, a Pied Piper whose intention was to lead the viewer away from what was really happening. The flickering light served to emphasise the confusion it represented, a skilful, alluring and powerful image, but nevertheless a clever pastiche of the truth. She picked up the phone.

'I wanted to apologise,' she told Badsha.

'And why would that be?' he replied, kindly, the calmness of his voice again sponsoring a tearfulness in her, just as Sharifa's had earlier.

'I didn't let you finish telling me about my family. I think it was Jamila you got to as I decided to leave.' It was the first time she had ever called her mother by her first name.

Badsha was somewhat taken aback by this turn of affairs for, however much he had promised Latif that he would tell his daughter the outline of the family story, Habiba's reaction in the restaurant had convinced him to wait indefinitely before finishing what he had to relay. Perhaps, though, the anonymity of the telephone might help if he took this opportunity given by Habiba to talk further.

'Sadly, Habiba, you did not have the chance to know your mother better. She was too desperately young to die and I know how much you would have benefited having her around as a buffer against your father, no matter how well-meaning he was.'

Habiba's memory of her mother was generic, sprinkled with specific moments which she recalled with great clarity. In many ways, she had been more traditional than her husband, never venturing outside unless she was covered and deferring to him in nearly all matters. Habiba had been ten years old when she died and looking back on it now, she wasn't sure if her recollections were about what her mother was actually like, or what Habiba wanted her to be. Did Habiba imagine that her mother understood the difficulties facing her daughter in England, caught between two cultures? Or was that the ideal mother she had created in her mind? And had she imagined that Jamila Popals was a beautiful woman whose looks were so often hidden behind a burka or shrouded by her hijab? Was it true that her mother had once told her that the future rested with Habiba and that it was important that she be loyal to herself? Or was that what she wished her mother had said to her?

'Are you there, Habiba?'

'I'm sorry, Uncle Badsha. I was thinking of my mother and wondering how many of my memories were accurate.'

'What is the overall impression you have of her, Habiba, the feeling you are left with?'

The question was obviously a prelude to learning something new about her mother and at first Habiba didn't know how to respond.

'I suppose I thought she was a very kind woman, traditional, too traditional, perhaps, but with an awareness of change, even if she couldn't have followed it herself.'

'She was all those things,' Badsha replied and Habiba could hear him preparing for what was to come next.

'She was all those things,' he repeated, 'and more. Her upbringing was rural and to arrive in London when she was barely out of her teens was a massive change. I never heard her once complain, even though, as I discovered later, there was plenty of cause for her to do so.'

'What do you mean?' Habiba asked, aware that there was something unspoken in what Badsha had just said.

'Jamila was sent to this country to marry your father, as I told you in the restaurant. It was an arranged marriage by remote control, from a distance of many miles.' He waited and Habiba could hear the atmosphere on the line, a faint buzz which may have been electronic, or his distant, low breathing.

'What you didn't know, don't know, was that it was a bad marriage, another bad marriage. Your father came from a fiercely orthodox family whose father ruled with a rod of iron. Latif was the elder of two sons who were born about twelve years apart. They lived in the same village as your mother's family and Kiran, your grandmother, knew them well.'

Habiba could hear the discomfort creep into Badsha's narrative, as if he was approaching a dangerous set of rapids which he wasn't sure how to navigate.

'When your father came to this country, the dynamics of the family changed and his brother, Ali, became suddenly more important. He lived nearby and, like his brother, he had never married. This was a pressure on their mother for she wanted to see them settled.' Badsha gave a small cough before continuing.

'Jamila was a beautiful young woman, both physically and as a person. It was Ali who first paid his attentions to your mother and he did this far beyond the eyes of his father, who would have been furious if he had known that he had made any gesture at all to any woman, let alone a neighbour like Jamila, still living at home. Ali knew that Jamila used to take her young brother to the banks of a nearby stream where, when the waters flowed, he would play in the pools and when it was dry, climb the boulders that over the years had been washed down. Ali would engineer meetings with Jamila on these visits and it was during one of these that it happened.'

Habiba listened, trying to imagine the encounter and wondering what was to come next.

'They had been discreetly talking, when there was a loud explosion. Jamila knew instinctively that it was her brother Salman and she rushed to find him.' He paused and she heard his slow intake of breath. 'He had picked up some shell, or mine, that had probably been washed down river in a previous storm. He had died instantly. She told me that he had been blown almost in half, although his head and torso were almost perfect. It does not bear thinking about, what your mother must have gone through. She lost her brother, but so much more than his blood seeped away from her that day.'

Habiba was holding the phone to her ear and shielding the side of her face with the other hand as if not wishing to see the picture Badsha had just described.

'She blamed herself until the day she died. She believed that she had been judged for talking to your father's brother, for stepping over a proscribed line. For merely talking to him, her life changed

165

forever. It all came out, of course, and the solution seemed obvious to everyone, even your mother. The dishonour was too great and she was sacrificed, sent to this country to marry your father, Ali's brother. It was a bizarre equation, a terrible logic.'

It was almost too much for Habiba to take in, for a considerable part of her was still fighting this overwhelming pressure of her past which demanded her attention like a spoilt child. But now she saw her mother differently and imagined her carrying around the memory of her mutilated brother and blaming herself always for what happened. She felt angry on her mother's behalf, at the unfairness of life and at what she had had to cope with.

'How much of all this did my father know?'

'Oh, all of it. That his young brother had made inappropriate advances to Jamila, during which Salman had died and that the local council had decided that a deal had to be organised between the families. It was awful. Your father believed he was being offered a woman who had been soiled and she, your mother, the penance of an older man for her sins. In some ways, if you'll excuse me saying it, Habiba, it is a wonder you were born. This, truly, was a bad marriage.'

Habiba's anger had strengthened. 'And so my father decided to take it out on me, to make me the scapegoat for his predicament.'

'I think he was frightened, Habiba. He wanted to protect you and that was the only way he knew how.'

'And my mother? Who was there to protect her?'

Badsha remained silent on the phone, as though weighing what he said next.

'I would have preferred to have told you this to your face, Habiba, but since we have started on the phone, I will tell you now. Ali continued to be in touch with your mother, although he never saw her again. He would write to me and I would show her his letters. I'm afraid to say, your father never knew this.'

'What would he have done if he had found out?'

Again there was silence.

'He would have killed her,' Badsha said eventually.

There seemed no way to end this conversation, so Habiba looked at the phone and turned it off and lay back on her bed. The ceiling danced with the reflections from the night lights and the tubes continued to rumble in and out of the station. There was too much to take in now and the information settled on her stomach like a bad meal. When sleep eventually came it arrived in its worst form, laden with images which, several hours later, caused her to wake in fear. The night lights were out and only the faint aroma of smoke lingered in the room.

Chapter 23

It was surprising how few people stopped to look at Messina's tiny portrait of Christ. In a gallery of towering canvases, its size made it insignificant and, day after day, people filed past without giving it a second glance. No longer was it a focus of devotion, public or private, although it was certainly the centre of attention of Giacomo Baldini. Overnight, he had felt slightly ill at ease about ordering such an extensive review of the CCTV coverage of the painting in Room 5 and his anxiety increased when it revealed very little from the current year.

'We do pick the girl up a few days before the theft and she appears to be sketching, or copying the painting. But it's nothing more or less than we might expect if, indeed, it was her that went on to do the job. She seems innocent enough, though,' one of his team told him.

He watched the sequences and Habiba Popals, wearing a hijab and scarf, appeared to be just another student of art engrossed in a project. It was difficult, if not impossible, to deduce from what they were watching that the project in question was the stealing of a picture from the collection.

'I want you to keep going back,' he encouraged. 'We have to find another connection between this woman and the picture. It's boring, gentlemen, I know, but please continue.'

Why he thought he would find the answer amongst a mass of digital imagery and not at the meeting he was about to have in his office, he couldn't really say, but the hunch remained strong in him. Colin Tyler was already sitting at the table in his office when he arrived.

'I've been with the anti-terrorist people all morning and they've run traces on both names, Habiba Popals and Anmar Ma'ab

Qadr without anything showing. They're somewhat astounded that we haven't got a complete image of her yet. The half-face we've been able to show them was universally rubbished. They were pretty sceptical that she's involved in a group but they readily accept that she might be what they called "part of the lunatic fringe" who want to show their devotion to the cause of Islam in their own particular way.'

'And we've got no reason to believe she wasn't,' Giacomo told him, 'although a little voice tells me that this is about something else that we've yet to discover.'

'Do you think we should release our picture of her, such as it is, to the press? Surely someone will know Habiba Popals?' Colin Tyler asked.

Unconsciously, Giacomo tapped his pencil against the wooden table and the irregular sounds it made might have been a message in Morse code. Why was he resistant to this very reasonable course of action? Someone would surely come forward with a photograph of the woman and details of her background. His mother would say, when she was faced with a decision, that her body would tell her what to do and right now his body felt uneasy at the thought of going public about Habiba Popals. There was a hinterland to this theft which remained hidden to him and which contained elements that might trip him up if he released what they knew about her.

'I would like to leave it for now,' he said to the policeman, who showed neither surprise nor disappointment. 'I don't feel confident that we have the right information to splash her name and face, even the little we have, all over the place. I may change my mind later.'

Giacomo Baldini was thinking about the dog he had had as a child, a cream-and-ginger pointer who would follow at his heels between the olives. One winter, when they were out hunting, he went missing and as the weeks went by there was no sign of him. When his father suggested going to the market to buy a replacement puppy, Giacomo had been alerted by a feeling inside him that the dog was still alive. He could remember the moment now, the certainty that to replace him would have been inappropriate and incorrect. A few days later the dog reappeared as if out of nowhere, his coat dusty and snagged with burrs but otherwise unharmed. Where he had been remained a mystery, but his arrival confirmed the accuracy of Giacomo's instincts. His body had been correct, just as he felt it was now.

'Give me until this time tomorrow,' he told Colin.

The memory of the dog, insignificant as it was, stayed with Giacomo and it triggered other thoughts about his days at home. He had been nineteen at the time and caught in a traditional struggle with his parents, who wanted him to take over the farm and the olive presses. Unusually for those parts, he was an only child and his reluctance to follow the family tradition seemed all the more shocking.

'Generations of Baldinis have built up this business, have farmed these hills,' his father told him.

'Your decision will kill him,' his mother implored at another time.

Was it merely the pressure to follow tradition that he had rebelled against, or was it driven by a more positive force? His father, whose hands and arms were the colour of the brown earth and whose face reflected and matched the lines and fissures in the dry land, was as much a part of the landscape as his ancient olive trees. From as early as he could remember, Giacomo had wanted a different environment and the occasional visits he had with his parents to the larger cities of the north excited him so much that he felt deflated when they returned to the farm. Now he was in London again, a city whose boundaries he barely knew, whose size dwarfed any city in Italy and he knew that the very anonymity of the place, the feeling that he could be himself here without observation, gave him great comfort.

His thoughts were interrupted by the ring of his mobile. It was one of the team looking through the old footage of Room 5.

'I've been looking at stuff from some four years ago, August that summer. I've found her again and a bit more besides. I think you should come and have a look.'

Suddenly Giacomo Baldini was back in the here and now, the dusty hillsides of his youth replaced by the sophisticated machinery in one of the finest museums in the world. In the control room he was presented with a close-up image of a girl with large eyes, dark hair and two flattened curls in front of her ears.

'Good heavens,' he said, under his breath. And, then, a little louder, 'it could be her.'

'Well, watch this,' the security officer said, switching to a different sequence. 'This is the day before, about the same time.' There was the girl again, only this time the camera was only offering a wide shot. 'I wouldn't have spotted this without the close-up the following day. Now watch.' Giacomo watched as the girl stood motionless in front of the painting for several minutes. At normal speed, she seemed to be there for an age and then, very slowly, she moved towards the painting until she was less than an arm's length away. And again she remained still, transfixed by what she saw in front of her. In all, she spent almost thirty minutes around the painting.

'Now, I'll take you forward to the next day again,' said the officer, cutting up the close-up image of the girl. 'Let me take you to the moment she arrives in Room 5.' He shuttled back the pictures and they watched as the girl reversed her progress to the open doorway to the room. He then played the footage at normal speed and the camera followed her in close-up to the painting.

'It's almost as if she was expected,' Giacomo said.

'That's what I thought,' the other man said. 'Now look at day three of the sequence.' And here again the girl appeared, this time the camera taking in the whole of her body.

'She looks quite different today,' Giacomo commented. 'As if she's dressed up to go out somewhere smart.' Her slim legs carried her once again without fail to the face of Christ.

'It's what the picture was for in the first place,' Giacomo said, having done his homework on the Messina. 'Devotion. And she certainly looks devoted. And rather pretty,' he said, as an after-thought. The image of the girl was paused and she was smiling, her tall body resting on one hip, the heel of one foot tucked into the instep of the other like a ballet dancer, her head cocked to one side. 'Beautiful, almost. Unusually striking, anyway. That's certainly what whoever was in charge of this room thought. Of all the people passing through Room 5, he certainly only had eyes for this one.'

'Maybe when he saw her get close to the picture on the first day, he worried that she might get too close the next time,' volunteered the officer.

'Perhaps. What happens the day after?'

'We don't see her again after that. It's just those three days in August.'

'Three days in a row suggests she might have been with a party, one of those study groups. Can we find out?'

'Sure.'

'Oh, and another thing. Can we pull out all the CCTV coverage for those three days. You've made things much easier for us. Thanks. Can you wait a moment? *Andare a passo di gambero,*' Giacomo Baldini said under his breath.

'I'm sorry, I missed that,' the security officer said.

'It's an Italian expression which means "to go forward like a crayfish, or shrimp". I think you say "to take one step forward and two steps back".'

And this is just how Giacomo Baldini felt. The more he learnt about the strange woman, the less he knew. The footage con-firmed the girl's unusual interest in the painting and it had given them a proper image of her, but it didn't explain why she might, four years later, have decided to steal it. The conundrum that faced him that morning was still waiting for an answer: should he release this clear image of the girl, or not? And still his body resisted the decision. He called the director's office and asked if she might come down to the control room. She rarely ventured into this part of her empire and when she arrived she appeared genuinely thrilled when she stepped into its dark interior.

Giacomo offered her a seat. 'Habiba Popals,' he said, pointing at the girl's face on the screen. 'It seems she became very interested in the Messina four years ago. Have a look.' The relevant sections of the recordings over the three days were shown to Miranda Goodheart.

'I see what you mean,' she said. 'She seems totally engrossed in the painting. It's like she fell in love with it. I think you suggested something similar in my office. In some ways, I'm not surprised because I have always thought that Messina had painted a very modern-looking man. You know, that unshaven look. And she's a good-looking girl, isn't she? Can I look at the close-ups again, please?'

Each of the monitors showed a different image of Habiba Popals from different angles, her long face, her proud nose and fierce eyes, the wide mouth and white teeth.

'Do we normally film our visitors in such vivid close-up?' asked the director. 'This is a positive screen test.'

Television tells us what to expect visually, so at first it didn't strike Giacomo as unusual that Habiba Popals had been filmed in such detail. It was the way she would have appeared in a television drama, or a Bollywood film. But for routine CCTV coverage of a museum, this wasn't normal and as this dawned on him he began to glimpse the new shape this case might take, one with sinister possibilities, at least for the gallery.

'I wonder if we can find out who the duty officer in this room was for those days in August four years ago? He might be able to help us.'

As if to round off his thoughts, the director, still looking at the girl, said, 'Why would such a good-looking woman want to commit a crime like this? It doesn't seem to make sense.'

Would an ugly woman have been more likely to steal the painting, he wondered, but he kept the thought to himself.

'Exactly,' echoed Giacomo Baldini instead. 'And that's why we won't be releasing her name or her picture until we know why.' He left the room and the frozen images of Habiba Popals, smiling and alive, went with him.

Chapter 24

There were two journeys that Habiba Popals took that early summer's day. The first was taking her at high speed across the rolling French countryside towards Paris. The second was gathering momentum inside her, a series of ideas which were gradually forming a shape that she recognised. It was some two weeks after her late-night telephone conversation with Badsha and the beautiful, sun-filled day lit up the French countryside in vivid detail. Habiba was changing, although she would have been hard put to define exactly how. In the simplest of terms, she was travelling in the opposite direction of a butterfly, in the process of discarding the bright, colourful clothing she had worn for the past four years, for something plainer, more pragmatic, which better reflected who she was and how she was feeling. It was a reverse metamorphosis. The trip to Paris she saw as the final act of the first part of her life and the place in which to launch the second.

From the Gard du Nord, she walked down the wide boulevards to the centre of Paris and the Seine. She crossed the geometric gardens of the Tuileries and took the Pont Royal to the Left Bank and the Musée d'Orsay. She imagined she was taking the last steps of her childhood as she entered the wonderfully ornate front of the one-time railway station. There was something deeply symbolic about Habiba's visit to Paris and there was nothing subtle about its purpose. Habiba had come to see *The Origin of the World* and if this was the ultimate act of rebellion against everything her parents had stood for, she did it now with no trace of anger. It was almost impossible to imagine the great hall filled with steam and the clamour of travellers and she crossed the marble floors in reverent silence towards the picture that had long fascinated her.

She stood staring at the mass of pubic hair between her splayed legs, the shape of her vagina emerging from the dark tangle, her nipples barely covered by the sheet, her face completely hidden. For her mother and father, this would have been the ultimate affront and it was impossible to imagine that they would ever have been able to stand in front of the picture, as she did now. There was a challenging lack of modesty about the woman who appeared to be showing herself both as an act of defiance and as a sign of indifference. This was the origin of the world and she was in charge of it, able to flaunt it when she chose to. Unexpectedly, the painting made Habiba think sexually for the first time in ages, encouraged by the apparently wanton freedom of the other woman in the painting. Courbet's picture represented the ultimate opposite of the proscribed life that her father had administered to her and from the moment Habiba had learned about this picture, she had wanted to see it. Now here it was, in the flesh. In her dark grey linen suit and black ballet pumps, she stood before it and admired the freedom it represented and knew that this was available to her as well. It wasn't the brazenness of the gesture, or the simple exposure of her body, but the fact that it was her decision to show herself in this way. It was in her gift, under her control. Despite its explicitness, what it represented in sexual terms was the exact opposite of what had happened to Habiba that summer four years ago. Then, she had been assaulted and something had been taken from her against her will. She had not been given the choice of the woman in the painting, the decision to expose herself dashed from her, ripped away and discarded. It was an act of vandalism that she could not and would not accept. The painting was a way of gently shutting the door on the past and an opening to the future. It represented the abandonment of her anger about her father and an impetus towards the resolution of what she had deliberately chosen to ignore over the previous years. The painting had restored and reassured her and she nodded a small acknowledgement towards the spreadeagled legs before turning away to leave the museum.

To begin with her mind was blank and it merely received the images she was being presented with as she walked slowly along the river towards Notre-Dame, crossing over to the Île de la Cité and then again to the Île St Louis. A process, though, was taking place behind the immediate sensations of the Paris views, a computer-like assemblage of logic which crackled away some distance beyond her conscious mind. She was in Paris for the day and it had already served one purpose. Before she boarded the train back, it would have helped formulate another. She walked up into the Marais, sauntering in front of the old-fashioned windows displaying fine stationery and wooden boxes of beautiful crayons. She sat on the curb of a raised pavement and knew that, despite the understated glories of the streets all around her, she wanted to be somewhere else. This brief invasion of the capital had served its purpose. She stood and looked into the window of the shop behind her, which contained an array of frames, some empty and others with pictures. And it was then, at the corner of rue Charlemagne and the rue St Paul, the component parts of the idea washed over her, missing details here and there but, nevertheless, complete. It seized her whole body, suffused it and filled every crevice. It was as if, like the woman in Courbet's painting, she had been given the freedom of unilateral action, of doing what she wanted without the approval of someone else. She continued walking northwards and the maze of narrow streets that made up this part of Paris, remained largely unseen by her. They were merely funnels for her thoughts and the accumulation of her ideas was kept in place and bounded by the ancient buildings of the 4th arrondissement. The more she assembled the plan, the more logical it became and, since she was her own council, she approved wholeheartedly the course of action that was being proposed.

For the first time in four years, Habiba Popals was facing in a different direction. Was it merely the passage of time that had turned her round, or the information she had received from Badsha? Would she have ultimately arrived at this state of thinking herself? She undid the tiny round of Camembert and poured herself a plastic beaker of red wine from the small bottle. The train had just begun the return journey and the woman it was carrying back had been transformed in the space of a day. Although the metamorphosis had been gestating for some time, in the gap between the two journeys Habiba Popals had stopped being a woman controlled by elements of her past. Now her sights were set on a specific goal in the future and she felt quite calm about what she had in mind. She sat and watched the suburbs of Paris scoot by, the graffiti-clad walls and the cheap apartments, cheek by jowl by the track. The sky was vivid pink as the sun dipped beyond the motorway to her left, a fluid line of cars silhouetted against the western sky. She sipped a little of the red wine and her tongue slowly licked her upper lip, like a lizard taking in the last of the sun. Beautiful and composed, if any man had chosen this moment to sit by her side and attempt conversation, he would have been put off by the look on her face, her mouth set in unsmiling determination and her eyes steadfast and unforgiving. This was a Habiba hardened over four years and suddenly aware of her power. On the journey, her mind repeated the plan over and over again, checking for weaknesses like a tongue seeks the jagged edge of a broken tooth. It was perfect in the simplicity of its purpose, its execution part of the journey of retribution. She, Habiba, had to work at getting the assault out of her system, a process of ridding herself of the guilt and doubt which had come afterwards. What she was about to embark upon was a pilgrimage, the route clear, the outcome uncertain.

She was leaving one picture in Paris for another in London. The face of Christ, which had so arrested her in the beginning, was at the centre of her attention. In her innocence back then, she had fallen for his beguiling looks and, when her defences were down, she had been lured into something altogether evil, which she could still only barely comprehend. She knew, though, that the picture would be the central part of her revenge and it would be given by a woman whose naivety had been replaced by a different wisdom and whose sense of purpose was unshakeable.

It was later that evening that Habiba wore a hijab for the first time in many years. It framed her distinctive features, emphasising the unusual shape of her face. She stared back at herself in the mirror and imagined her father seeing her now, demure and traditional, all traces of femininity suppressed. He would assume that Uncle Badsha had made her see the error of her ways, the history of the women in the family fair warning not to transgress. She could see him standing behind her now, nodding approval, his arms folded and his face for once joining in and matching his permanently smiling eyes. How wrong he would have been, she thought, as she added a further scarf, sweeping it around her face so that her nose and mouth were hidden.

'No, Father,' she said to the mirror. 'This is not for Anam, Noreen and Kiran and not even for my own mother, Jamila. This is for me, Habiba Popals. For that is who I am.' She now tied a red scarf, like a bandana, under the hijab, so that she had three layers of protection. She dropped her head so that her eyes looked directly back at her, clear and unblinking, the only part of her face visible. She held her own gaze, but there was nothing questioning in the cool eyes, merely a calculated certainty.

In the course of the following week, she scoured the Internet and spoke to estate agents until she found the flat in Whitcomb Street. She was wearing the hijab when she met the agent and she watched the sour expression on his face as they agreed the deal. Was it merely the colour of her skin, or her partially hidden features, or both?

She left her flat in Shepherd's Bush and moved in a few days later. She sat in the living room and looked at the great blank western wall looming across her windows and at the cameras mounted on the corners. Not for an instant did her resolve falter and she never doubted the justness of her cause, nor the wisdom of its purpose. In some ways it seemed preordained, but it was only much later that she gave this thought any real credibility.

The following week, wearing the same outfit that she had tried on in front of the mirror, she returned to the National Gallery for the first time since the events of four summers ago. The rain was sweeping across the broad pavement in front of the building and the wind carried the spray from the fountains towards groups of unwary pedestrians. Now the two parts of her life, so forcibly kept apart, were closing together and for the first time in four years, she felt in charge of her own life.

She entered the doors with no fear but with all her senses alert. This was the beginning, the first stage in taking control and she left the pretence of the previous four years behind as she stepped into the building. Like an animal, she was coming back to a place that she knew, scenting familiar territory but, unlike before, she was aware of everything around her. She knew now that she was being watched, that her every movement would be tracked, but this time she was one step ahead, she had grown. A different Habiba Popals walked between the masterpieces. The entrance to the National Gallery was a portal to the next stage in her life, although Habiba did not consider what this might be like. In fact, she deliberately chose not to, concentrating solely on what was directly ahead of her. Had she known what would unfold over the following months, she would have smiled and shaken her head.

PART TWO

One Life

Chapter 25

He lay on the sofa, the remote control in his hand, the television reflecting on his face in the darkened room, dancing shapes over and around his eyes. There were no curtains in Sean Dunmore's living room and he enjoyed watching the late-night cavorting on the screen, knowing that he couldn't be seen and that he was above everyone else. He surfed between the porn channels, searching for the right ingredients to satisfy his hunger that night. The television was also reflected in the big window, flaunting the images that it projected into the night. He flicked away from a blonde woman with a well-endowed white male, to a couple of women alone in a bedroom, stripping for one another with pantomime exaggeration. Moving on again, he paused for a moment longer, to take in the woman masturbating, her face contorted in what he thought was faked pleasure, until he arrived at a scene which seemed to match what he had in his mind. A black girl, wearing a short leather skirt and a tight white T-shirt, was alone in a house. She wandered from room to room, stopping at a succession of mirrors to adjust her clothing. A ring at the door brought another black girl, similarly dressed, and a scenario he had watched a thousand times, in one form or another, began again. He wondered whether he preferred dark flesh, the more accentuated curves of the black girls, the larger arses, the bigger breasts. He had been trying to distract himself from thinking about the Indian girl, but the sight of the dark nipples in huge close-up once again resurrected her image and he immediately pointed the control at the television. The pictures were extinguished but his mind continued to circle around the tall Indian girl he had known briefly four years ago.

The spill of light from the city was now defining his body as he lounged along the black leather sofa. He saw himself as a bird of prey, returning to this room, his nest, perched above everyone. From here he felt he could survey all those around him, unseen. In one of the men's magazines he'd bought he had seen an article about the golden eagle and he had liked the image of the great bird, standing at the centre of his nest, looking down over a distant valley, a predator, imperious and untouchable. He stood in the window and watched the frosted outline of a figure in a bathroom in one of the flats opposite and below him. To his left, a line of bright red brake lights defined the main road and to his right, the inky waters of the Clyde picked up the occasional flickers of yellow from the banks. Sean Dunmore had a natural instinct for danger, a highly developed sense of cunning which, over the years, had served him well and kept him clear of trouble. He was now weighing up what to do first about the Indian girl. His logical mind had arrived at a conclusion which, contrary to the evidence he was being presented with, he didn't believe. A painting is stolen from the National Gallery, the very picture that he'd seen the Indian girl so obsessed by. Part of the modus operandi was the use of smoke grenades to disguise the theft and, a few days later, he thinks he sees the Indian girl and is then involved in an incident with a smoke bomb in a pub. And, to add to the mix of events, he loses his keys. Earlier, when he got into the flat with the help of the locksmith, he didn't at first think to find out if anything was missing. It was only later that it dawned on him that the Indian girl might have taken the keys and he quickly searched the flat. It was evident that nothing was missing, which brought him full circle and to question once again the improbable scenario. Why construct such an elaborate plot? What if he had been mistaken and the girl had been someone else and the smoke bomb merely an odd coincidence? That animal part of Sean Dunmore that was always alert, though, wasn't convinced.

Sean Dunmore recognised that he had to keep ahead of himself. The pattern of behaviour that now accompanied the taking out of a girl was gradually becoming more extreme and demanded that he cover his traces even more carefully. The Japanese student, for example, had been more difficult than he expected but, then again, the pleasure had been that much greater. She had come to see the new exhibition of installation art and he had picked her up under a series of figures hanging from the ceiling like deformed stalactites. He had followed the same routine and the seduction, as he liked to call it, had taken place further along the Clyde towards Govan, amongst the ruins of what had been a shipyard. She was barely conscious by the time he had driven her there and it had infuriated him that she did not put up more of a battle when he began to play with her. He lifted her short tartan skirt and she appeared not to notice. Her breasts were tiny and when he undid her tight, orange-checked shirt, she offered no resistance. Was it worth it, for this flat-chested child? He slapped her hard across the face and it was only when she began to come to her senses, that he became aroused. She tried to keep his hand away from the tops of her legs but she wasn't strong enough and as he inched his fingers forward his excitement increased. He hit her again, as he came, and he registered the twin satisfaction. She was still drugged and he took her back into Glasgow and left her outside one of the big bars where, even in the dead of winter, girls went out drinking with flimsy dresses and high heels, often to end up vomiting in the gutter outside. The Japanese girl was no different to any of them, good for only one thing. Even if she went to the police, which he doubted she would, his story was watertight. He had taken her to have a drink and left her early in the evening to return home. That she'd had too much to drink was her fault. The drug would quickly dissipate in her system and all trace would be gone by the following day.

His thinking came back to the Indian girl and he felt a familiar stirring at the thought that she, too, might be offering him resistance. He imagined taking her again and the idea of hitting her across the face, striking her hard in punishment for making his life difficult, filled his mind. She needed to be taught a lesson and he began to work on how he might make this a possibility. Tracking her down shouldn't be difficult, although he had yet to find her name. He wondered if Armpitts's secretary still worked at the gallery. She'd been a pretty girl and he was certain that she had found him attractive. Perhaps he could get a name and address from her? The difficult stage would come later, for he would have to work out carefully how he could get close to her again. He laughed, for he could barely remember her face and the only clear memory he had was of her large, dark nipples which, even as he stood looking out of his apartment years later, he could recall, profiled against the window of the car as he ran his hands roughly over them.

It was then that his senses were alerted to another possibility and one that posed real danger. If he was looking for her, so would the police and this fellow Baldini at the gallery. He was faced with the decision that confronted him as soon as he had seen the photograph of the painting in the newspaper. Should he pre-empt everything and go directly to the Italian and tell him of the connection? If they caught up with the girl, what would she accuse him of? She couldn't prove assault or rape, but it might be messy and he would rather not risk this course of action. No, he had to find the girl first and then, one way or the other, make sure that she didn't speak to the authorities about him. His argument was circular, for it brought him back to his original question: why should the Indian girl have gone to such elaborate lengths to get her own back on him?

The following morning, as he took his coffee break, he called the gallery in London and asked for Dr Ruth Pitts' secretary.

'Hello,' he said. 'This is Sean Dunmore, from the Gallery of Modern Art in Glasgow. Is that who I think it is?' He had forgotten her name and he hoped that it was the same girl he remembered.

'Oh, hello, Sean,' she said enthusiastically. 'This is Diana. Gosh, it seems ages since you were here.'

'Well, it is getting on for three years, Diana, but I remember you clearly. How is Dr Pitts?'

'Oh, she's fine,' the secretary said, enjoying the flattery, 'although she's in a bit of a spin about this theft.'

'I read about that,' Sean said. 'Wouldn't have happened in my day.'

They both laughed and Sean chose the moment to pose the question.

'Listen, I need your help. We're trying to put together a database of schools and contacts in London who might consider it worth their while coming up to Glasgow on study groups, like you do down there. We're keen that it should be representative, you know, diverse, and I remember a particular party that Ruth showed round a few summers ago, not long before I left. Any chance you could give me a list?'

To the PA, this seemed a particularly harmless request and she promised to e-mail him details of the groups and schools that her boss had looked after that summer. An hour later, the list came through. There were only two parties that August and the first was a mixed group of boys and girls which he dismissed. The other group came from an all-girls' private school in Wandsworth. The names of the six girls who took part were listed and he was able to eliminate four of them immediately since their names seemed too English. He was left with Sharifa Khan and Habiba Popals. He stared at the two names and for a moment was stuck, his eyes resting on each as if expecting a clue to somehow emerge from the strange combinations. But this is what Sean Dunmore liked, the tracking down and pursuit of a woman. It was no different from sitting in the control room at the gallery, his eyes scanning the floors until they came to rest on an anonymous girl. Then the slow zoom-in, the getting closer until, in the end, they were drawn right into his net.

He sat back at his desk and put himself in her position, arriving in Glasgow to look for him. He was certain she would have come by train and he made the assumption, as he imagined the police would, that she stayed in a hotel. He Googled Glasgow hotels and made a list of those within the proximity of the station. He started with the cheapest and worked upwards, asking if he could speak to a Habiba Popals or her friend Sharifa Khan who he believed were staying at the hotel. It was logical and pains-taking, the phone equivalent of a fingertip search, tedious and apparently futile until the moment of discovery. The list of ticks against hotel names became longer and Sean Dunmore's lunch break was extending beyond the hour when his weary slouch suddenly changed and he sat forward, hunched over the phone.

'We don't have a Sharifa Khan,' a voice told him. 'But a Habiba Popals checked out earlier today.'

Habiba Popals. He had a name and she had come to find him. The realisation slowly sank in and it made him look up and around him as if he expected her to be there, standing over him. The vague concern that he had felt earlier had now spread through his body, a sensation that was an uncomfortable mix of excitement and fear. He stood and walked into the main collection, passing between the installations until he came to the strange figures hanging from the ceiling. Why he should have done this, he didn't know, but somehow, under the jumbled collection of limbs and torsos he was able to think and a calmness descended on him. He had a name and now he would find her. Quietly, he spoke the two words, using the same pronunciation as the Glaswegian receptionist.

'Habiba Popals.'

Chapter 26

'What's in a name?'

Habiba Popals' name was ringed at the centre of his lined pad and he spoke her name quietly to himself. He remembered what the director had said in the control room. 'Why would a beautiful woman want to steal the painting?' He wished, now, that he had replied, 'Are you suggesting only ugly women can be thieves?' but it wouldn't have seemed right at the time. He had a printout of her face alongside the pad, taken from a freeze-frame from the digital footage. He had chosen it himself, an instant when she had turned and appeared to be looking up at the camera, her eyes wide and caught slightly at an angle, so that the whites were more pronounced against the dark pupils. Her mouth was slightly open and the white of her teeth seemed to complement that of her eyes. Only one of the scimitar curls was visible, hooking down along her jaw line. Her look was inquisitive, almost demanding a response and Giacomo Baldini held it in both hands and the look from her eyes seemed to go straight through him to a place he barely knew existed. He put the photograph down and turned to her name on his pad. From this, Giacomo Baldini had drawn another line at the end of which was an empty circle. Into this he placed a query. He had a location, the control room, but not a name and, as was his habit, his pencil continued to tap on the empty box leaving a pattern of grey dots. Was there an axis, he wondered, between Habiba Popals and whoever was in the room? Could the theft of the precious painting have been an inside job and, if so, how? He entertained the thought for a moment, allowing the possibility to exist, testing it to see whether it held water. It sank almost instantly. Why wait four years between a recce and the job and why would a young girl – she appeared to be no more than twenty – want to steal the picture in the first place? The fact remained, though, that she came back to the gallery, to the same picture, and stole it. What was her motive? The box with the query was now a dark grey balloon, a doodle that accurately reflected the state of Giacomo Baldini's thinking. It was as if Habiba Popals had been watching him throughout this process, her eyes and the slight smile on her face, almost mocking him.

'Habiba Popals,' he repeated. 'What's in a name?' Over the next few hours he was to find out. First came the arrival of Colin Tyler, the policeman holding a sheet of paper with yet more names.

'A strict rota of staff using the control room didn't exist in those days,' he explained, 'but only certain people were allowed in there and this is the list.' There were seven names on the paper that joined the other two sheets laid on Giacomo Baldini's desk, three neat rectangles that represented the state of their thinking. Three of the names were staff who had been sifting through the CCTV footage and both men believed they could be discounted.

'What about Brian McMasters?' asked the Italian.

'Why not?' the policeman responded.

Both men looked at each other, each trying to work out in what ways the ex-head of security might have been able to engineer the theft of the picture.

'He was retiring, somewhat weary with the years he had spent here. Perhaps he wanted one final pay day, Jack?'

Baldini was already shaking his head. 'I can't see it,' he said. 'He could have removed that painting without all the palaver that went with it. He had special access and keys to all the security systems.'

'He might have wanted it to appear that way, Jack. The girl was maybe a decoy to take our attention away from him. Perhaps he's put the picture away in a secure vault somewhere. He would certainly know a few villains who would buy it for a knock-down price. It's a possibility.'

Baldini nodded, accepting the validity of his colleague's remarks. 'What of the other names?'

'We've been chasing those up,' the policeman said. 'One of them, sadly, has died. She had to leave last year on doctor's orders and the other went to work in New Zealand. Which leaves us with Sean Dunmore.'

'Tell me about him.'

'Very capable and extremely good at his job but he was only here for about eighteen months.'

'Why did he leave?'

'He was offered a better job in Glasgow.'

Giacomo Baldini looked up. 'Does that seem likely?'

'Well, he's got the equivalent of your job at the Gallery of Modern Art up there.'

'And that's a big place, is it?'

'Not really, but at least he's in charge, if you know what I mean?' Colin Tyler smiled as he said this.

Giacomo Baldini was tapping his pencil again. 'It doesn't seem a very long time to stay at this place, does it? What was he like, this Sean Dunmore?'

'Good-looking boy, quite pleased with himself, obsessed with all the gadgetry here and full of good ideas on how to improve security. He was a fellow traveller with you. Believed we needed airport-style protection here and that some sort of incident was inevitable.'

'He was right there, then, wasn't he? Could he have master-minded this with the girl? If he knew the systems here so well, he would have known what was possible.'

The second incident which was to bring him closer to Habiba Popals came with the ring of his phone and the somewhat excited voice of Dr Ruth Pitts.

'I've just seen something rather extraordinary,' she said, 'and I don't know what to make of it.'

'Go on,' encouraged the Italian.

'Well, I'm not really up to speed with some aspects of the web, but I was doing some further research on the Messina when I saw a link to YouTube, which, I must say, I didn't know much about. It was under the title "Devoted to Messina?" I had a look and I think you should too. I was going to forward you the link, but I thought you'd like to see it with me.'

A few moments later the two men gathered around Ruth Pitts' computer. Her arms were wheeling as she repeated how she'd come across the piece of video she was about to show and they waited patiently for her to access the link.

'Now watch,' she ordered, 'and tell me what you make of this.'

She clicked on 'play' and enlarged the small box to full screen. The quality wasn't good and at first it appeared to be nothing more than the interior of a modern flat. Even when the painting came into view, neither man registered it at first and it was only when Ruth Pitts pressed 'pause' that their focus moved to the picture on the wall.

'It can't be the painting, can it?' Colin Tyler said disbelievingly. 'Isn't it the photograph from the newspaper pinned up?'

'No,' answered Ruth Pitts, animating the footage. 'You will see that the frame is three-dimensional. See, it casts a shadow as the camera moves round.' She replayed the short sequence.

'And it is unlikely,' added Giacomo Baldini, 'that there would be a second, identical fake, in existence. We have the original fake here. By default, then, this must be the original painting.'

Ruth Pitts turned to look at him, as did the DI.

'We were clearly meant to see this. It's as I thought. There is more to this than we are seeing. So we need to know, in this order, where the footage was shot, by whom – although I think we can guess who that might be – and where she uploaded it from. Does the site give us any clues?'

'I'll get on to YouTube,' Colin Tyler offered.

'Yes,' said Giacomo Baldini distractedly, as another thought began to take hold.

'We are being led to the painting in a very deliberate way. The picture is a means to an end and we have to find out what that is.'

Back in his office, the three rectangles of paper were still lined up on his desk reminding him of the link between the control room and Habiba Popals.

'What's in a name?' he said, yet again, drawing another line from Habiba Popals' name and creating another circle, alongside the one he'd filled with grey dots earlier. Into this he wrote Sean Dunmore and, after the name, a query. He then called the Gallery of Modern Art in Glasgow and, explaining who he was, asked to be put through to the head of security.

'Mr Dunmore is not in today,' his PA told him. 'He phoned in earlier to say that he'd been unexpectedly called away on business.'

Giacomo asked for his mobile number and an address where he could be contacted.

'I'm sorry, but because of this protection of data business, I'm not able to give out these details.'

And then she heard him ask what seemed to her a very strange question. 'Do you happen to know if he lives in a modern flat, with a large flat-screen television?'

'I'm not really sure what you mean,' she said uncertainly. Giacomo waited.

'Yes, he does live in a new block of flats,' she said finally and it was clear she was going to give no more details.

Moments later, he called again and spoke to the director of the museum and explained why he needed urgently to contact Sean Dunmore. He didn't tell him the full story, merely that he needed the skills and information that Sean Dunmore had to help find the missing Messina painting.

Under the bubble containing Sean Dunmore's name, Giacomo Baldini now wrote the address before picking up the phone to speak to Colin Tyler.

'Meet me down in Room 5.'

Giacomo Baldini was standing in the corner where the Messina portrait had once hung. In its place there was another small religious picture, but he wasn't looking at it. His eyes roamed around the room, taking in the position of the camera high on the far wall and he imagined the two Habiba Popals, the one who first saw the portrait of Christ and who had stood just where he was now, enthralled, and the second, who came here with her face wrapped and hidden. Something had happened to turn one Habiba Popals into the other and, as he stared back across the room to the camera that was recording his movements, he felt curiously protective of the tall girl with the proud features.

Colin Tyler interrupted his thoughts. 'The YouTube footage was uploaded from an Internet café in . . . '

Baldini finished his sentence ' . . . Glasgow.'

The policeman nodded. 'And we have the name of the woman who placed it.'

'Let me guess,' said the Italian, again interrupting his colleague. 'Anmar Ma'ab Qadr.'

Colin Tyler smiled in surprise.

'I think we're going to be making a journey to Glasgow, don't you?'

With this, he handed the policeman the piece of paper with his doodles. It took Colin Tyler a few seconds to realise what he was being asked to read and by the time he found Sean Dunmore's name with the address underneath, Giacomo Baldini was on the other side of the room.

Later, as the train pulled out of King's Cross and disappeared into the tunnel under the Regent's Canal on its long journey north, Giacomo Baldini placed the image of Habiba Popals on the table in front of him, spreading his hand across her face to flatten the paper.

'What do you think, Colin? Why would this woman,' he gestured at the picture in front of him, 'why would she want to lead us to the painting, for that is surely what she is doing?'

'Maybe it has nothing to do with us, but someone else. We're just pawns in the game.'

Giacomo Baldini nodded in agreement. As the train emerged from the tunnel and began to gather speed another train flashed by in the other direction, the squeal of its brakes indicating its approach to the terminus. On board, Habiba Popals wrapped her scarf around her face and took the artist's carry case down from the overhead rack. It was empty.

Chapter 27

It quickly dawned on Sean Dunmore that he had moved from being hunter to hunted. The predator was now prey and with it came the uncomfortable sensation of being followed, perhaps even watched. Without being able to comprehend the whole picture, he was cunning enough to realise that he had little time to spare. Habiba Popals was a loose cannon and he had to trace her quickly. He still found it hard to believe that she had involved him in a plot as complex as stealing a picture from the National Gallery, but he wasn't going to waste time trying to fathom her motives.

It was eight o'clock on a grey Glasgow morning and, looking at his watch, he gave himself until midday to find her address. He sat at his computer and if he hadn't felt so concerned, he might have enjoyed the next few hours as he become the pursuer once again. He had followed this path before, tracking down individuals and if his mood had been different, he would have laughed at a society which was able to champion data protection alongside freedom of information. He entered the labyrinthine world of the Internet with confidence, clicking through the gates and layers towards the information he sought. Sean Dunmore loved the impersonal world of the Internet, where nothing is sacred. He wove his way through the chuntering search engines, sifting through the electoral register and details of community charge payments. His work had taught him the new language of investigation but it was his insatiable desire to observe others undetected which honed his skills. To Sean Dunmore, guilt and shame were words in a foreign language and he fed on the private lives of others.

It didn't take him long to find the old address in Tooting Bec, where she had been living when he first encountered her. It had been her father's house but it was the next address that interested him, for six months later Habiba Popals had moved to Shepherd's Bush. He made a note of the details and then, after a call to directory enquiries, he had her land-line number. He phoned but there was no reply. Using the information he had gathered, further enquiries to the mobile phone service providers enabled him to track down her mobile number. It was barely ten o'clock and he felt he was within touching distance of the tall Indian. His highly developed instinct for self-preservation was giving him two apparently conflicting messages, one stressing caution, the other, speed. In the former column he deduced that Habiba Popals would not have used her Shepherd's Bush address as the base for the robbery. And, for the moment anyway, he was not sure what he would say to her if he called her mobile. In the other column, though, he heard the distant feet of other pursuers for, as sure as the sun sets in the west, she would be followed up here to Glasgow.

'Think. Think,' he ordered himself, glancing at his watch and telling himself he still had two of his allotted hours left in the pursuit of the whereabouts of Habiba Popals. He put himself in her position. What would he have done if he had been planning to steal a painting from the National Gallery? He snorted at the thought, shaking his head in disbelief. He sat on the edge of the leather sofa and looked out of the window from which he could just see the flagpole which topped the strange, columned dome of the building where he worked. Would Habiba have taken a flat like this, near the National Gallery? He got up and pressed his face against the glass, feeling its cold against his skin. If so, would the details of her address have already been fed through to any of the existing databases he had been exploring? He doubted it. He returned to the computer, leaving a smear of saliva in the centre of the window, and quickly brought up the names of letting agents for WC2. He groaned at the number and another quick glimpse at his watch told him that time was fast running away from him. He was quite blatant.

'My name is Sean Dunmore,' he began. 'I am part of the investigating team looking into the recent theft of the painting from the National Gallery. We are trying to locate a woman called Habiba Popals who may have rented a property nearby. She might not have used that name, but perhaps a similar, Indian name.'

He was systematic and relentless, ticking off the names on his list as the hands of his watch turned closer to midday. He had arbitrarily chosen the deadline, but his internal detectors were already registering alarm. It was important that he maintained his methodical approach and continue working down the list with the same calmness and, at seven minutes to midday, his patience was rewarded.

'Bopals, you say?'

'No, Popals, with a P.'

'Yup,' the voice told him. 'Habiba Popals, took a flat in Whitcomb Street a couple of weeks ago. And only yesterday she gave us notice on it. What's she been up to, then?'

'Probably nothing,' Sean Dunmore lied, watching the sweep of his second hand. The news made it even more crucial that he got down to London as soon as possible. 'Would it be possible to meet at the flat? Final thing today? It is of the utmost importance and we really would be very grateful.'

No persuasion was necessary. By chance, Sean Dunmore had spoken to the agent who had done the deal with Habiba Popals and he was only too intrigued to discover what the mysterious and rather strange Indian might have done. It would quite liven up his afternoon.

Sean Dunmore packed a bag with the odd certainty that when and if he returned to the apartment, his life would not be the same. His stood in the middle of the room and looked around him as the bell of the nearby church began to chime. By the end of the twelve strokes, Sean Dunmore was pushing open the main entrance to his block and making for the station.

* * *

On the wide concourse of Glasgow Central Station, where each year thirty-four million passengers cross the pale stone floor under the modern latticework of white girders, Giacomo Bandini and Colin Tyler passed within a few metres of the man they had come to see. The train that had brought them north was being prepared for the return journey, which would take Sean Dunmore to London. If, at that moment, the two men were lagging behind the unfolding events, by the end of the afternoon they would have caught up, although their discovery would present them with a new and more pressing problem.

From the train, DI Tyler had spoken to colleagues in the Glasgow police and obtained a warrant for the search of Sean Dunmore's flat. Both men had made the assumption that he wouldn't be there and on the train northwards Giacomo Baldini had outlined why.

'Either she's an extraordinarily arrogant and confident woman who is deliberately leading us on a wild goose chase while she disappears with Sean Dunmore and the picture, or,' and he hesitated before continuing, 'or she has a score to settle with Sean Dunmore and wants us to be part of the dance.'

'What sort of score?' the policeman asked.

'What would you think, Colin?' said the Italian, looking across to his colleague. 'Why would a woman want to take revenge on a man?'

'A woman scorned?' he answered. 'She went out with him and was then dumped?'

'Possible, but it seems a bit of an over-reaction, doesn't it? No, I still think something else happened to this young girl.'

He pointed at the picture on the table, his finger on Habiba Popals' forehead as she continued to stare up at him as she had throughout the journey. He tried calling Sean Dunmore's mobile, but it was constantly engaged. He wondered where he was and what he was doing.

The colour of the buildings in Glasgow seemed to intensify the gloom of the day and although it was only just past midday, it felt as though an early dusk had already arrived. They picked up the warrant from Strathclyde police and continued on foot to Sean Dunmore's address in the company of a sergeant who was more than just a pathfinder. There was no response from the external buzzer, so they rang several others before finding someone who would let them in. They stood outside his flat and knocked on the door but the silence was no more than Giacomo Baldini had expected. He nodded at the sergeant who took a bunch of keys from his pocket and began to work at the two locks. Before the three men entered the apartment, they each stretched on pale latex gloves.

Seconds after stepping inside, they knew the picture wasn't on the wall. Giacomo Baldini walked forward and peered at the place where it should have been, taking hold of the film poster and putting it down by the sofa.

'She hung it here,' he said, almost to himself. 'She wanted to lead us here.' He looked around the room, taking it in for the first time.

'Jack.' Colin Tyler was standing in the kitchen area, his gloved hand on the kettle. 'It's still warm.' The faint aroma of toast hung in the air.

In the bedroom, the bed was unmade and a wardrobe door hung open.

'I think he may not be long gone,' the DI said.

'Right,' agreed Baldini. 'We need to systematically search this place. It's not big, so it shouldn't take long. I think we know what we might be looking for.'

They began in the living room and kitchen, pulling open drawers, removing pans, taking the cushions off the sofa, checking every space in or behind which something might have been concealed. Colin Tyler moved into the hallway and was standing on a chair looking into the cupboards above the door.

'Jack,' he called. 'Take a look at this.'

Colin Tyler stepped off the chair and Baldini took his place. The smoke canister was at the back of the cupboard and he carefully lifted it out and examined it.

'It's the same as the type we picked up in the gallery,' he said. 'This one is red.'

From his position on top of the chair, he looked around the small lobby. 'I wonder what else we are going to find.'

They both knew to what he was referring and as they continued to search a feeling of excitement began to grip Giacomo Baldini. It wasn't so much the anticipation of finding the painting, more the sensation of being part of an elaborate and unusual story, the end of which he couldn't predict.

He opened the broom cupboard to the right of the front door and began to remove the untidy jumble piece by piece. Even when he had taken out most of the junk, he almost missed it. It looked like a fuse box, or even a container for hanging keys. It was only the grey colour that made it stand out and immediately Giacomo Baldini could see the grey walls of the gallery and, in his mind's eye, the rectangular box fixed innocently on the bridge.

'It's here, Colin,' he said quietly. 'I think we can assume it's stuck on to the side of the cupboard in the same way it was attached to the wall at the gallery.' He looked back at the policeman. 'And I think we can say with some certainty that the painting will be inside.'

He leaned into the cupboard and, placing his hands at the top and bottom of the wooden box, pulled forward from the top, his bottom hand supporting and pushing into the wall. It came unstuck easily and he carefully lowered it forward, before taking it out of the cupboard. The painting was face down and he gently lifted it out, so the face of Christ slowly appeared.

'Well, I'll be . . . ' Colin Tyler muttered under his breath.

Giacomo Baldini carried the painting through to the living area to place it on the hook where the film poster had hung. The two men stood and looked at the five-hundred-year-old masterpiece.

'Well done, Jack.'

'Yes,' said Giacomo Baldini, 'but we're only halfway there. The painting is found in the cupboard of an ex-employee of the National Gallery, a man who would have known many of the security procedures. And yet . . . '

Christ's eyes were looking upwards to the right, fixed on a spot just beyond the frame and he appeared to be about to speak, his lips slightly parted. It was an unreal moment and the two men stood there in silence, an act of devotion and thanks for the completion of one part of their task.

'Why couldn't he have organised the whole thing?' the detective asked. 'Why shouldn't she have been working for him?'

'Why then would she have posted – if, indeed, it was her – the footage on YouTube? We've been deliberately fed the clues. She's the one in control.'

It troubled Giacomo Baldini that he could already sense that this Habiba Popals was beginning to touch him somewhere he found deeply unsettling. He should have been delighted that the painting had been recovered safely and he should now be setting in motion, along with Colin Tyler, the procedures to secure the site and pursue the investigation. He was, though, hesitating, responding to some voice inside him. Who was this Habiba Popals and why had she created this elaborate dance? With this thought came a faint warning, a distant ringing which told him that even though the painting, in all its miniature glory, hung on the wall in front of him, he was only just at the beginning of a journey. And he wasn't quite sure where it was taking him.

'The question is, Colin. Who will find Habiba Popals first?'

Chapter 28

Habiba had wept on the train, quietly crying in the first-class carriage taking her back to London. These were not the tears she had tried to hide from Sharifa, tears which spoke of desperation and uncertainty. These tears seem to have sprung from nowhere, risen quite naturally, like water from a hillside, seeping out along a spring line and flowing abundantly down her cheeks. She was glad that she was alone and could indulge them, allow them free passage, happy for the moment that they came without reference to their origins. Habiba was aware that she had been expecting them and so it was no surprise that they appeared now, as one part of her strange adventure came to its conclusion. It was only in the physical stillness that followed that she was able to unpick their sources and examine them for the first time. She had slowed down, her breathing deeper and as the countryside swept by and the stations came and went, she felt calmer. She could see herself now, sitting curled up in the corner, her feet on the seat to her side and could acknowledge, for the first time since the death of her father, that she was alone. She was mourning for herself first, a young girl abandoned. With this came the fleeting awareness that she also missed her father who for so long had been the dominant influence in her life. They had been two sides of an arch, and the act of pressing hard against each other had maintained the shape of their relationship. In one way, his death had automatically brought about her own collapse, although she had not been able to see it at the time. She had wept because she could see now that his certainties, although profoundly different, had helped define her own.

The tears, she realised, were also for the girl who had spent almost four years denying the dreadful events of one night. She had deliberately navigated around the consequences of the assault so much so that her life had become distorted and disfigured. She had cried for the girl who'd been pretending, who'd built a carapace to defend herself against the truth and to keep others at bay. Carrying it around had worn her out but if she hadn't quite shed it yet, she was well into the process of discarding it. The tears, then, were for the vulnerability which now followed, bringing with it the awareness that the full confrontation had still to come, the proper balance yet to be put back into her life. The wild sociability of her days at St Martin's had hidden her loneliness and her tears had helped wash away that very necessary pretence. She was more open now for whatever might follow, but this new status came tinged with fear for Habiba Popals had no clear idea of what lay ahead of her.

'Sharifa, it's Habs.'

Habiba had called her friend from the train, needing both to hear her voice and to ask for help.

'I need somewhere to stay for a while,' she asked and the very tone of her voice alerted her friend to Habiba's state.

'Of course,' Sharifa said. 'Rafi has missed you.'

By the time Habiba arrived at King's Cross, her tears had restored her equilibrium and helped reaffirm her next course of action. She took the Northern Line down to Charing Cross and deliberately walked in front of the National Gallery on her way back to the flat. This was neither an act of bravado, nor of flaunting her achievement, but a way of gauging the new perspective which had begun to align itself after the tears. She wondered who would find the painting first. If it was Sean Dunmore, she imagined the confusion that would follow; if it was the police, or this man Giacomo Baldini, she knew that it would cause them to hesitate. Either way, Sean Dunmore's position at the centre of events would be highlighted.

On the way to the flat, she stopped at an Internet café and sent a note to the estate agents giving them notice that she was leaving the flat as from tomorrow, and that her deposit should cover the normal notice period of one month. Afterwards, she went and bought some blank cards and envelopes.

It was strange to be back at the flat, now that its usefulness was over and the small living room smelled stale, even though it had been barely a day since she left with the painting. Perhaps, before, she had been too pre-occupied to notice the faint aroma of damp and decay. The newspaper cutting was still pinned above the fireplace but now the power of the face seemed diminished and she could see the reproduction for what it was, as useless as the paper on which it was printed. She wrote on one of the plain cards and tucked the message into an envelope and placed it, upright, on the mantelshelf beneath the cutting. She looked around the flat one final time, spending a few minutes in the bedroom, before stepping out onto the street and clicking shut this chapter of her life.

Half an hour later she was sitting in Sharifa's living room and the tiny flat in Whitcomb Street was forgotten. She was surrounded by the fresh smells of baking and on her knees she rocked the tiny figure of Rafi under the watchful gaze of her friend.

'So how have you been, Habs?' she asked, without preamble.

'I've been busy,' she replied, burying her nose into the back of the baby's head. 'Busy getting my life back.'

'You might have to explain. The last time you were here, you looked awful.'

'I think you'll find out soon enough,' Habiba said quietly.

Sharifa frowned and looked at her friend. 'How?'

'I can't tell you just yet, Sharifa. Would you mind? I know I am asking a lot, to come and spend some time with you here, but could you wait?'

Sharifa noted the differences in the woman sitting opposite her, the smile on her face as she played with the child, the eyes which had lost their puzzled hurt, and her clothes which no longer shouted her identity. But the fact that Habiba would not confide in her concerned Sharifa.

'What's happened to your flat in Shepherd's Bush?'

The question lay between them and it was moment before Habiba spoke.

'I can't go back there for a while. I will, soon, but for now there is part of me that needs to be hidden. It's not for long. Please understand.' She held up the baby so that he was facing her and the broad smile on her face brought a similar response.

'And, think how much babysitting I will be able to do for you.'

'Are you in trouble, Habiba?'

'I was in trouble, Sharifa, but not any more,' she said simply and, despite the denial that this statement represented, for Habiba it was true.

'Well, you look a lot better,' Sharifa said, but in a way that suggested she had suspicions about her friend's behaviour.

'You could say that I am on the road to recovery, although I still have some way to go. Don't I, Rafi?' The baby looked back at her, his big eyes dark and innocent.

'Rafi's as much in the dark as I am, to tell the truth,' Sharifa said, with a shake of her head. 'Does Badsha know what is going on?'

Habiba looked at her friend and wondered what he would think when the story came out? Would Habiba be seen in the same light as Anam, Noreen and Kiran and her own mother Jamila? Was she the next in a line of doomed and unfortunate women whose destiny was decided by others?

'No, he doesn't, Sharifa. But I don't think he'll be surprised when he knows.'

'Habiba Popals. We can't sit here all night and talk in riddles. Make yourself useful and go and bath my child otherwise we will simply go round and round in circles for ever.'

*   *   *

He was barely twenty-four hours behind Habiba, Sean Dunmore estimated, and his job now was to whittle away at that gap, gradually drawing her closer and closer to him. He was agitated and made several journeys to the buffet car, angrily pulling the tabs off a succession of beers, impatient as the hours of the journey stretched ahead of him. He was looking out of the window, rubbing the small scar on the back of his right hand. He didn't register the scenery, for his mind was attempting to give some logic to the events which were now propelling him towards London. Sean Dunmore hated loose ends and this Habiba Popals was just such and needed to be brought under his control. He took a swig from the can of beer and tried to imagine what power he could assert over her, at how he might frighten her. His mood turned uglier as the train sped southwards for, just as he had sensed as he left his apartment, the damage caused by the Indian might be extensive. Sean Dunmore's childhood was used to only one sort of woman, that represented by his mother, who had protected and cosseted him and would still be wiping the food from his mouth if she had the opportunity. Her son's behaviour was always excusable and she defended him to the point where his father left, realising that he couldn't compete. Sean Dunmore was raised without the normal boundaries of right and wrong. To him, women were there to do his bidding. He remembered the girl next door and how she had started wearing the tight tracksuit bottoms and T-shirts which showed off her breasts. They had both been about fifteen and he used to watch her in the garden from his bedroom window, walking around in that flat-footed way she had, her arse stuck out behind her, her breasts out front. One day, when her parents were at work, he went round to see her. She let him in and took him through to the kitchen where she handed him a Coke. He could remember watching the gap of bare flesh at the base of her back and it seemed perfectly normal to slide his hand down inside and feel the rounds of her bottom. When she pushed him off, he took no notice and continued to help himself to what he assumed she really wanted. Only when she stabbed the back of his hand with a pair of kitchen scissors did he stop, a look of astonishment and anger on his face. Later, when the girl's parents came to complain, his mother berated them for having a daughter who had deliberately led on her son, accusing her of flagrantly trying to seduce him. 'You should just look at the way she dresses,' she yelled at them. 'She's only got one thing in mind, that girl.' There was no mother to defend Sean Dunmore now and to justify his actions but he had already guessed what stand she would have taken. Habiba Popals was a woman scorned, so upset that her son had decided not to continue their relationship that she had taken the unbelievable step of stealing a valuable painting with the intent of trying to implicate him in the theft.

It was only then that a shocking realisation came to him and he jumped to his feet and looked behind him, back along the carriages, desperately hoping that there was some way the train had not left Glasgow Central. 'Damn, damn, damn,' he said under his breath, but loud enough for the passengers on the other side of the aisle to give him a strange look. He suddenly knew, with absolute certainty, that she had left the painting in his apartment. He cursed his own stupidity and, as the panic rose in him, he asked himself just how carefully he had searched the flat the previous evening. And he knew, even as he recalled his movements, that he had been cursory and slapdash and had not fully thought through the situation. Now he was racing the wrong way when he should have been sprinting back home where, he was sure, he would discover that she had deliberately and maliciously hidden the painting. His frustration turned instantly to anger, at himself and at the girl. She was no longer a tall and attractive source of physical pleasure but an object of hatred. He slumped back into his seat as another thought occurred to him to counter his previous logic. Was it him she wanted to discover the painting? The answer was immediate and he sprang to his feet again, so that now his fellow passengers were showing concern at his behaviour. She wanted someone else to find the painting and, just as the earlier thought had arrived with absolute certainty, so now another struck him with the same force. She would lead the National Gallery and the police to his door and no matter what he said, he would be deeply compromised. For all he knew, they were walking around his apartment at this very moment. He looked at his mobile and, for the briefest of seconds, wondered if he should call the gallery, this man Baldini, and pre-empt the situation. Would they assume that he had stolen the picture with her? Surely not. It was best that she remain isolated and that any contact he had with her should be alone and private. Very private.

There were two hours left of the journey, one hundred and twenty minutes for him to play with the idea of what he would do to Habiba Popals when he found her, and find her he would. In his mind she had ceased to be a woman and by the time he arrived at the house in Whitcomb Street to meet the estate agent, she was merely an object in his path that had to be removed. When the man let him into the flat, Sean Dunmore told him curtly to wait outside and he pushed past him into the small living room where he came face to face with the newspaper reproduction of the painting.

'What a bitch,' he said.

And then he noticed the envelope. He opened it carefully, slowly drew out the card and stood looking at the words Anmar Ma'ab Qadr. He shook his head in irritation, flinging the note into the fireplace and turning impatiently to look around the dreary room. He pushed open the door to the bedroom and was taken aback to see what at first he thought was a real baby lying against the pillow on the bed. It was wrapped in a white blanket, its dark eyes staring back at him so that, even after he realised it was only a doll, his heart continued to beat loudly in his chest. The small sash window was darkened by the larger buildings crowding around the tiny terraced house and he remained motionless in the gloom of the interior. Was this another message to him? With a sudden jump of defensive logic, he remembered that he had not penetrated the girl that night and so he couldn't have got her pregnant. When he slammed the bedroom door, the whole house shook and the baby toppled slowly onto its side and a veil of dust was released into the grey light.

* * *

From the train, Giacomo Baldini and Colin Tyler had set in motion the same process that Sean Dunmore had followed to track an address for the young woman whose picture the Italian now carried folded in his jacket pocket. The flat in Shepherd's Bush drew a blank but, using the same logic as Dunmore had earlier, by the time they trundled over the Manchester Ship Canal, they had the address in Whitcomb Street, although the Italian knew it would be empty when they arrived. His fascination with Habiba Popals increased in direct proportion to the merry dance she was leading them. The painting, which they had left behind for forensics to examine, would be returned to the National Gallery in due course, thus completing a strange journey which, he realised, he had watched like a passenger. Since he'd arrived in London, he had had barely a moment to himself, to reflect not only on his new job, but his new life. He was living in a hotel, without his familiar possessions, with no routines and plunged into a strange limbo in the pursuit of the stolen painting. Part of this excited him, for it contrasted so sharply with the ordered succession of events which dominated the lives of his parents and their parents before that, the predictability of the seasons, the specific routines of farming, the comfortable familiarity with the land. They were not part of Giacomo's life now and the strangeness of the journey from Glasgow, the passage of unfamiliar territory outside his window, fed a need in him which he didn't question.

'He's there before us,' Colin Tyler said, breaking into his thoughts. Giacomo frowned.

'Sounds like Dunmore has been to the house already. The estate agent I spoke to tells me he took a fellow round earlier who said he was investigating a theft.'

'And, I imagine,' the Italian added, 'that he found that the girl had been there even before him. Now we just have to make sure that he doesn't get to the next piece of the jigsaw before we do.'

'Where do you think she's gone?'

Giacomo pondered the question, as night began to fall on the heart of England, obscuring the details of the country which, for the moment, he had chosen to adopt. A number of thoughts occurred to him and he placed them in order, as he would do on a desktop. Now that the picture had been recovered, he could simply hand over the operation to the police. He pushed that to one side as he pulled out the picture of the girl and looked at her wide eyes. He imagined releasing this image to the newspapers, knowing that it wouldn't take too long for her to be flushed from wherever she was hiding. However, that course of action seemed illogical to Baldini for it appeared to him that Habiba Popals had been deliberately leading them towards her all along, the painting merely a means to an end. Then a third option came to him, one which he put to the policeman.

'Wherever she's gone, Colin, I rather think we need to find her before Sean Dunmore does. What I would like to do, I think, is release a picture of myself along with the news of the recovery of the painting. This, I hasten to add, has nothing to do with my taking credit for getting it back, but because I want to include a passage which would run something like "Giacomo Baldini and the police are pursuing a particular line of enquiry and would be grateful for any help from the public." At the same time, I want a response posted by the YouTube footage of the picture at Dunmore's flat. It should run something like "Is one's fate the place where the leopard always returns?" And then my mobile number.'

Colin Tyler looked at his companion, not doubting him, but waiting for an explanation.

'The name she leaves behind her undoubtedly means something along the lines I've just said. I want her to come to us, to me, and this is the only way I can think of to make her do it.'

'But you couldn't leave a number, could you?'

'Yes, and for all the people who phone, there is only one name I will be looking for. Anmar Ma'ab Qadr. It will be a password. Anyone who is unable to give me that, we don't bother with.'

It was almost midnight before they got to the house in Whitcomb Street, where they were met by a constable who had earlier picked up the key from an increasingly puzzled agent. The thought that he must have walked past the painting a couple of days ago made Giacomo smile as he climbed the stairs to the first-floor apartment. The smile remained on his face when he saw the newspaper cutting pinned on the wall and widened as he read the three words on the card he retrieved from the fireplace.

Colin called him through to the bedroom where the doll lay face down on the bed.

'The baby who never was,' the policeman said.

'I wonder when she decided not to take it in with her,' Giacomo Baldini added, constructing in his mind the sequence of events which resulted in the doll being left in the flat.

'In hindsight, it was a very good decision,' he added, almost to himself.

He walked over and gently unfolded the blanket which shrouded the doll. It didn't surprise him to find the envelope within the white bundle.

'Do you have your gloves?' he asked the detective, who pulled out of his pockets a ball of white latex. Once he had them on, Giacomo carefully opened the unsealed envelope and took out the note. He looked up at Colin before handing it to him, along with the one he had read earlier.

'Anmar Ma'ab Qadr.'

He smiled. 'Let's do what I suggested,' he said to the detective. 'And let's just hope that she finds us before Sean Dunmore finds her.'

Chapter 29

The darkness that closed around Sean Dunmore was not just the London night, corrupt and incomplete as it was, but a more profound blackness which became increasingly intense as the early hours ticked by and his mind picked over the line of events which led to his lying on a hard bed, in a cheap hotel just off Smithfield Market. He could hear the release of air brakes as the big articulated lorries backed into their slots to unload their carcasses, a jagged symphony of noise which accompanied his insomnia. The hotel, used by drivers who had made the long journey down from Scotland with their cargoes of prized beef and marsh-raised lamb, was nothing more than a dosshouse, its Crittall windows covered by cheap nylon curtains hanging crookedly in the orange glow of the sodium lights. The surroundings suited his mood, stark and ugly and, as he watched the torsos of dead animals carried from the trucks, increasingly violent. The heavy rear doors of the refrigerated trailer banged shut and the driver shouted to the white-coated porters who milled around like chubby ghosts. Sean Dunmore knew that the longer he failed to speak to the police, or to this man Giacomo Baldini, the more doors would shut behind him and the further he would implicate himself. It was imperative that he found the girl soon and as he waited for the interminable small hours of the morning to unwind, he considered the address he had on a scrap of paper by his laptop on the chair at his bedside. He was a pursuer again now and his nose was to the wind as his logical mind tracked down the girl who threatened his neatly organised life. He had worked on the assumption that Habiba Popals would be staying with a friend and the only name he had was Sharifa Khan, the girl who had been with the group at the Gallery. She had an Indian name as well and they all stuck together, he reasoned. His trawl through the databases had given him an address in New Cross, along with a telephone number and although he had considered calling it earlier, he figured he didn't want to alert her. He decided he needed to be nearer the address before he phoned and so all he could do now was wait and listen to the ancient market go about its business.

Four hours later he sat in a hire car not far from the house, his line of sight somewhat obscured by the spreading arms of a dishevelled buddleia in a garden to his side. He punched in the number, only too aware that this was the only option available to him and that, if she wasn't staying here, his task would become much more difficult.

Sharifa was feeding the baby when the phone rang and she wiped the mix of pureed pear and apple from Rafi's mouth before lifting the portable.

'Hello, is that Sharifa Khan?'

'It is, but if you're flogging something I'm not interested.'

'Oh, no,' the voice said brightly, 'far from it. I'm actually phoning to speak to Habiba Popals.' It was the momentary hesitation that Sean Dunmore picked up on, that tiny trip in time which gave so much away.

Habiba was sitting in the front room, using her friend's computer and Sharifa could see her through the crack in the door. Too many replies came to her mind at the same time for her to choose the correct one quickly enough. How did anyone know Habiba was here? She was instinctively cautious.

'No one here with that name,' she said.

'But you know her, I believe?' came the immediate reply, which again caught her out and a second, infinitesimal pause, betrayed her.

'I was at school with someone with that name, but that was a long time ago,' she replied.

'Do you know where I might find her?' the voice jumped in, before she could put down the phone.

'No, I'm sorry I don't,' Sharifa said, slightly relieved. 'Who wants to find her, anyway?' This was another mistake.

'Oh, it's a small legal matter. Not to worry.' And the line went dead. Sharifa laid the phone on the table and walked through to her friend whose back was turned to her.

'Does anyone know that you are here?'

The question caused Habiba to swivel in the chair and look at Sharifa, with a shake of her head.

In turn, Sharifa nodded back. 'I think they do.'

Habiba got up and walked to the window and stood looking up and down the road. From his position beyond the weeping buddleia, Sean Dunmore saw her shape appear in the bay of the house. She was too far away to be recognisable, but he knew it was her. If she hadn't been at the house, Sharifa's response to his initial question would have been quite different. 'What do you mean?' she might have said, or perhaps even 'Gosh, I haven't heard that name for a long time.' But the momentary confusion told him everything he needed to know. All he had to do now was wait.

Inside, Sharifa asked two questions.

'Who is it, Habiba? And what does he want?'

Habiba kept her back to her friend.

'He stole something from me,' she said quietly. A fly buzzed against the window and outside a car went silently by. Sharifa heard Rafi complaining and went to the kitchen and returned with him in her arms. She was happy to wait for Habiba to say more.

'And now I am in the process of taking something back from him,' she continued.

'What's that, Habiba?'

'His freedom. And the freedom he's denied me for the past four years.'

Perhaps the baby had picked up on the atmosphere of anticipation in the room, for he became still in his mother's embrace. Habiba turned and went over to the computer where she had been working when the phone had rung. Earlier that morning, the newspaper had arrived and she had read the piece about the recovery of the painting which had been accompanied by a photograph of Giacomo Baldini. He looked as she had imagined, solid and unsmiling, conveying the necessary ingredients for his job, although, she noted, his eyes were not those of a man dulled by life. They were alive and questioning and complemented the copy in bold under the picture which explained that he was following a particular line of enquiry and was calling on the public for help. She had Googled his name and amongst the various pages of links that appeared for him, there was one that had caused her to frown. Leaning forward, she had clicked through to the material she had posted on YouTube. When Habiba had begun this elaborate, but nevertheless instinctive, way of putting a sense of balance back into her life, she had been unsure how it would play out in the end, merely trusting that the sincerity of her aims would naturally find a way through. She saw her footage frozen at the beginning of the pan across Sean Dunmore's room and her eyes registered the number of plays the material had received. But it was the comments box which held her attention for it declared the name of the one sender who had bothered to leave his reactions: Giacomo Baldini.

She might have written the words that she read out loud: 'Fascinating. How very clever and intriguing. It should lead to something much bigger. Perhaps you would get in touch to discuss the implications. Is one's fate the place where the leopard always returns?'

Giacomo Baldini had left a mobile number, which Habiba was about to call. She looked across to her friend, still patiently waiting an explanation for Habiba's strange behaviour.

'If you listen, Sharifa, you will learn a little more.'

The air of expectation still cast its spell over the mother and child as they watched Habiba make the call.

'Hello. Mr Baldini?'

'Yes?' She could hear the wariness in his slightly accented voice.

'I think you wanted me to contact you?' She paused, but there was no response and she knew that he was waiting for a sign that this was not a hoax.

'Anmar Ma'ab Qadr,' she said, carefully pronouncing each word.

'Habiba Popals,' he replied and, if it is possible to hear a smile, she did. She caught her breath, the slightest intake of air and her shoulders dropped as she registered this moment of connection.

'I am not sure whether I am talking to you, or you're looking to talk to me,' she said. She watched as Sharifa sat on the arm of the sofa, adjusting the child on her lap, the puzzled look still on her face.

'The picture is safe,' Baldini told her, which had not been his intention but the sentence had somehow emerged.

'It always was,' Habiba replied. 'In a way, the painting doesn't matter in this, however beautiful it is.'

'I know,' he said, and Habiba could hear a trace of warmth in his voice, the merest hint of sympathy.

'How do you know?' she asked.

'It was an instinct, I suppose,' he said, surprised the conversation was taking this turn, although, if he had stopped to think about it, his feelings had started when he had first seen the four-year-old recordings of her.

'You didn't look like a woman who would steal a painting for money,' he continued and immediately regretted it, for it was not what he really meant. Before she had time to respond, he changed his approach.

'Something happened, didn't it?'

There was a silence on the line and Habiba felt the rise and fall of her chest and knew that Sharifa, sitting opposite with the baby, could see the change in her demeanour.

'Yes.'

'Something that I don't know about, something to do with Sean Dunmore. And something you don't want to talk about on the phone.'

'Yes. And yes. And yes,' she said, slowly repeating each affirmative. This is not what Habiba Popals had expected either, although her ideas of what form this episode of the unfolding events would take had always been unclear.

'We should meet,' he said after a pause and added, as if anticipating her response, 'somewhere you feel comfortable. And safe,' he added, and again the tone of his voice conveyed to Habiba a level of concern she had not anticipated.

'What I set out to do is not yet finished,' she said and her assumption that he knew what she was talking about was quickly confirmed.

'I know,' he said. 'But you should be careful.'

How curious, Habiba thought, that Giacomo Baldini should be acting as a protector and not condemning her for what she had done, as if he, too, understood that the painting was a side stall in the story that was unfolding.

'Sean Dunmore,' she said.

'Sean Dunmore,' he repeated.

It was as if Giacomo Baldini had absorbed the key elements of Habiba's story so that they could now talk a sort of shorthand, each half-predicting what the other might say.

'He's not far away, is he?' she asked, rhetorically.

'I believe not,' he confirmed.

And in an instant Habiba's body gave her a peculiar and unwelcome memory which was now released to assail her, one that thrust her back to a blurry place in her past, a dark night she could barely remember. Habiba Popals could smell the distinct and cloying aroma of Sean Dunmore's deodorant as surely as if he had been standing at her shoulder.

'I will be alone,' Giacomo said, sensing a sudden uncertainty. 'I am not interested in entrapment.'

'I know that,' she said, although she could not give any logical reason why she chose to believe him. She just knew that Giacomo Baldini was telling the truth and the comfort of that fact seeped into every part of her body.

'Do you know Greenwich, Mr Baldini?' Habiba wanted a location close by, one that was reasonably open so that she could observe it beforehand.

'Vaguely,' he said.

'There is a pedestrian tunnel which leads under the river, from near the old ship called *Cutty Sark*, across to Island Park, which looks back on Greenwich. I will meet you there this afternoon at three, on one of the benches by the Thames.'

'Be careful,' he said. It was a warning he need not have given, he realised, aware, once again, of the invisible line he had crossed with this woman who, though he had never met her, seemed increasingly familiar.

Habiba continued to hold the phone, before looking up at her friend and her baby.

'Come here,' she said and moved aside so that Sharifa and Rafi could sit in front of the computer. She then animated the sequence in the YouTube video box and clicked it to full screen. As the sequence developed, she pressed 'pause' and directed Sharifa to the screen with her finger. She didn't speak and waited as Sharifa absorbed the implications of what she was seeing.

'It's that picture, isn't it,' she said, 'the one that was stolen?' There was a pause as various stages of comprehension fell into place.

'Did you take it?' And then, looking at Habiba's face. 'You did take it.'

Sharifa's own face was a mask of astonishment, a mix of query and shock, her furrowed brow reflected in the narrowing of her eyes which, in turn, caused the corners of her mouth to lift in a grimace.

It was strange to feel that the truth, or at least one part of it, had escaped and was now a tangible entity for more than just her to consider. Habiba knew that she owed Sharifa more of an explanation, but she was unable to give it, partly because she wanted to talk first to Giacomo Baldini and secondly because she couldn't. One part of the reason why she had chosen to take the painting still lay hidden to Habiba Popals.

'Yes, I took it. I didn't see it as stealing and I still can't use that word for what I did. He stole something, I didn't.'

'And you aren't going to tell me what caused you to do this, are you?'

'Not yet, Sharifa. Please be patient with me. You don't deserve this silence but it is not ready to come out yet.'

'I worry about you, Habs. Who was the person who called and what does he want?'

Perhaps, at this stage, the baby registered the worry in his mother, a certain tension in her body, her attention diverted from him, for he gave a small murmur of concern and his hand came up to touch her lips.

'Rafi knows,' she said and kissed his cheek, nuzzling his face into her own and then, looking up with her eyes, 'what have you got yourself into, Habs?'

Habiba stood and walked over to the window again and looked out and knew that somewhere in the apparently benign suburb of New Cross there was a very real danger to her, an animal which, wounded and in pain, was twice as angry as before. She sensed him, but couldn't see him, knowing only too well his cunning and doubly alert to his ways.

'You will know soon enough,' she said, before softening her blunt response by adding. 'I think you knew from the start, from the point it began. Rafi takes after you, I can tell.'

And then a pause.

'Someone is trying to hurt me and someone is trying to help me. If you can order me a cab for half-past two it will take me away from one in the direction of the other.'

She could see the concern, tinged by fear, in Sharifa's face and she was glad when she picked up the phone without any further questions.

Later, when she climbed into the cab, she might just as well have been stepping off a cliff for, no matter how much of what had gone before had been instigated by her, the next hours were a mystery that not even she could predict. The black cat which scuttled across the road ahead of her gave her no comfort.

Chapter 30

Sean Dunmore's lack of remorse was both his strength and his weakness, for whilst it enabled him to commit certain acts without fear of their consequences, it left him without the ability to imagine other scenarios which might hamper his progress. As his car pulled out to follow the taxi, he knew he had to find Habiba Popals before the Italian. It never occurred to him that Habiba Popals might have spoken to Giacomo Baldini and that there might exist between them an accord, however ill defined it was, that could prove a barrier. He could only see the Indian as a criminal, albeit one with dangerous knowledge about himself, and in this way he thought he was on the same side of the fence as Baldini, two men in pursuit of a thief.

The taxi was heading north, down towards the Thames, threading its way through the streets of Deptford before turning east into Greenwich. During his brief spell in London he had come here a couple of times, visiting the Naval Museum as part of his training and drinking at the riverside pubs. The cab pulled off the one-way system and stopped in a cobbled cul-de-sac close to the *Cutty Sark*. Cursing, he had to drive past and around the one-way system, to avoid the possibility of detection, and by the time he had done the loop, she had paid her fare and was walking quickly in the direction of the Thames. It was as he squeezed into a parking bay that he realised where she might be going and he slammed his door in anger. She was walking quickly towards the glass-domed lift shaft which took pedestrians down to the tunnel which connected Greenwich with the Isle of Dogs. He knew that she was going to trap herself, for there was no way she could get through the white-tiled subterranean passage before he caught up with her. He began to jog in her direction, hardly daring to believe his luck.

Just before she reached the round building which held the old wooden lifts, Habiba glanced behind her, cursing her foolishness at suggesting such a vulnerable place to meet Baldini. She caught her breath when she saw the figure moving steadily towards her, perhaps two hundred metres away. She ran to the lifts but just as the doors parted, she realised the peril she was putting herself in and she turned and began to sprint in the direction of the pleasure-cruiser pier, where a string of passengers was filing on to a boat. She hadn't wanted it to be like this. She saw herself as the pursuer now, hedging him further and further into a corner, trapping him in a place where there was no escape. Instead, he was hounding her, getting closer and closer as she arrived at the stern of the boat. She was the last to go aboard and she was helped on board by a man with a naval cap pointing at a jaunty angle.

'My, we are keen to see the sights, my dear,' he said. 'Wish they was all like you.'

As she looked back, the crewman's eyes followed in the same direction, but by this time Sean Dunmore had stopped running and could only watch as the boat pushed slowly off from the floating quay. He was close enough for her to see the coldness of his eyes and the stillness of his face. It was an image she knew only too well and, involuntarily, she shook her body in revulsion. She watched him enquire at the kiosk, no doubt asking where the boat was stopping, for some went straight to Westminster Pier and others had dropping off points en route. At that moment she wasn't sure herself, but for now she enjoyed the relief of watching the Thames stretch between the two of them, the churning yellow-grey waters pushing her further and further away from his heartless stare. It was only now that she wondered how he had found her, and the memory of his eyes, dead and expressionless, told her that she wasn't safe. She had pulled the tail of a bear and it would hunt her down. She took her mobile phone out of her shoulder bag.

'Baldini.' He answered before she had spoken.

'He's following me.'

'Where are you?'

'I'm on one of those pleasure cruisers. I jumped on at Greenwich.'

She was cross with herself, for she hadn't wanted it to be like this. She wanted to humiliate Sean Dunmore, to confront him with what he had done and now she felt at a disadvantage again.

'Hello? Habiba? Are you still there?'

This was the first time he had called her by just her Christian name and she registered the fact as the boat slowly followed the river around the wide bend in front of Canary Wharf.

'I think the boat is going to Westminster Pier, but it might stop on the way, I'm not sure.'

'Well, don't get off until then. I'll be there.'

And he was gone and she was left with the residue of concern in his voice. When the man in the sailor's hat approached her for the fare, she asked him if the boat stopped in between here and Westminster.

'Want to get off already, do you, miss? We'll be pulling into Butler's Wharf by Tower Bridge and then again at Tate Modern. Any good for you?'

Even as she paid for her ticket to Westminster, she knew what she was going to do. Her four years in purgatory had given her a fierce desire to free herself of the feeling of being a victim, whether of her father, or Sean Dunmore, or, most of all, herself. As the boat pulled into Butler's Wharf, its engines reversing against the tide to enable the craft to delicately nudge the pier, she queued up to leave. She made sure she was at the end of the line, standing as close to the side of the boat as she could in order that she could be seen from the shore. As she went to step off on to the jetty, the last to disembark, she paused and, looking at her friend in the hat, said, 'Oh, I should be getting off at Westminster, shouldn't I? How stupid.'

She was helped back on to the deck even as the boat moved

away from the pier. She was sure that Sean Dunmore would have been watching her, hoping that she would disembark. Habiba reckoned, though, that no matter how fast Sean Dunmore drove, he could not get to Tate Modern quicker than the boat and even if he did, he would have to park and walk, for there was no road alongside the Thames at the Gallery. As they slipped under London Bridge, she called Giacomo Baldini again.

'Change of plan,' she said without preamble. 'Meet me at Tate Modern, Room 2, Floor 3.' She had visited the museum many times as a student and this was her favourite collection. She rang off, suddenly glad to be back in control.

*   *   *

Habiba Popals' confidence was misplaced. Sean Dunmore, furious at the dummy he had received at Butler's Wharf, drove at frightening speed around the front of London Bridge station and cutting down to the side of Borough Market, abandoned the car by the Anchor pub where he was just in time to see the rear of the pleasure boat pass under Southwark Bridge. He jogged along the Embankment, keeping the boat in view, but slowed to a walk as it came alongside the pier. From a distance he watched her get off, striding up the long walkway in front of the Globe Theatre. He noticed that she was confident enough not to look back and he imagined that she assumed that she had thrown him off her track. She entered the side door of the gallery, the one facing the river, and entered the bowels of the vast brick building. He hurried after her, making sure that he kept groups of people between himself and the entrance. Even before he had entered the gallery he saw her slide through his vision on an escalator taking her to a higher floor. He quickly followed the signs to the stairs and taking two and three at a time began to race upwards, glancing occasionally at the escalator which he could see through the gap on each landing. He arrived at the top just as she did but he was protected by the corridor which led from the stairs and was long enough to include the toilets. She didn't hesitate as she stepped off the escalator but continued straight on towards a room which announced 'Poetry and Dream'. He had to be careful now, for he was not sure of his sightlines and the geography of the floor. He snatched a folded guide from a rack on the wall and quickly tried to orientate himself. The sweat was beginning to run down his face and drop with distinct plops on to the floor plan. Only now did he wonder whether she had come here to meet someone and he looked up and around him. He had established that the only way down from this floor was through this central area which contained the lifts, stairs and escalator. Removing his jacket and keeping his face down to look at the guide, he made his way forward to the rooms which contained the collections. He did not see any of the pictures as he sidled past the various entrances and he continued to use other visitors as camouflage, joining in with them or standing just beyond them. And then he caught a glimpse of her from behind. Like him, she was in a group and he almost missed her. She was standing in front of a tall picture, the sort he hated, a mass of peculiar shapes that looked like mad puppets dancing in a broken jigsaw. It was easy to observe her and for a moment he was taken back four years to the first time he had tracked her across the floors of another gallery. She looked different, still tall and striking, but now somehow harder and less available. He recalled the lazy smile she had had in the car when he was taking her out of London, the wetness of her lips and the hooded droop of her eyes. He was jerked back into the present when he saw the man standing behind her. He leant forward to say something in her ear and she turned to face him.

*   *   *

'Miss Habiba Popals?'

She hesitated before angling her body in his direction.

'Giacomo Baldini.' She was tall enough to look him in the eyes.

They stood for a second in front of Picasso's *Three Dancers* as if absorbing the strangeness of the situation. For him, it was as if he had known her for a very long time and he was not quite sure why or how. And then, irrationally, for he had not meant to begin talking to her in this way, he asked:

'Is this a particular favourite of yours?' nodding upwards at the painting.

'Sort of,' she said, still looking at him. 'There's a madness in the dancers which I came to understand.'

He absorbed this, knowing somehow that she had not chosen by accident this place to meet.

'You're not going to ask me what it was I came to understand?'

'I think you will tell me,' he replied calmly, as if he did not want to disturb the metre of their exchange.

'You see the face of the woman on the left, the one with the mad mask who looks as though she is carrying a builder's saw?'

He took his eyes from hers and looked beyond her to the painting and saw the wild and bewildered look of the dancer who appeared to hold in her hand a white saw.

'Is that how you felt?'

She nodded.

'And you'll tell me why?'

She nodded again.

And, again, Giacomo Baldini wondered why their exchanges had taken this form since, standing in front of him, was a woman who had stolen a painting from the gallery of which he was the director of security. He gave a brief smile, and whether she understood where it came from, he couldn't be certain, but he imagined she might.

'And what about him?' he asked.

'I don't think he followed me here,' she said, aware that she had barely looked around her since arriving in the gallery. She did so now, scanning the various entrances to the room, expecting to see the bulk of Sean Dunmore framed in a gap.

'I wanted him to think that I was getting off the boat just up river, at Butler's Wharf. Instead, I stayed on until here. I didn't think he would be quick enough to get here ahead of me.'

Giacomo Baldini wasn't so sure and it was his turn now to look around the room, his eyes resting on each of the individuals in the open space. Then he took her by the arm, placing his hand under the crook of her elbow, and led her out of the room.

'We should talk,' he said, not looking at her.

'In the café,' she replied.

'In the café,' he agreed.

*   *   *

Sean Dunmore had sat on a black banquette which allowed him a view into the room. He watched them stand, face to face, eye to eye, and make their exchanges. He couldn't understand their body language for, as far as he was concerned, this was the moment when the policeman would have put his hand on the villain's shoulder and informed him that the game was up. Instead, it was as if they were friends and had organised to meet at the gallery and then take lunch afterwards. When Baldini smiled, Sean Dunmore frowned, unable to fit this gesture into the scheme of things, trying to force it into the jumble of events but finding it didn't fit. He saw them look around, perhaps surveying the surroundings for him and then, in a movement which he again found out of place, he saw him hold her arm and lead her away, talking to her as though she were a colleague, or someone even more intimate. His puzzlement was in equal proportion to his anger, the one fuelling the other. It appeared that he was on her side, open and willing to listen to her, sympathetic to whatever she might have to say. The indignation rose in him unfettered, an illogical expression of the unfairness of the Italian's behaviour and what it might mean to him. Instead of Habiba Popals' being isolated and condemned, the Italian appeared to be colluding with her. Suddenly, Sean Dunmore felt very exposed and like any animal cornered, his defences were put on full alert and the adrenalin pumped around his body. He discreetly followed them and as they began to climb the stairs he deduced that they might be going to the café on the top floor. Their tread was slow and they continued to talk, the Italian leaning in towards the Indian, as if they were discussing the finer points of one of the paintings. He took the lift to the top floor and by the time they arrived he was sitting in the corner of the room, looking at the view down over the Thames and closely studying a menu in front of a wall which appeared to be covered with giant liquorice allsorts. He watched them arrive and sit at the bar stools which lined the long picture window and afforded huge views northwards over London. He knew that Baldini would check out the room and so he made sure his back was turned and that he was writing an imaginary note as he allowed them to settle down. The bar restaurant was busy and there were more than a dozen tables between them so he could observe them in some safety. She was talking now and he was listening, again leaning towards her almost deferentially, his head cocked at a slight angle. It was as if he had suddenly taken on the role of investigator and was watching the collaboration of two suspects. He could guess what she was saying but he was impotent to intervene and put his side of the story. The unfairness of what was happening in front of his eyes infuriated him and he gripped the arms of his metal seat in frustration. Not for one moment did the alluring shape of Habiba Popals, her long legs encased in her tight jeans, the high-collared white shirt which revealed the curve of her neck and the set of her face, the slow, mute movement of her mouth, give him any sensual pleasure. All he felt now was a cold and black hatred, which lay on his chest like an uncomfortable weight and which, with a gesture of his hand over his breast, he knew he had to remove.

Chapter 31

Even before Giacomo Baldini had walked with her through the gallery and up the stairs to the restaurant, he knew that many of his old certainties were evaporating before him. It was as if every script he had prepared had been caught in a swirling wind and sent spinning in the air around him, tantalisingly close but entirely out of his grasp. He registered again that he could not account for this, because whatever exchanges were taking place with this tall young woman at his side were entirely easy and seem to follow logically, without effort. Watching her face as she spoke he could see how she had the resolve to accomplish what she had just carried off, for if determination is defined physically, he could see it now, the sharp lines of her nose and jaw and the calm look of her eyes, a clear reflection of her mind. Those wide eyes that had looked up to him from the photograph which was now in his inside pocket, were different today, cooler, less believing, and the impetuous licks of her hair had been replaced by a style altogether less obvious. Because any more recent picture of her had been shrouded by her hijab and scarves, he was still getting used to these changes, absorbing a woman who had been transformed in some ways but carried something of the previous young girl close beneath the surface.

But why should he care, why had he embarked on this series of thoughts and at what point had they begun? And he smiled again, as he had done in front of the Picasso painting, a small eruption of mirth bubbling up from he knew not where and catching him by surprise. The wind continued to agitate the old scripts around his head and he imagined what he might have said in different circumstances with someone else, the cold procedural exchanges, the satisfaction of a job completed, the impatience to see the loose ends tied up and the report presented to the director. All that now seemed so remote, so far away. He was part of a play he hadn't expected to like but which had drawn him in so that he had abandoned his desire to try and catch it out and instead given himself up to the story.

When they sat down, she looked at him again, the clear steady look of confidence which seemed to say to him, 'Go on, ask me.' He held her stare before glancing around the busy restaurant, momentarily coming out of his shell to see if Sean Dunmore might be there watching them. He knew what he looked like from the records back at the gallery, but he had no sense of him as a person except what he had picked up by instinct and from the appearance of his flat.

'Something happened,' he said.

'Something happened,' she repeated, still holding the gaze of the man opposite her. If it is possible for a voice to be justified by an appearance, she thought, this was it, for the sympathy she had detected on the phone was now reinforced by his physical presence. She had never allowed herself to think as far as this stage and she realised, even before she began to speak, that the completion of her journey, the offloading of the unfinished business, could not be entirely complete without Sean Dunmore, but even as she thought this she realised the simplicity of her thinking. Revenge isn't that neat and it dawned on her that Giacomo Baldini, sitting calmly and watching her, knew this already.

'Something happened,' she said again and he could see her drawing in the air ready to tell him, or at least to fill in the details, for he felt he could guess the outline of what she might say.

'A long time ago, now,' she began, 'when I was a different person in a different world, a part of my life was taken from me.' She looked up at him but he remained quite still.

'The worst thing is,' she continued, 'that I can't remember much about it. Or perhaps that is fortunate, for perhaps the details would have been too great for me. And then again,' she said, dropping her head and her voice, 'imagining what those details might have been has also been torture. Do you know what it is like to be brought up and feel that you are not part of your family, that everything you do runs counter to what is expected of you and is never enough?'

Again, he remained still, although the impulse to join in and agree with her rose spontaneously in him.

'My father didn't want me to go, worried that I would dishonour the family and bring shame on his name. Well, he was right and, of course, I couldn't tell him, or anyone else for that matter. These things get trapped, don't they, Signor Baldini?'

He gave the smallest of nods, a slow dropping of his head whilst his eyes remained on hers.

'It is curious, but I now realise as I sit here and talk to you, that my father used to watch my every move, just as he did.'

'Sean Dunmore.'

She returned his slow nod and continued. 'When I arrived on the course, he must have tracked me from the start. I thought our meetings were accidental, but I now know he was tracking me.' As she said this, she ran the palm of her right hand down the sleeve of her left arm, as if brushing off some residue of the memory.

'He drew me in, asking me for out for a drink, and I was unaware what was going on.' She remained quiet for a moment. 'I still don't really know what happened.'

He wanted to put his hand on her arm, the one that she had brushed clean, but he stopped himself. Down below, unseen to him, two men on stilts were performing in front of the crowds of tourists, wobbling to and fro, pretending to nearly fall off their lofty perches.

'I still don't know whether he actually raped me,' she said absently, leaping several stages of logic. 'He hurt me though. My body showed that.'

And now he did put his hand on her, lightly and then withdrew it. She looked up at him, brought back into the present from some dark place a long way away.

'As I say, he took me for a drink. Took me for a fool. Why did I change? Something happened. I can't remember much, if anything, about leaving the bar.' She had again retreated and he could see her eyes casting around for some firm memory of that day.

'Later, I remember being by the road and the bright white and yellow lights, the noise and a terrible sense that something awful had taken place. I was staying in a hall of residence in Mile End and I remember the porter telling me off, as though I was some common or garden drunk. The following morning was the worst of my life.'

Again, the pause, as the memory was recalled and weighed, its awfulness revisited.

'It has stayed with me for four years. Do you know how I tried to ignore it?' she said quietly to him. 'But it was always there, hovering on my shoulder, calling me away, distracting me no matter how hard I tried. After a while I realised it was indelible, a permanent stain whose presence could not be ignored. Sometimes it would defeat me and a huge lethargy would take over. Other times, no matter how much I laughed or partied, it was still there. But I tell you this again, I cannot remember what happened.'

Again the silence, which he knew he shouldn't fill.

'I wasn't pregnant. I didn't have Aids. And, for this I suppose I should be grateful.' She was about to say, 'and I'm alive', but she stopped herself for, in some ways, she knew that she had been half-dead ever since the assault took place.

'When I first came into the gallery, when the excitement of the place swept through me, I saw the painting, the face. I didn't know it was Christ, but I saw something in the face that I recognised, perhaps wanted. I returned many times to look at it, to marvel at the expression he had, the indifference to me, the viewer. I didn't see him as Christ, or perhaps I did and my very attraction to him was a sort of revolt.' She looked directly at him to see if he understood what she was talking about.

'I understand,' he said and nodded for her to continue.

'It wasn't until much later, years later, long after the assault, that I understood that my feelings for the picture represented what I was before . . . before, before it happened. Sean Dunmore took something away from me, no, tore it away from me and had no idea what he did. He was only interested in one thing. So I thought I would give it back to him, to remind him of what he had done or, perhaps, to *tell* him what he had done. It has been my therapy, I suppose.'

She raised her head to him now, looking down her nose in defiance, expecting him to chastise her perhaps and reveal her foolishness. But he remained silent, his eyes still holding hers, waiting for her to finish.

'I knew I wanted to place it into the centre of his life, to show his ugliness against it. He had no right to do what he did to me.'

As she spoke, he was more and more astonished. She had created a simple equation, a moral balance and had seen it through. There was not one shred of guilt or embarrassment in her and her eyes challenged him to contradict or belittle her.

'I understand,' he said. 'I understand.'

'When I was at his flat,' and she looked away as she recalled the smell that had greeted her, 'I saw some bottles in his bathroom.'

'Rohypnol,' he said. 'I saw them, too.'

She looked at him before continuing. 'I looked it up. It's a date-rape drug, isn't it?'

He nodded.

'Even knowing that didn't help, for I realise the memory of those moments is lost forever. I want to see him, you know? It cannot stop here, with you.'

'I know,' he said. Habiba Popals had been unable to speak of the criminal act which she had suffered and instead had taken her own revenge. It was a form of personal *omerta*. This, indeed, was an unusual woman.

'You didn't want me to think he had stolen it, did you.' It was a statement, rather than a question.

'No, that wasn't the point,' she said in agreement.

He waited.

'I was frightened he might damage it. From the little I know of him, he would have no regard for art.' She paused. 'But, then, for a while nor did I.'

He finished what she was in the process of saying. 'What good is art if you feel as you did, as you do, perhaps. In these situations art, beauty, is a luxury shorn of its value.'

'And so,' she said, 'the picture is a catalyst. Messina's little painting had no value except to expose what had gone on.'

'Has it done that?'

'Up to a point,' she said, 'but it's not finished yet.'

The more he heard of her story, the less certain he was of what he should do next. He was allowing the situation to unfold slowly but in truth she was leading the way and he could not be certain quite where they were heading.

'He knows where you are living, doesn't he?'

'Yes, he followed me to Greenwich.'

'What do you want?' he asked her.

'I want to be rid of the way I feel,' she said. 'I want to know what happened. I want to release the memory, set it free so that I can see it, touch it and discard it if I want. I want my years back, do you see? Precious years that weren't his to take.'

There it was again, the look in her eyes saying that her terms were unconditional and not open to negotiation, and he was swept along in the current of her fierce determination. There was something primitive, elemental, in her thinking which he recognised only too well, even if it did disturb the practised logic he had come to understand and follow.

235

'You know why he wants to find you?' he asked.

'I imagine he wants to keep me quiet, to stop me talking to you.'

'You want to see him, don't you?'

Habiba looked hard at the man sitting opposite calmly appraising her, and she realised he understood, that he wasn't going to stop her now, cut her off before she could complete what she had set out to do. He was helping her define the next stage. She nodded.

'How are we going to do that?'

And for the first time in as long as she could remember she smiled with the whole of her face.

*   *   *

The process of their conversation, the ease with which Giacomo Baldini sat with the woman who had stolen one of his precious paintings, continued to infuriate Sean Dunmore. When he saw him gently touch her forearm he almost stood and shouted his complaint. They were colluding, forming a pact against him, one in which her criminal act seemed to play no part. And, finally, when she smiled, it seemed to be in acknowledgement of his compliance, as if he had agreed to her terms. He watched them leave the café and take the long, slow escalator down through the floors. As before, he sprinted down the stairs so that he arrived at the street level well before they did. The rise and fall of his chest matched his mood. It was as if the anger was trying to escape, to find a place to land and create mayhem and burn itself out. And it would soon, he declared to himself, aware now that he had been isolated, that the Indian girl would have told Baldini everything. How dare he take her side of the story without knowing his? His sense of injustice was instantly metabolised into hatred as he followed them out of the Turbine Hall into the startlingly bright day.

Chapter 32

It was all too easy.

He followed them back along the Thames but when they turned in from the river, he knew he had a problem. He watched as the Italian opened the passenger door of his grey BMW and allowed the tall girl to fold herself into the front seat. At no point did either of them look round in his direction. In fact, they showed a remarkable lack of concern. He accepted that he would lose them here, for he had abandoned his own car on the other side of Southwark Bridge. His only hope of staying in touch with them rested on Baldini taking her back to the New Cross address and it was only when, half an hour later, he saw the BMW outside the house, that his well-developed sense of self-preservation was alerted. They had wanted him to follow and so far he had done their bidding.

He parked in the shadow of the buddleia once again and considered his position. The anger was still very much alive in him but for the moment it had been pushed aside and sealed. He needed to think clearly and he began to list his options and they began with a simple statement: he had done nothing wrong. A demented woman was trying to implicate him in a crime entirely her own doing because he didn't continue their brief relationship, one which had finished nearly four years ago. There was no truth, indeed no evidence, in any allegations she might make against him. As far as he knew, the picture had not been discovered, although he was certain it might have been placed in his apartment. But he wasn't to know this, for he had come to London following a hunch that the Indian girl might have been implicated in its theft. Yes, that was it. He didn't feel he had enough evidence to be certain, so he had come to London to see her. It was all entirely plausible. As his tortured logic developed, it took him along a path he at first refused to contemplate, but the more he allowed it to play in his imagination, the better it became. He continued watching the house until Baldini left and drove away. Sean Dunmore felt the suppressed anger pushing against his ribs as he thrust the car into gear and turned away from the house in the opposite direction to that taken by the grey car.

Giacomo Baldini had entered a vacuum of his own creation. He had deliberately suspended the normal routines of investigation in order to accommodate the wishes of a woman who had just committed a major crime. Although he could justify this to himself, to anyone else his course of action might have been more difficult to explain and to some, might appear downright suspicious. He was, in fact, colluding with Habiba Popals, deliberately delaying the moment when she would be publicly revealed as the woman who had successfully stolen a major work of art from the National Gallery. To answer the question why was more difficult and it was this that preoccupied him as he drove past the Rotherhithe Tunnel and turned on to Tooley Street, heading towards central London. Of course, he believed her story entirely, but it was more than that. He wanted her to complete her elaborate plan, for it to reach the conclusion she had set for herself. He had read about cases of slow-burn provocation, where women – it was always women – committed serious crimes against their husbands, or members of their family, after years of provocation. Somehow the case of Habiba Popals was similar, the reverberations of an assault progressively wearing her down over the years to the point where she had to take extreme action. He shook his head in astonishment as he wove through the railway arches in front of London Bridge station. To have created such an elaborate plot and carried it off perfectly demanded singular determination and enormous focus and for this he could not help but admire her. Habiba Popals:

he had found out about her, of course, looking up her name and tracing her background. As far as he could gather, her family was from Pakistan, from near the Khyber Pass, where three countries seem to collide and their boundaries, artificial as they are, seem to have no significance. He wondered if she had ever been to Pakistan and he imagined the landscape as similar to his own in Sicily. Although less mountainous, Sicily was also the victim of fierce heat and similarly fierce people, who defined themselves by honour and family first and region second. And so, what did all this tell him about Habiba Popals? It told him he had never met anyone like her, that he was drawn to this woman as never before and that her face, first revealed to him partly disguised by a headscarf and hijab, then later, more fully, by the still-frame image of her with the luminous white eyes and teeth, and then, finally, in the flesh high up in Tate Modern, was more beguiling than any he had ever seen in his life. He had not expected this, not sought it and yet the images of Habiba Popals dominated his thoughts.

*   *   *

When Habiba had introduced Giacomo Baldini to Sharifa Khan it had been without explanation, except to add a line about his job. There was too much to say, too much still to unravel and then settle, for anything more profound to be said. Even when the Italian had left and they were alone, Sharifa kept her counsel, waiting for her friend to tell her more. Habiba thought it might have been easier to talk to Sharifa, but when the moment came she discovered the opposite. The baby was asleep and they carried coffee to the table in the window of the front room where they sat, at first in silence.

'You were right in the beginning, Sharifa. You noticed that I was different, but I couldn't talk to you then. It has taken me four years to begin to account for what happened.'

She told her story to Sharifa, as she had to Baldini but when she saw the tears in her friend's eyes, she, too, began to weep. Sharifa could understand the scale of the repercussions of the assault and would know that looming over the event, even now, would be Latif Popals, ready to condemn his daughter rather than the perpetrator of the rape.

But the second part of the story brought laughter as Sharifa erupted in astonishment when she heard about the theft of the painting.

'How did you manage it?' she shouted and both young women laughed at the audacity of the act. Sharifa was even more wide-eyed when Habiba told her about breaking into Sean Dunmore's apartment and leaving the picture for the authorities to find.

'I don't believe it,' she said, her eyes wide with amazement. And then, just as quickly, the same eyes narrowed and her face changed.

'It was him who phoned, wasn't it? This Sean Dunmore?'

Habiba nodded as she was brought back to the here and now by the tone of Sharifa's voice.

'I know, I know, Sharifa, it's not fair on you and Rafi that I am here. I have thought about this and I will go back to my place. I don't want you to be in any danger.'

Sharifa looked at her friend and acknowledged the truth of what she said. She had detected the whiff of evil when she had answered the phone to Sean Dunmore and she wanted him nowhere near her child.

'Thank you, Habs. But stay for lunch and we will drive you over to Shepherd's Bush. It's not that far.'

While they chatted in the kitchen, while Rafi sat in his high-chair and banged away with the assortment of toys he had in front of him, from time to time Sharifa glanced at her friend and worried for her safety. Dishonour was a condition they knew only too much about and Habiba had deliberately and methodically exposed Sean Dunmore for what he was. He would, she knew, strike back.

*   *   *

If Giacomo Baldini had not quite worked out what his next moves would be, the decision was taken away from him not long after he arrived back in his office. He was wondering what to say to the director, how to couch the events of the previous twenty-four hours, when his phone rang.

'There's a call for you, Jack,' his PA told him. 'He says it is urgent and it is about the missing painting.'

'Who is it?'

'He says his name is Sean Dunmore.'

Baldini paused, looking up at the expanse of brown wall ahead of him, and wondered what this would bring.

'Put him through.'

'Hello. This is Sean Dunmore. I used to work at the National Gallery a few years ago and I think I might have some information about the recent theft which might interest you.'

'Really?' said the director of security.

'I wonder if I could come and see you about it?'

Giacomo Baldini had not really expected this and again he hesitated, absorbing the brazenness of the man's suggestion. The voice he heard was light and chatty, that of a mate phoning to arrange a meeting in the pub.

'Fine,' he said. 'Are you nearby?'

'I'm not far away,' said the jaunty voice. 'Shall we say four o'clock at the gallery?'

He agreed and put down the phone. He had an hour to wait, sixty minutes to stay in the bubble of his own creation. He went over to his briefcase and clicked it open, taking out a small digital recorder. He replaced the batteries and returned to the desk, where he rearranged the papers on the side closest to the chair opposite his own, to hide the small device. He saw from his computer that he had an e-mail from Miranda Goodheart and he opened it to find that she wanted to see him later in order to prepare an announcement about the safe return of the painting. For the moment he ignored it and paced the airless room as he tried to prepare himself for the meeting with Sean Dunmore. He had to be careful, for he had information that Dunmore might not suspect that he had. But, more than that, he was aware of his anger and if this should show itself in any form, it would be a mistake.

By the time he was shown into the room, Baldini had started the recorder and made sure that he was sitting down. He merely gestured to Dunmore to the chair opposite, for he had no desire to shake the hand of this man and although the visitor's arm was half-raised in greeting, he withdrew it and took the seat as directed.

'Gosh, the place hasn't changed much,' the younger man declared. 'How are you finding it?'

The rounded good looks of Sean Dunmore's face, the lightly gelled hair teased into casual disarray merely served to deepen Baldini's dislike, and his cocksure stance, legs apart and stretched forward, were no more than he would have expected.

'I believe you have some information for me,' Baldini said, leaning forward to look more closely at the man he already felt he knew so much about.

Sean Dunmore looked back at him and Giacomo Baldini could see the wariness in his eyes as they tried to second-guess how much he already knew.

'I assume you haven't got the picture back, yet?'

'I thought it was you giving me information, rather than the other way round,' Baldini answered quietly.

Sean Dunmore now adjusted himself on the seat, still keeping his eyes on the other man and allowing himself a second or two to absorb what was happening.

'I used to work here as you know . . . '

Baldini's face remained unresponsive.

' . . . and when I saw the missing picture in the paper, at first I didn't recognise it.'

Baldini continued to look at him, thinking that he was probably lying.

'And then I recalled that it was a painting that had aroused particular interest in a visitor to the gallery during my time.'

Baldini's silence was beginning to unnerve him.

'She was an Indian woman, more a girl really. I was in the control room when she first came in and I really didn't take much notice of her. But she spent a long time in front of the Messina and I thought this was a little unusual, particularly when she stepped in close to look at it. It was then that I started to examine her movements a little more carefully.'

'I know,' said Baldini. 'We have seen the footage.'

Sean Dunmore wasn't going to let anything show as he received this information and he barely skipped a beat before he continued.

'So you know what I am talking about, then? It wasn't normal behaviour and given that she was, well, of foreign extraction and maybe a Muslim, I thought it was worth keeping an eye on her.'

'Lots of people spend time in front of individual pictures, Mr Dunmore. I wonder what it was about this particular young woman that aroused your interest?'

At this point, Sean Dunmore realised that the Italian was ahead of him. He needed to go on the offensive.

'She was part of a study group,' he said in an offhand way, 'and I gave her some extra information about Messina, the artist.'

'I didn't know you were an expert.'

'Oh, you'd be surprised what you absorb when you work in a place like this,' he said, not taking the bait. 'But you know that. I asked her for a date,' he went on, making the information appear incidental, 'and put her in the picture, as it were.'

'And then what happened, Mr Dunmore?'

'Call me Sean. Well, I drove her back to the place she was staying, and that was that. I wasn't interested in taking things further, but then, up in Glasgow, where I now work, I saw the painting in the newspaper and I suddenly remembered her. I thought it would be useful if I told you.'

'Did you, now?'

He nodded, their eyes locked on one another.

'Tell me, Mr Dunmore, have you seen this footage before?' He turned to his computer and brought up the YouTube sequence. He moved the screen so that he could see it more easily. He pressed play and watched the man's face as the camera panned across the room, the slow realisation that this was his own apartment and then the momentary confusion when he recognised the painting on the wall.

'But that's the Messina, isn't it?' he said in disbelief. This was easy to do, for he couldn't believe what he was seeing.

'Did you put it there, Mr Dunmore?'

'No, of course not. Why would I put a stolen picture in my apartment and then film it for everyone to see?'

'Precisely, Mr Dunmore. Who would want to do that? And why?'

'You cannot suspect me of taking the picture, can you?'

Baldini remained still, wondering in what direction this dislikeable man would take now. He could see him organising the next act in this charade, rearranging the information to put himself in the best light.

'You don't think,' he said, and Giacomo Baldini could have finished his sentence for him, 'that she put it there, do you?'

Baldini raised his eyebrows. 'Why on earth would she do that?'

'Well,' he said, leaning forward, as if to take Baldini into his confidence, 'I think she was rather keener on me than I was on her.'

'I don't follow you, Mr Dunmore. Are you suggesting that, as the result of one date, this woman would steal a picture from the National Gallery and leave it in your room as an act of thwarted love?'

'I suppose I am really,' he said conspiratorially. 'You can never tell with those Indians. You know, the honour of the woman and all that.'

'No, I don't. Tell me about it.'

'Well, you know, I did kiss her a bit, and the rest of it. She maybe thought I was more committed than I was. For me, it was just a bit of fun, but for her, well . . . '

'We recovered the picture from a box in your broom cupboard, Mr Dunmore. Hidden.'

There were two pieces of information that Sean Dunmore was receiving now and he fought to put them in order of importance.

'You've been to my apartment?'

Baldini nodded.

'And the picture's back here?'

Sean Dunmore was keeping his composure, continuing to play the innocent part, expressing surprise at the unfolding events, a look of boyish innocence on his face.

'Well, that's good news, isn't it? And was I right? Did she have something to do with it?'

'What do you think?'

'Well, you know what I think. Yes, she did.'

They had reached an impasse and both men knew it. Giacomo Baldini was not going to reveal that he knew what had happened four years earlier and Sean Dunmore knew that there was no evidence to support any claim by the Indian woman against him.

'My colleague, Detective Inspector Colin Tyler will want to talk to you. He came with me to Glasgow.'

'Fine, bring him on,' Dunmore replied.

'You're not telling me the whole story, are you, Mr Dunmore?'

'Any more than you are, Mr Baldini.' He got up to leave.

'I came here to try and help and all I get is suspicion and evasion. I'm sorry I bothered.'

He walked over to the door and paused. 'From what I can see, Mr Baldini, she's got her teeth into you now. You should be careful. You might find a Rembrandt in your bedroom soon.'

And with that, he was gone, the door clicking shut in his wake.

Chapter 33

For a moment, Giacomo Baldini didn't know what to do. As parting shots go, it was perfectly aimed, hitting him somewhere just beneath the waterline. The truth always hurts, especially when it is hurled by someone as corrupt as Sean Dunmore. Giacomo Baldini knew that he had created a dilemma for himself, deliberately keeping Miranda Goodheart and Colin Tyler in the dark about Habiba. Sean Dunmore was only too aware of this, giving Giacomo Baldini further proof, if he needed it, of the fact that people with the least social conscience have an unnerving ability to detect where you are most vulnerable. Sean Dunmore knew that he was protecting Habiba – he had probably seen them together at the Tate – and that his relationship with her, if viewed from a certain angle, might be perceived as compromising. The truth was, Giacomo Baldini did feel that his priority was Habiba Popals, in a way that he was finding entirely disarming. The director of security of the National Gallery should not be seen to help a woman who had recently stolen one of their works of art and he was walking a tightrope in not issuing proceedings against her. But, as he had done almost from the start, he knew that he couldn't. Habiba had to be allowed to complete her unfinished business with Sean Dunmore. He made his choice and called her mobile.

'Habiba, it's me. Where are you?'

'I'm still at Sharifa's, but she's going to take me to my house in Shepherd's Bush.'

Baldini felt an immediate concern and he quickly flicked back through the pages of his notebook to reassure himself that he had this address.

'You might be surprised to hear that Dunmore has just been

to see me.' He waited for the information to sink in. 'I think you can guess what his story is. He blames you for everything, saying that you stole the painting to get even with him for having ended your relationship with him.'

'I don't suppose he mentioned assaulting me, did he?' she said with casual sarcasm.

'And he accused me of having an inappropriate relationship with you.' He could hear her pause and take on board this accusation.

'He is an unpleasant man. An evil man, Signor Baldini.' Habiba Popals said this quite calmly and he imagined her face as she spoke, recalled it in great detail, the certainty of her cause reflected in every contour, and it discomforted him to know that Sean Dunmore had recognised this.

'This is a difficult equation,' he said, aware of the ambiguous nature of the statement. 'It will be very difficult to prove that the assault took place.'

'No,' she said, 'it is really very simple. I know that it happened to me and I'm the only one that matters.'

Now it was his turn to hesitate and he gave a small, silent laugh, an invisible smile.

'So how can I help?'

'You're smiling, aren't you?'

'Yes, I am.'

'Good,' she said. 'You have helped. You listened.'

'You know what he is going to do now, don't you?'

'He'll come and look for me. He's angry. I have made a fool of him.'

It was what she wanted, he knew, a denouement of her own making, deliberately drawing Dunmore towards her despite the danger involved.

'You could make it worse for him,' she said quietly. 'You could release the news that the painting has been retrieved from his flat. He wouldn't like that. It would provoke him.'

'And in the meantime?'

'He's waiting to see which way you turn. You've not detained him, you haven't arrested me. He'll come after me, but I don't think he will commit himself just yet.'

'You're happy that he might follow you to Shepherd's Bush?'

'What is he going to do?'

'He's going to frighten you, Habiba.'

'You care, don't you?'

'I do.'

Gradually Habiba Popals was beginning to hear Giacomo Baldini more clearly. It was a sign that she was starting to emerge from the fortress that she had erected around herself since the assault. This had been a selfishness forced by necessity, but her obsession with self-protection had dulled some of her other senses, so that the empathy that the Italian had shown at the Tate had taken some time to work its way into her system. And now, in the middle of the phone conversation, she was once again picking up a certain tone of voice, an element of concern which, for so long, she had learnt to live without. She sat back and absorbed its significance, trying to see Giacomo Baldini as a person rather than as someone who could help her complete her task. He had loosened her defences without her being aware of it, allowed her to talk to him, enabled her to speak to Sharifa, and now she was conscious that parts of her were being called into play that she had deliberately put out of bounds a long time ago. It was dawning on Habiba that she didn't have to explain herself to this man, that he seemed to grasp what she was about even when she wasn't entirely sure herself, and the realisation took her by surprise.

'I'm sorry you find yourself in this strange position,' she said.

'I'm not,' he said, although he wondered if Miranda Goodheart or Colin Tyler would understand his position. At some stage, he would have to find out.

'Thank you,' she said and contained within this generic response were more feelings that she could quite understand.

'You will be deliberately putting yourself in danger,' he told her again, not in admonishment but simply as a matter of fact.

'I know,' she said, 'but it's the only way I can think of finishing it. I think you know that.'

'I do, but don't underestimate him, Habiba.'

Simply in the way he said her name, she could detect an intimacy which was new and different to her, a clear message which she was only just allowing herself to read.

'We haven't got long.'

'We haven't,' she replied, conscious that she had used the first person plural.

'You'll be nearby?'

'I'll be nearby.'

* * *

Sean Dunmore knew he had to be careful for he had engineered himself into a precarious corner of safety. He didn't waste time congratulating himself on his encounter with Giacomo Baldini, although in the end it went better than he had expected. What he needed to do now was second-guess what the director of security might do next and the more he thought about it the more he knew that he would announce the recovery of the painting. He could see the headlines, the precious masterpiece in the broom cupboard of a former security officer of the National Gallery. The malevolence that was gathering and expanding in his chest caused him to push his hand violently against the steering wheel and swear at the windscreen. Why hadn't he paraded the woman who had stolen the painting? Because he fancied her, didn't he?

'Bastard!' he shouted out of the window to no one in particular as he drove angrily back to New Cross to pick up where he had left off a couple of hours earlier. He assumed she would still be there and he imagined what he would do to her if he could get her alone. She would have to pay for what had happened and as he thought through the possibilities, his face took on the blank, distant look that Habiba had seen from the Thames, a face capable of the worst cruelty, a face devoid of even the slightest hint of sympathy. In the cold darkness of his mind he assembled the various elements of his bizarre logic to turn the world in his favour, to justify his actions. By the time he arrived at the house and parked under the dishevelled buddleia, he had found another way to further protect his position. He took out his mobile and, with the calm assurance of someone who knows he is right, called the National Gallery and asked for the director.

'It's Sean Dunmore,' he told the PA. 'I used to work with the security team at the gallery. I have some important information about the Messina theft.'

Miranda Goodheart's voice was typically bright when she came on to the line.

'Well, Mr Dunmore, thank you for calling. Miranda Goodheart here. I believe you have some news for me.'

'I do, indeed, Dr Goodheart. I think you should ask your new director of security why he hasn't organised the arrest of Habiba Popals, the woman who stole the painting.'

When Miranda Goodheart replied, her voice was slightly less jocular. 'I'm not sure I follow you, Mr Dunmore. I'm sure Mr Baldini is doing everything he can to draw this affair to its proper conclusion.'

'Affair may be exactly the right word. Baldini spent a good part of today with Popals and then allowed her to go. Why would he do that, Dr Goodheart?'

'I'm sure he had his reasons and that he will tell me those reasons in due course. I'm not clear why you are telling me this, Mr Dunmore.'

'Aren't you? I'm surprised. I would have thought it was quite clear. But I leave you with the image of Giacomo Baldini and Habiba Popals, sitting in the café of Tate Modern, with his hand on your thief's arm. They might just as well have been lovers.'

'You can't possibly be suggesting that he had something to do with the theft,' she said, knowing the idea was preposterous.

'I am suggesting that his judgement is clouded. His relationship is inappropriate and he has a clear conflict of interest.'

And with that he snapped shut his phone.

Miranda Goodheart sat holding the phone, looking out of the window at the plane trees along Charing Cross Road dancing in the wind, the shadows of the leaves shimmering on the Portland stone façade of the building opposite. She had achieved her success in life by a natural ability to separate the important from the trivial and to approach delicate issues in careful, flanking movements which would not leave her too exposed. She had been the recipient of much misinformation in her life, rumour with mischievous intent, political and personal, and she was adept at filtering fact from fiction. Her instincts now told her to wait, to draw breath before calling Giacomo Baldini and she continued to watch the trees and listen to the buses rumble towards Trafalgar Square.

If she had phoned, she would have found Giacomo Baldini's office empty.

*   *   *

Habiba Popals came out of the house at around half-past six, followed by a woman holding a baby. He assumed this was her friend Sharifa and he was disappointed to see that she was carrying a baby. They climbed into a white Ford Escort estate, the child strapped into the back seat alongside Habiba, the mother driving the car. It still seemed unreal to Sean Dunmore that Habiba Popals was a free agent and as he followed them through the now-familiar streets towards the Rotherhithe Tunnel, he began to see himself more and more as the enforcer of the law, his anger against the Indian laced with indignation, to produce a powerful blend of self-righteousness. Her freedom, which earlier in the afternoon he had viewed with suspicion, was now a red rag to his sense of unfairness. The toxic blue air of the tunnel further reflected his mood and he watched the car, four vehicles ahead of him, negotiate the narrow bends which led up to the north bank. He thought they were making for the Mile End Road and he began to think back to their session in the car park. He realised how tame it had been, a lost opportunity, for he had missed the chance to really hurt her. Back then, he was still only developing his taste for the exquisite conjunction of pain and sexual pleasure.

They didn't turn along the Mile End Road, but continued northwards towards Islington and then west on the Euston Road. It wasn't until the elevated section that he thought they might be making for her home in Shepherd's Bush, the address he'd first found when trying to track her down. The white Ford turned into a street of small terraced cottages not far from the tube. Eventually they pulled up and he was careful to drive beyond the white car as they manoeuvred to park. He watched them go into the house and then, a few minutes later, Sharifa re-emerge with the baby. He watched Habiba embrace them and dislike seeped out of him like lava from a volcano, corrosive and indiscriminate. He had no plan, but he was restless and impatient, goaded by this woman's continued freedom. He wanted desperately to get her alone, to see the fear in her face, to make her accountable for what she had done. And as he sat in the quiet street, his mind worked his way over her body and he imagined her resistance as he moved to touch her breasts, to slide his hands between her legs and he saw, with utter clarity, the look in her eyes when he slapped her across the face, the intake of breath at the shock, the fear of what was coming next.

She was alone now and he had to decide what to do. A tube rattled by and he felt the vibrations through the body of the car.

Chapter 34

It was strange to be in the flat again and its atmosphere closed uneasily around her, the stale air of emptiness, the faint smell of decay. She lit two candles and opened a window, keen to impose herself on the place again. So much had happened since she was last there, experiences which the flat seemed too small to contain. She began to clean the living room in a vain attempt to establish some normality in her life. It was only when she moved the big self-portrait to wipe the top of the mantelpiece that she was reminded of Uncle Badsha and the call she had made to him late that night that now seemed a thousand years ago. She would have to talk to him again soon and she put her hand to her forehead as she imagined his face when he read the news of what she had done, the sense of betrayal that he would feel that she hadn't confided in him. Something stopped her calling him now for she reasoned that, even if the morning papers carried reports of the recovery of the painting, her name would not be involved. It was only later, as she placed the picture of herself back in place, that she wondered if there were other reasons for her reluctance to speak to him. She looked up at the woman in the picture, a woman she barely recognised, her hair blowing in the wind, her eyes wild and lost, and considered her as she might a separate person. She could see the desperation in the face, apparently thrown back in exhilaration but in truth an expression of anguish, not dissimilar to the face of Christ. It was the first time she had recognised the similarity between the two pictures and she found it disconcerting that she should only see this now. What else was she likely to discover? Her perceptions were in the process of being realigned.

She was suddenly aware of the silence around her, turning in fright to look at the door to the living room and then quickly glancing to the window. Somewhere in the distance she could hear the sound of a drill and the faint tapping of a hammer. None of the tiny sounds she now heard were innocent and they all carried with them the possibility of re-interpretation. Again, the smell of Sean Dunmore came back to her, a Pavlovian memory triggered by fear and association. She returned to the picture to reassure herself. This was the person that Sean Dunmore had created, haunted and desperate, a woman crucified by his desires. Sean Dunmore, the lone predator, was out there somewhere and the picture, a permanent memory of what he had done to her, would help her hold her nerve until he arrived. Darkness fell on Shepherd's Bush.

He waited and watched, but no one came and no one left. Only the trains rattled to and fro and the cars hunted for places to park. A West Indian woman walked slowly towards him carrying bags of fruit and vegetables, the sway of her large backside emphasised by the tight white trousers she was wearing. She passed the car and looked down at him, her wide face smiling. He stared coldly back at her, his eyes following her until she turned out of his vision. A dog cocked his leg against the street name and trotted after her. This was a grubby part of the world and he despised being here. It was almost dark now and he climbed out of the car and walked to the end of the road and back, checking the other vehicles. As every second ticked by, his field of vision was narrowing and the other parts of his life – his job, his flat in Glasgow, the women in the bars on the quayside – were receding. This moment was the only one that mattered to him and he was driven forward by a desire that burned deep inside him, a cocktail of sexual desire and raw brutality. The boy who had brazenly slipped his hand into the tracksuit bottoms of his neighbour's daughter, was now the man capable of much blacker indiscretions. As he approached the front door his breathing became shallower and the stillness that came over his body was one that reflected complete confidence. What he was about to do was entirely justified. He looked at the two bells on the door-frame but decided against pressing either of them. He had seen that one of the windows in the bay was half-open and he silently moved to his left. The room inside was dark and it was impossible to see if anyone was inside. He moved back to the door and pressed the bottom bell, immediately moving back to the side of the window. The moment he saw the light go on in the hallway, he pushed the window further open and climbed through. He heard her demand at the door.

'Who is it?'

He could now make out the shapes in the room, lit by two candles on either side of a tall portrait of the Indian woman. He sat in a chair opposite, to one side of the door, his legs outstretched as they had been in Baldini's office. He heard her slide the security chain in place and the sound of her feet walking along the hall. She came into the room without noticing him and he looked at her from behind, aware once again of her height. She was wearing black tights over which she had a short dress studded here and there with pale sequins which reflected the flickering yellow of the candles. Even in this pale light he could see her shape, the graceful curve of her back and, as she turned slightly to pick up a cup from the table, the faint rise of her breasts. And then she froze, sensing that she wasn't alone, and as she completed her turn, she returned the cup to the table.

'You're here,' she said. She had smelled him before she saw him.

He merely looked at her, alive to the intimacy of the room, the closeness of her body and the suppressed anger that was inside him.

'You've been to a lot of trouble for me,' he said slowly and she heard the tension under his voice, the words issued under pressure. She said nothing. She knew that just behind her, in a scuttle by the fireplace, there was a brass-handled poker.

255

'Why?' he asked. 'Why?' Just a little louder this time.

Logic doesn't apply to this man, she knew, but she wanted to tell him anyway.

'You raped me,' she said.

He stood up suddenly and took a step towards her. She held her ground.

'And so you stole a picture from the National Gallery and put it in my flat. Let me ask you again, why?' He was shouting at her now and she felt his spittle on her face.

'You wouldn't understand,' she said and was too slow to avoid the open palm that swung in her direction and slapped her face with a stunning crack. She fell across the table and held her cheek.

'Think you're so clever, don't you? You wanted to humiliate me, didn't you? Well, no one can prove what happened years ago. They're going to put you away, girl. All that trouble for nothing.' His eyes were wide and he was pointing at her.

Her face was hot and stinging and it felt lopsided. Her thoughts were clear, though, and the sight of Sean Dunmore swaggering in front of her made her realise what she had wanted to do ever since that fateful night in Mile End.

'Not for nothing, Sean Dunmore. I'll bring you down with me, you and your disgusting ways.'

This time she was quick enough to avoid a second blow and in the instant that Sean Dunmore lost his balance, she picked up the poker from the fireplace. She looked at him now, her eyes daring him to move towards her, the poker motionless in her right hand.

'You wouldn't dare.'

She said nothing.

'A major theft and now GBH. You won't be out for a long time, will you?'

'You're not very brave, are you, Sean Dunmore? And not really that attractive. You needed to use drugs to get your way with women. How pathetic is that?'

He lunged forward again and she smacked him across the side of his head with the poker, feeling the contact against the bone and the skin. He grunted and clutched the side of his head with his hand, staggering into the bay of the window. Then, with an awful roar, he picked up the chair he had been sitting on and rushed at her, the second blow she aimed at him merely splintering the wooden frame. The chair knocked her backwards and he was able to grab the end of the metal poker. She aimed a kick between his legs and he doubled up in self-protection. Then, triumphantly, he rose up, the poker in his right hand, tapping it against his open palm.

'Take your clothes off,' he demanded and banged the poker hard against the table. 'Go on. Start with your tights. Go on.' He jabbed her in the ribs and she collapsed to her knees. Habiba scanned the floor, a bloody drool dropping on to the boards. He came behind her and put his arms around her, pressing his hands into her breasts.

'C'mon Habiba Popals. Not quite so clever now, are we?' He yanked at the dress and ripped it off, revealing a pale silk vest. She instinctively covered herself, but he rapped her knuckles and she dropped her arms. He lifted the hem of the vest with the end of the poker, pushing it higher and higher until he could just glimpse the bottom of her breasts. She pulled away and tried to grab the poker, but he dodged and thwacked the top of her arm. She winced and fell to her knees again.

'Make it easy on yourself, Habiba. You don't want me to hurt you any more, do you?' He was goading her and the way he spoke the words made it sound as if he was encouraging her to fight back.

He came round behind her again, the poker raised to strike her. With his free hand he felt under the silk shirt, touching her nipple. She flinched and kicked hard against his shins but he pushed her forward so hard that she collided with the wall, bringing down a picture, which smashed against the floor. He raised the poker to strike her across the neck, but a voice called from the window.

'Don't. Put it down, now.'

Sean Dunmore froze, the poker above his head, Baldini's voice ringing in his ears, and turned to see the outline of the Italian framed in the bay window. In one movement, he adjusted his position and hurled the poker towards the profile, watching it turn end on end until it struck the glass which then shattered over the shadowy body. He heard the exclamation of pain from the other man and then moved to the door, which he assumed led to the kitchen and then out to the back garden. He ran across the small yard and leapt over the fence at the back on to a group of plastic dustbins, which absorbed his fall. A dog barked next door and a group of cats scattered around him. He continued running along the dark passage towards the sodium lights he could see in the distance. There was no noise behind him and looking back he could see that he was not being followed. He slowed his pace and kicked another plastic dustbin, which erupted and released an explosion of rubbish into the air.

Baldini took off his jacket and placed it around her shoulders before putting his hands gently on either side of her arms. He was not interested in Sean Dunmore, only the woman in front of him.

'Let me see your face,' he said and she looked back at him. The bruising was emerging around her left eye and a dark blue wheal stained the top of her right arm.

The relief he felt was palpable and it mingled with the residual fear that if he had been just seconds later the poker might have smashed across her face, the proud face which was now inches from his own. It was all he could do not to embrace her.

'I want to get him,' she said.

'You will,' he said. 'We will. Put something on.'

She was beginning to shake now, but there was no fear in the eyes that had looked back at him. She changed into jeans and a pullover, his jacket still around her shoulders. His mind was racing ahead, the fury he felt being channelled into planning what they should do next.

Whilst she was in the other room, he blew out the candles and when she returned he asked her to turn out the lights. She followed him to the front door and then along to his car, where he opened the door for her.

'I think he'll come back for his car,' he said. 'We should wait.'

And they sat in the half-light of the grey BMW and he waited for her to speak.

'What if he doesn't come back?' she asked.

'We'll find him, don't worry.'

She looked even more beautiful to him now, her lower lip slightly swollen, her hair dropping across her forehead and her eyes staring through the windscreen, scanning the street. When he had seen Dunmore standing behind her with the poker he had never before felt so impotent in his life, but never more sure.

'You know why we have to find him, don't you?'

'Oh, yes,' he said, 'I know why we have to find him.' She glanced across to him and looked at the shape of his face in the light of the streetlight. She had caught that tone of voice again, but this time she wasn't surprised and was quite ready to receive it. Habiba Popals fully realised that she didn't need to explain to Giacomo Baldini what she was doing and that, to him, this whole elaborate adventure was perfectly normal and entirely understandable. The pain of her bruises seem to recede and she pushed back the strand of black hair that had dropped across her eyes.

Sean Dunmore crept back to his car just before four o'clock, keeping to the shadows of the street, before starting it up and driving it away, lights unlit, towards a deserted Shepherd's Bush Green. It was difficult to follow him across London because Baldini suspected that Dunmore knew he drove the grey BMW. On the near-empty roads he kept his distance, but when they arrived at Smithfield, the market was in full swing, so it was relatively easy to observe Sean Dunmore park his car and enter the hotel. Baldini watched the front of the cheap building until a light came on in a room on the second floor.

At the same time, they turned to face each other. This was not one person leading another, but a partnership, unofficial and without contract, but mutually understood. Somewhere, in the short time she had known him, a line had been crossed. She looked at him, and the noise of the lorries, the shouts of the porters and the paraphernalia of the market seemed to emphasise the moment, containing them at the centre of the activity, an opera in which they were the stars. For Baldini, the line had been crossed a long time before, perhaps even before he met her, when he first began to comprehend what drove this woman with the remarkable face and piercing eyes. He didn't have to ask her if she was prepared to do what had to come next and for a moment they sat silently in the centre of the wall of sound around them.

'You have taken my side,' she said after a while.

'There was no side to take,' he replied after a while. 'You may find this hard to believe, but the moment I stood in the gallery and looked at the space where the picture should have been, I sensed something different. The smoke was still in the air and I knew this wasn't what it appeared to be.' He looked across at her. 'It wasn't.'

'And you, Giacomo, I know nothing about you.'

'Oh, I think you do, Habiba. Of this I am certain. Whether you like what you see, what you know, I cannot say.'

He looked down at her hand and saw the blood bubbling up through the bruise which Sean Dunmore had caused. He knew he shouldn't hold this hand, that it was too soon, and the wound that lay between them was not only the reason that they were together at the beginning of a cold dawn in the shadows of the ancient market, but the reason, too, that they were still apart.

Chapter 35

They called to her as she and Baldini crossed the market to the hotel.

'Bit late for this sort of thing, isn't it, love?'

'Was you the black sheep of the family, darlin'?'

The aroma of damp meat hung in the air and a rack of pigs' torsos was wheeled in front of them, the porter giving a low wolf whistle at Habiba.

The hotel's clients were nocturnal, coming and going from midnight to the early hours of the morning, and the reception desk of the brightly lit lobby was manned by a balding man with a ruddy face. He'd seen everything in his time so the arrival of a smartly dressed man and a tall Paki girl didn't strike him as particularly unusual.

'I need to talk to one of your guests,' Baldini told him and he noticed the look of surprise on his face. It was a long time since any of the drivers who dossed down there had been called 'guests'.

'He's on the second floor,' Baldini added and with that they moved towards the stairs and the night porter returned to scrutinising the runners and riders for later that day at Folkestone.

They stood together in the dimly lit hallway in front of the door he estimated to be Sean Dunmore's and before he knocked he beckoned Habiba to one side so that she wouldn't be seen when the door was opened.

'What is it?'

'Porter.' Baldini said.

He heard the door unlock and saw the handle turn and even before Sean Dunmore had time to peer through the crack, Baldini had put all his weight behind it and forced his way in. The two men stood looking at each other.

'We meet again, Mr Dunmore.' Baldini said and by now Habiba had followed him into the bedroom.

'This woman, Habiba Popals, has some unfinished business with you.'

He watched Dunmore dart a glance across to Habiba and he could see, almost hear, the process of justification and denial taking shape inside him. The violence that had been in Dunmore's eyes when he burst into the room was being replaced by the familiar sly look of confidence. He pulled the chair out from the table next to the bed and sat down, crossing his legs and brushing an imaginary speck of dirt from his trousers. A thin blue line of bruising was visible along his left cheek.

'I went to see her and she attacked me,' he said, pointing at Habiba, 'with a poker.'

'Why would she do that, Mr Dunmore?'

'I told you, she's cross with me, you know, for letting her down before. What do they say about a woman scorned?'

'Oh,' said Habiba, adopting a mocking tone, 'I don't think we are talking about scorn, Mr Dunmore. I think the word is abuse. Perhaps you would help me remember exactly what went on.'

'You can't remember because you were drunk,' he replied, offhand, looking first to her and then across to Baldini for affirmation. 'I'm not surprised you can't remember.'

'Now, then,' she said, with exaggerated slowness. 'Wasn't there a drug involved. Rohypnol, I think it's called? You have plenty of it in your flat in Glasgow.'

Sean Dunmore did not change his demeanour. 'You broke in, didn't you?' He was smiling, leaning back in the chair. 'You put it there.'

'I didn't break in, Mr Dunmore,' Baldini interrupted. 'I had a warrant to search your apartment. I found it.'

'But she could have put it there in the first place, couldn't she?' he said, looking again at the Italian. 'This is entrapment.'

'I saw you attempt to strike this woman,' Baldini said, but

knowing in advance that Sean Dunmore would have an answer.

'Is your dick so small you don't want girls to see it?' Habiba Popals said. 'You quite clearly have a problem in that area. Girls don't fancy you normally, do they?'

Baldini was surprised and looked across to Habiba. She was goading Sean Dunmore, speaking with an extreme south London drawl, a deliberately mocking tone, sneering and insolent. She was smiling at him, her face tipped forwards, daring him to respond.

The smile was still on Sean Dunmore's face but it only related to the shape of his mouth. His eyes looked at her menacingly and Baldini knew that if he had not been there, Dunmore would have struck Habiba to the ground.

'You see,' Habiba continued, 'you are a weak man, a weak man who doesn't like women and who women can see through. Isn't that right? I should think you're a mummy's boy, aren't you, Sean Dunmore? You think that all women adore you like your dear mummy. I expect she wanted to have sex with you, didn't she? Perhaps you're gay, really.'

He lunged at her now, his fist raised to smash into her face, but the bulk of Giacomo Baldini blocked him, catching him across his chest and stomach below the flailing arm. He went sprawling sideways across the bed and when he stood up he was leaning back against the wall.

'She let you think you could do anything and get away with it, didn't she, Sean?' She was still talking like a street girl from Tooting Bec, her hands on her hips and her head tilted backwards.

'And that's why you have become a pest. You don't care about the lives you destroy, do you, mummy's boy?'

Baldini watched her goad him, making the phrase as pathetic-sounding as she could, taunting him with it.

'You bitch,' he said. 'Who'd want you, anyway? Skin and bones.' He spat the words at her.

'Well, apparently you did, Mr Sean Dunmore. Because you

followed me, didn't you, across the floors of the gallery? Lapping me up on the monitors, weren't you? Getting your fill without me knowing. That's your style isn't it? Safer that way. You're a twisted nonentity, Sean Dunmore. Nothing more, nothing less, than a mummy's boy.'

And as she said this phrase again, she leant forward and spoke the words into his face. He rushed at her again and grabbed her by the shoulders even as Baldini held on to the top of his arms and pulled him back.

'I'm glad I didn't put it into you, you pock-ridden bitch,' he screamed. 'You weren't worth the effort. You were only good enough for me to wipe my cock on.'

And with this, he pushed violently back at Baldini, who fell against the bed and hit his head on the metal frame, loosening his grip on the man. As he stood and turned to the door, Sean Dunmore made to strike Habiba again, but she ducked under his fist and lashed out with her leg and felt it disappear into the soft flesh of his stomach. And then the door slammed and he was gone, clattering down the stairs into the first streaks of dawn.

Neither of them moved as they regained their breath and took stock of what had just happened.

'Thank you,' she said quietly.

The drama of the market continued beneath them, the raw meat coming and going, as another one was being played out above, in the dismal room in which the smell of Sean Dunmore still lingered

'You let me do it,' she continued.

'I wouldn't have known how to,' Baldini said. 'You knew how to get under his guard. I didn't.'

'You did. You knew,' she said simply, and he looked over and saw that she was smiling.

'He said it, didn't he?'

'He did.'

Her smile was wider now, but it was fragile and he watched as it was transformed into tears. She began to weep, the strength leaving her legs, but could not bring herself to sit on the bed, a bed in which he had slept. At first she just stood there, her shoulders shaking, her face hidden by her hands. He put his arm around her and led her to the chair. After a while she stopped and looked out of the window at the accumulation of trucks under a grey-pink sky.

'I know what happened.'

'You know what happened,' he echoed.

'I would have killed him,' she said, looking at him.

'Oh, I know that,' he said quietly. 'You still can.'

And she laughed, the tears rolling down her face, and she knew with absolute certainty that this was the first time she had laughed properly for four years, laughed with the whole of her body. The joy was indistinguishable from the tears, each the product of relief, and as they continued the image of Sean Dunmore began to recede, bit by bit, imperceptibly at first, but as the sun came up, his retreat was undeniable.

'Is there any need to know more?' he asked her.

'Do you know what it means to me to know that he has not been inside me?'

He nodded.

'I cannot have those years back but I will trade them for that small piece of information.'

The sun was now touching the ornate metalwork on top of the market building and the white-coated workers began to melt away, like so many Draculas. He took her down to a café and they drank coffee as the porters continued to observe them with open curiosity, looking directly at her black eye and the wound on her hand. They swapped stories of what might have happened but none came close to the truth. In this case, life was stranger than fiction and had they been party to the true story of Habiba Popals, they would have laughed it away in disbelief.

His phone rang and he noticed it was seven o'clock as he

pulled it out of his pocket, seeing that it was Miranda Goodheart. He registered that he had received half a dozen other missed calls and several texts. He knew what they were about, and for now he ignored them all. He took her hand and laid his paper napkin across its back and watched the beads of blood seep into its whiteness. He didn't want to think beyond this moment for he couldn't condemn himself for anything he had done. He didn't even want to alert Colin Tyler about Sean Dunmore, nor justify himself to the director of the gallery.

'What now, Giacomo?' she said.

He didn't want her to call him Jack. Ever.

'Ah,' he said. 'So much.'

And she smiled at him, his hand still resting on her hand, the specks of blood now dried into tiny dots on the napkin.

'It's been a long journey for you, hasn't it?'

'Why do you support me?'

He shrugged. 'It's been the easiest thing to do in my life. Perhaps I recognise something in you.'

And he felt her spread her fingers, just a little, so that they accommodated his hand more easily.

'So, shall we go and face the music?'

'Of course,' she said and the porters watched them as they left, the tall woman from Pakistan and the stocky Italian with the greying hair. If they had continued to watch, they would have seen him take the underneath of her elbow, as he had done in the Tate, before helping her into his car.

*   *   *

They didn't rehearse what they were going to say and in the car Giacomo made calls to Miranda and Colin and arranged to meet them shortly after nine. He was perfectly pleasant on the phone but clear that he was not prepared to discuss anything until he met them. Miranda Goodheart told him that she would assemble as many board members as she could and, for what he had in mind to do, this seemed appropriate. Afterwards, they settled into an easy silence but later, as they nosed their way into the underground garage opposite the National Gallery, and were swallowed into the darkness, Habiba suddenly sat forward.

'This is where he brought me after the pub. I know it.'

He watched her as she shook her head, desperately trying to accommodate this shred of information into a larger whole. He parked the car and turned off the ignition and he listened as it ticked and settled into silence.

'They will come back to you, these fragments of memory,' he said, not looking at her, but into the darkened windscreen, 'perhaps all your life. What you have to do is make sure that . . . '

' . . . that they don't spoil that life,' Habiba said as she, too, stared directly ahead. They stayed like this for a few minutes, in silence, before they set off to the gallery.

They were waiting for them, fanned out around the large table in Miranda Goodheart's office. The director was flanked by Colin Tyler, and the various members of the Board, whom he had met only a few days earlier, sat in mute expectation. Miranda Goodheart was in her element, fully aware of the importance of this meeting and determined to orchestrate it in such a way that she emerged unscathed.

'Well,' she said brightly, 'we had begun to wonder what had happened to you.' And with this she looked at Habiba as if to say 'and I know this is the person who detained you.'

'This is Habiba Popals,' Giacomo Baldini began. 'Miranda and Colin,' he continued, nodding at each of them, 'you are familiar with her.' Then, turning to the members of the Board, 'Familiar because we have all been viewing CCTV footage of her recorded recently and four years ago. Four years ago she also attracted the attention of a man who worked here at the National Gallery . . . '

' . . . Sean Dunmore,' added Miranda Goodheart.

Giacomo Baldini glanced across to Habiba, who, in return, looked back and gave him the smallest of nods. She knew he had been seeking permission to tell her story.

'Sean Dunmore went on to rape Habiba and I wouldn't be surprised if he'd used the gallery to pursue other women as well.'

Habiba noticed that he continued to look at her, rather than the others in the room.

'For the next four years Habiba suffered the psychological reaction that many victims of rape experience and it was only recently that she decided to do something about it.'

And now he turned to face the others.

'She decided to take a picture from the gallery and leave it in Sean Dunmore's flat in Glasgow.'

'To make us think that he had stolen it?' a member of the Board asked in disbelief.

'No,' Giacomo Baldini said, with a weak smile. 'No, not at all. She wanted to tell the world about the man who raped her. She wanted to confront him with the consequences of his actions.'

'For goodness' sake,' he heard the man mutter.

He was still smiling, though, as he continued the story. 'Four years ago she had fallen in love with the tiny Messina and, correct me if I am wrong, Habiba, you took this as a symbol of something that Sean Dunmore had destroyed, a certain innocence, I think.'

There was silence in the room, a quietness emphasised by the noises in the street outside and Giacomo Baldini paused in this calm, as if waiting for the information he had just given to percolate through.

'An eye for an eye,' Miranda Goodheart said, wanting to establish the reality of what had taken place.

'Not entirely, I think,' Baldini countered. 'This was much more sophisticated.'

'It sounds as if you are on her side,' said another member of the board, a woman with wild, curly black hair and a large necklace of wooden beads. Baldini chose to ignore her.

'Habiba had no intention of harming the picture. Its return to the gallery was always assured. She recorded sequences of it at Sean Dunmore's flat, images she posted on a website to emphasise the incongruity of its presence in Sean Dunmore's world. As Habiba told me, the painting was a catalyst, a means to an end. And you have it safely back now.'

'Are you suggesting, Giacomo, that we do nothing about this?' Miranda asked innocently and her remark opened a floodgate of indignation from the great and the good gathered around her table.

'We can't be seen to encourage this sort of behaviour,' said one.

'Surely this primitive form of revenge belongs to another era,' said the woman with the large hair and big beads.

'What do you have in mind, Jack?' asked Colin Tyler, aware that Baldini would have predicted these responses.

'The gallery has a problem, I concede,' he said. 'It has to be seen to respond to a criminal act but it has also to acknowledge that it allowed one of its staff to use its resources to commit at least one rape and perhaps more.'

'Quite, quite,' said Miranda Goodheart, who moved uncomfortably in her chair. 'I should say at this stage that I have received two phone calls from Sean Dunmore, one yesterday and the other this morning, just before you arrived. You might not be surprised to learn that he views proceedings in a somewhat different way from you.'

She waited for a response, but there was none.

'He denies rape. He believes that you, Ms Popals, acted out of revenge because he didn't want to continue the relationship you started four years ago.'

'Stop this.' Giacomo Baldini held out his arm and the director look startled at the sudden interruption. He took from his top pocket the small recorder which he had used in his office and which he had taken to Smithfield. He tossed it to Colin Tyler, who caught it neatly.

'He admits it on tape. It's towards the end, but don't listen to it now. You need to call your friends in Glasgow and get them round to impound his flat.' He looked at the director now. 'He used a date-rape drug which we found there and will still be there, unless he gets to it first.'

Miranda Goodheart absorbed this information quickly, as she was trained to do, and Colin Tyler got up to use his phone at the far end of the room.

'Sean Dunmore aims to make things difficult for you, Giacomo. He tells me that you are having a relationship, a compromising relationship, with Ms Popals.'

When she said this she didn't look at Habiba, but slightly tilted her head as she spoke to Baldini, her eyes still fixed on the Italian.

He smiled again, a small one, acknowledging that private thought somewhere deep inside him.

'Sadly,' he said, 'this is untrue. I cannot pretend that I have not been mightily impressed by Habiba Popals, but it is entirely untrue to say that we are having a relationship, compromising or not.'

Habiba Popals watched Giacomo Baldini, still weighing the word 'sadly'. She had felt strange standing in front of these people who regarded her, from time to time, as if she was an item in an auction whose provenance was uncertain. And now he had cut across all of this by hinting at something that was way beyond what they were discussing. She looked over to him and he was regarding her evenly.

'This is ludicrous,' the woman with the beads exclaimed. 'You cannot be the director of security and take sides with the thief who stole one of our paintings.'

'Yes, it is the perception that counts here,' Baldini continued, 'for no matter what I do, we do, Sean Dunmore will let it be known that I did not arrest Habiba as soon as we knew that she had taken the painting. Neither did we bring in Sean Dunmore. Habiba needed the freedom to confront him, which she did last night. You will hear what happened on that tape and you'll be able to form your own opinions. However, it will be easier for you to do so if I step down and so I am offering my resignation. I will deliver it in writing later today.'

If a silence can double, it did so now and, by the same scale, the noises from outside increased. It was Habiba who spoke first.

'This is entirely wrong. You have your painting. You have the reasons I took it and protected it. And you know, or you will do soon, that Sean Dunmore is a vicious and dangerous man. Why should Giacomo Baldini have to suffer for us?'

Miranda Goodheart knew exactly why and she was grateful that her new appointment understood the curious way these situations were handled. Nevertheless, a doubt was nagging her and since she found it difficult to put flesh on it, her instincts told her she should take heed.

'If that is your wish, Giacomo, but if you would allow us some time to consider the matter. Perhaps Ms Popals could give us a moment or two together.'

Habiba was incensed, hearing the sing-song tones of the gallery's director, the political manoeuvring that was taking place around Giacomo Baldini. More than that, she was absorbing the fact that he had offered to sacrifice his job for her.

She walked towards the table and looked at them all and the fierceness of her gaze made one or two of them look away.

'I'm sorry, young lady,' the woman with the hair and beads said, 'we don't do things like this here. We don't take the law into our own hands.'

'It wasn't law that I took into my own hands,' she said, 'it was my life. I would like to talk to Signor Baldini. Now.'

She turned and walked to the door.

'Why did you do that?' she demanded outside.

'It's the way things are done,' he told her as she approached him, her eyes carrying the fury she felt.

'Ha!' she said. 'You would sacrifice your job for me?'

'I believe I would,' he replied. She let this information settle on her.

'I don't have long, do I?'

He shook his head. 'They will have to make this official and it all depends if charges are made. That will be a police decision.'

'I have to go somewhere, now,' she told him. 'Later, you will be able to find me at home.'

When Colin Tyler came out of the director's office, he found Baldini standing there staring along the corridor towards the stairs where, a few moments earlier, Habiba Popals' silhouette had slowly disappeared out of his sight.

Chapter 36

She was on the Central Line again, the stale warm air reminding her of the journey she had taken that morning so long ago, the day after the event that had split her life into before and after. Now another divide approached, one which she could sense but not quite put a shape to yet. It had begun to emerge as the train rattled back from Glasgow, after she had left the painting in the flat, but now it was beginning to take a more potent form, at the centre of which was Giacomo Baldini. He had never questioned the tortuous way she had decided to expose Sean Dunmore and now, somewhere after Chancery Lane, this fact began to open doors which she'd thought had been shut, or had not even realised were there. The first of these led directly to the Italian. The assault had arrested her sexuality, dealt it a blow from which she thought she would never recover. She had spent four years denying it, circumnavigating it, replacing it with hectic activity and fierce creativity. It was not surprising, then, that this door had been shut and that even now she entered it with some apprehension. By Old Street she had begun to see Giacomo Baldini differently, as a man, rather than as a champion or guardian. She thought about his words again: 'sadly not'. She knew now what he meant. It was perhaps the realisation of this which pushed her towards another door. Why had she, an intelligent woman, about to start a prestigious and well-paid job, jeopardised it all with the elaborate and outrageous theft of the painting? Only now, as the train approached Mile End station, did she consider, for the first time, the consequences of her actions and this, in turn, brought her right back to Giacomo Baldini. He had never once made her think of these, letting her believe that her cause was just and her actions appropriate.

The escalator carried her upwards and the stale air pushed her out of the station on to the dirty pavement and the roar of the main road. Just beyond this clamorous thoroughfare, beyond the terrace of dilapidated houses in front of her, lay an unexpected oasis of quiet and beauty. At the centre of this was a garden square of imposing Georgian terraced houses, proud behind their iron railings. Habiba had spoken to Badsha on the phone and so he was pre-warned that she wanted to speak to him about something serious. They kissed and he led her to the upstairs drawing room, dominated by two floor-to-ceiling sash windows which looked on to the square where an autumn sun was just catching the yellowing leaves. The gentleness of the light and the beauty of the square were at odds with the story that Habiba told Badsha. It was the third time she had explained her actions and this, combined with the quietness of the room, made it less of a confessional and more a dispassionate recounting of fact. Habiba reasoned that she wanted Badsha to know what had happened before he read about it in the papers or saw it on the television news, but the more she spoke the more she understood that this wasn't just an act of politeness. She knew that he might help her understand what she had done and that it would allow her to talk about this man Giacomo Baldini for the first time.

Badsha's face barely changed as the story unfolded although she noticed his eyes narrow when she told him of the assault that had taken place not a stone's throw from where they were now sitting. She told him everything, the theft, the placing of the painting in the Glasgow flat, the involvement of Giacomo Baldini.

'For so long,' she explained, leaning forward with her elbows on her knees, 'I didn't know what to do. I tried to suppress my feelings hoping that they would somehow disappear with time. In fact, the very opposite happened and I began to dread the arrival of each day. I thought if I shouted loud enough, I could blot out the thoughts that kept coming back to me, but they were always there, waiting for me.'

As she spoke, Badsha was shaking his head, tiny movements which accompanied her words.

'I knew I couldn't go to the police,' she continued, 'for quite apart from the fact that they wouldn't have believed me, or had any sympathy for a Pakistani, I knew it wouldn't have been enough. My reply to the man who did this to me had to be slower, more complete. It had to mean more, for me. Do you know what I mean, Badsha?'

'More than you know,' he said.

'The idea to take the picture came to me perfectly formed, as if it had been a plan lying in a drawer waiting to be discovered. I recognised it immediately and never doubted that it would work. It is only now that I wonder where it came from.'

Now it was her turn to shake her head and she stared out of the window as if looking for a sign that would answer her question.

'As soon as I started, it felt right. I was at last addressing the problem that was inside me. It was out in the open, in front of me, and I could deal with it on my terms. It wasn't a question of making Sean Dunmore understand. He could never do that. It was about helping me understand, helping me claw back what I had lost, helping me catch up with my life. My father would never have understood, would he?'

Badsha was looking at her, watching her calm and careful manner, the certainty which radiated from her, and he stood up and went over to the window. The square, neat and ordered, lay before him, the flower beds perfectly symmetrical, the footpaths exactly dissecting the space.

'Ali, the man who should have been your father, would have understood,' he said, turning to face Habiba. 'Your mother spoke of him often, to me, in private. I told you, he kept in touch by letter, which he would send to me for Jamila. It is a tragedy that these two were kept apart. Perhaps what you did was for her as well. You may have been righting two wrongs.'

Habiba frowned, imagining her mother with this other life, one she, Habiba, knew nothing about, unable, or unwilling, to do anything about it, and she glimpsed the impossibility of Jamila's position. Her mother was still bound by the conventions of a society which, even though it had expelled her, still kept her firmly in its grip. Secretly, though, she had maintained a lifeline for herself and Badsha had been a go-between, keeping her mother in touch with the happiness she had been forced to leave behind.

'I was lucky, wasn't I?' she said quietly to Badsha, who gave the tiniest shrug of his shoulders. She was a child of Tooting Bec, a south London girl, who had been given freedoms unknown to her mother, freedoms that had allowed her to fight her own demons. He looked at the bruising on her face, the darkness that spread from her eye down through her cheek and at the dark blue patch on the back of her hand and he could see the warrior in her, far removed from the urban landscape of a big city, at home in a different landscape.

'And what of this man, Giacomo Baldini?' he asked.

'It is as if I have begun to see him for the first time,' Habiba said. 'He seemed to understand what I had done without me explaining, but I didn't see this at first. He has risked his job for me. Don't you think that is remarkable?'

Badsha had listened to Habiba's story and the part that Giacomo Baldini had played in it and he could see how she couldn't quite account for his growing importance.

'Perhaps not,' he said. 'Perhaps he needs something from you and you can't quite see it that way round.'

Habiba looked up at him, waiting for Badsha to continue.

'Perhaps,' he said, 'he has fallen in love with you.'

Habiba could not help but smile at this statement, for in so many ways she immediately felt it was the truth. The circumstances in which this had taken place had meant that she could not properly acknowledge the fact until now. The moment she heard

Badsha say it, she allowed it to become a reality for the first time.

'He sees something of himself in you, I think,' Badsha added. 'I know you won't like me saying it, but you are both driven by forces that you sometimes would rather deny. What do you feel about him?'

'I have not been able to think about that, Badsha,' she said, still smiling. 'Until last night, when I finally confronted Sean Dunmore, my mind had been closed to those thoughts. It was impossible to think in that way. But now . . . '

She thought about his very public declaration, in front of everyone at the gallery, that he was sad that he was not having a relationship with her and she smiled even more. She knew that the next time she was with Giacomo Baldini, she would see him very differently.

'Come,' Badsha said, 'let us go and have that lunch we couldn't enjoy last time.'

As they walked down the stairs he wanted to think that Habiba Popals was a natural successor to the women he had described at that last lunch, but he couldn't, for in so many ways she was different. This was a woman who had taken destiny into her own hands and his admiration for her was unlike that which he afforded her predecessors. It was true that her father could only see the line of women that came before his daughter as bringing disgrace on the family. He had been unable to see the daughter developing in front of him, to understand that she was a wise and resilient Londoner, a product of an environment that was entirely natural to her as much as it was alien to him. And that was a pain they both had to endure.

Habiba looked back at him, her wide eyes alive and the smile a reminder of how she used to be.

*   *   *

He made two razor slashes across the eyes, the canvas peeling back to produce two voids. He then stuck the poker into her body, several violent thrusts each puncturing a hole in the painting before finally smashing it into her face. He swept the objects off the top of the mantelpiece and, with the heel of his shoe, crushed the lustre saucer which had been holding a candle. He looked back at the painting, the girl eyeless, her stomach a gaping hole. He should have done this to the painting of Jesus.

It had been easy getting into the flat, stepping through the broken window which he had smashed the day before. He could feel the bruise on his stomach where she had kicked him and he pressed it so that the pain would remind him of what he would like to do to the girl. It was dangerous to come back to the house but he wasn't prepared to take the train back to Glasgow, his tail between his legs. He still believed right was on his side but he had moved beyond logic now and all he wanted to do was severely punish the Indian for all she had put him through. He went into her bedroom and began pulling her clothing out of the chest of drawers. When he came to her underwear he ran his fingers over the cotton and silk before using the razor to cut the crotches out of the knickers and the fine lace of the bras. He then went out to the road, as he had several times already, knowing that there was a chance that Baldini would return, perhaps even with the girl. He walked to the top of the road, by the tube station, and sat in a pub with a view of both the tube exit and the road opposite. He waited and watched, occasionally rubbing his hand over his stomach, a predator once more.

Chapter 37

'What's going on, Jack?'

Colin Tyler was sitting on the edge of Giacomo Baldini's desk, in the terracotta room. In the short space of time they had worked together, he had developed a real respect for the Italian but he was finding it difficult to understand the recent turn of events.

'I've listened to the tape, so we have a case against Dunmore,' he continued. 'He's not returned to the flat, so they've got it cordoned off. We just need to bring Habiba Popals in. I'm not sure why you let her go.'

Baldini screwed up a piece of paper and rolled it into a ball and tossed it towards a bin by the far wall, where it fell short.

'Precisely, Colin. That's why I have resigned. As far as this place is concerned, my action is illogical and I'm not sure that any explanation from me would help.'

'What explanation is that, Jack?'

Giacomo Baldini looked up at his colleague and for an instant wondered whether his motives should remain private. In the end, though, he believed that Colin deserved to know why Habiba Popals was not sitting in this office with them.

'I don't know where she went, Colin, but I do know it will be to finish what she set off to do when she took the painting. You see,' he said, standing and putting his hands in his pockets, 'mad as it may seem, I don't think Habiba committed a crime. Or, if she did, it was a crime under duress and to a large degree ultimately excusable. I know, I know, it's an indefensible position. But what makes it worse, what makes it impossible, is that I have fallen in love with Habiba Popals.'

He saw the look of surprise on the policeman's face.

'Let me tell you, though, that she doesn't know this and that nothing, I repeat, nothing has happened between us. Nevertheless, you can see that my position is untenable.' He retrieved the ball of paper with his foot and flicked it into the bin.

Colin Tyler remained silent.

'You see,' said Giacomo Baldini with sudden animation, 'it was a way of purging what had happened to her, an extraordinarily sophisticated form of revenge. The picture was never in any real danger, but she had been in the aftermath of the rape. She denied the impact of the assault for as long as she could and then chose her way of releasing it. Amazing, really. Imagine, stealing a painting of Christ, one that both represented your innocence and your anguish and depositing it in the flat of the man who raped you. And then, on top of it all, posting a video of it on a website for the world to see.'

'It's still a crime, though, in the eyes of that world, Jack.'

Giacomo Baldini nodded. 'I know, I know.' And then, suddenly stiffening. 'You know he attacked her, twice. If I hadn't been there, he would have done her some real damage. Where are we on bringing him in?'

'We don't know where he is, Jack. He didn't return to Smithfield. His hire car is still there. He might be on a train to Glasgow, but I doubt it. He'll be down here still.'

Giacomo Baldini thought for a moment, his body still, his face to the brown wall, his back to his colleague and he could see exactly what was going to happen next. A good lawyer would get Sean Dunmore off by claiming provocation and unreasonable behaviour on the part of Habiba Popals. She would be forced to endure a humiliating court case during which his own compromising position would be revealed. The bigger crime, the sexual assault on Habiba, would be obfuscated with the evidence on tape open to interpretation. No one would even be able to prove that he had used the drugs that had been found in his flat. Habiba's private solution to her grievance, her own system of justice, was one that wouldn't be understood by the rest of the world, as Colin had said.

'We need to find them, both of them,' he told Colin, his mind still in the future, counting the difficulties that lay ahead for Habiba.

They drove to Shepherd's Bush, the Italian outlining what had taken place there and at Smithfield, and Colin began to see the true picture of Sean Dunmore.

'What a nasty piece of work,' he said. It was a phrase he repeated when he clambered into the flat through the broken window and saw the painting hanging crookedly on the wall of the living room, the eyes blank, the body destroyed. But it was in the bedroom that a real fear gripped Giacomo Baldini, a pervading sense of evil, and at once he felt hopeless. Why did he let her go so easily? Had Sean Dunmore already got to her? The panic rose in him and he picked up his mobile to call her, his eyes betraying his anxiety.

*   *   *

Sean Dunmore watched the grey BMW turn into the street opposite and he smiled at his foresight. If Baldini was here then it was a fairly safe assumption that she would not be far behind. He wandered over to the bar and ordered another drink, whilst keeping his eye on the tube station exit. He was in a cocoon of time which related only to now and which allowed no access to the past and no entry to the future. He felt impregnable, untouched by doubt or consequence, and he waited for the arrival of Habiba Popals as a lion waits in the long grass by a waterhole.

It was twenty minutes later when she emerged from the tube, turning quickly down her street without glancing behind her. He had to catch her before she reached her house and he ran down the road, using the parked cars as cover. Just as he got to her, he heard her phone ring and she was picking it out of her shoulder bag when he grabbed her around the arms, pushing her violently against a corrugated iron fence which dented with their weight.

'C'mon, you fucking bitch,' he hissed at her, dragging her along the side of the fence, her body bounding against the dirty metal grooves, towards the brick arches of the tube line. She made to break free from him and he struck a blow to her stomach which caused her to double up.

'That's for the one you gave me yesterday, you little fucker. Not quite so fucking lippy now, are we?'

He had pulled her into a car breaker's yard, a jumble of wheels, car body parts and dirty oil cans, forcing her towards the darkness of the interior, yanking her hair back so that she yelled in pain. Up above, a train rumbled by and he hit her again, her cry lost in the noise.

'What is it, Jack?'

Giacomo had suddenly stopped moving, the phone to his ear, his hand supporting himself against the open door. He had heard Sean Dunmore's voice and now all he could hear were muffled sounds, followed by a grunt. Then he heard the train and at first he wasn't sure whether it was on the phone or outside. And then he realised it was both and he bolted for the door and out into the street. He saw the train and began running in the opposite direction to the way it was travelling. He was desperate and his eyes were wide with terror, the fear that he would be too late. The rattle of the train disappeared and he cursed the noise of his breathing as he gasped for air. He was still holding his mobile and he heard Sean Dunmore's voice again, the single word 'bitch'. He turned to his left and made for the darkened arch, stepping between the oily puddles until he could see them on the far side, Sean Dunmore's body looming over hers, his hand wrenching back her neck, his knee between her thighs. Baldini ran and hit him as hard as he could, his fist sinking into his solar plexus, the air expelled from the man's mouth in a roar.

Dunmore let go his grip, bringing his arms behind him for protection as Baldini hit him again, a glancing blow across his face which sent him further into the darkness. Colin Tyler had arrived now and seeing this Dunmore turned and ran towards a door at the far end of the arch. He crashed it open and disappeared. Baldini reached the door seconds later to see him clambering over a gate protecting stairs which led up to the tracks. He was almost at the top before Baldini had scrambled over the gate. He took the steps two at a time, his chest hurting as he fought for breath. A narrow concrete walkway ran along one side of the track, like a tiny platform and Baldini could see Dunmore about fifty metres ahead of him, running with careful tiptoe steps towards the station in the distance. As he followed he registered the red tube train pulling out of the station and coming towards them. When it arrived alongside Dunmore he had to stop, fearing the train would knock him on to the tracks, which allowed Baldini about ten seconds to get closer before the tube clattered by him.

'Stop, Dunmore. Stop now.'

But his words were lost in the rush of the train just centimetres from his body. Dunmore was on his way before Baldini could move, but the distance was shorter and he was gaining on the blue-suited figure. Dunmore turned to see his pursuer and almost lost his balance on the narrow ledge. Baldini called to him to stop again, but he ran on, reaching the platform of the station. Sprinting between the people, he made for the exit, leaping over the steel barriers and down the stairs into the street. As he took the stairs after him, Baldini could hear the sirens of the police vehicles that Colin Tyler must have called. Halfway down to ground level, he watched as Dunmore made to cross the road and then changed his mind, looking up the high street towards the sound of the sirens. In that fatal moment, that second of hesitation as he changed direction, he was hit by the front a bus which launched him against a taxi coming the other way. And in an instant it was over, the body broken in the road, the pedestrians staring, their hands to their mouths, the police arriving and, above it all, the sound of his own breathing.

He felt nothing for the man whose blood was now flowing slowly to the gutter, the life already departed from the body.

Colin Tyler had now arrived and was speaking to a uniformed officer in one of the cars. Habiba Popals stood by the side of the road, very still, looking at the body of Sean Dunmore crumpled in the road. He began to walk towards her and she looked up, registering his slow approach to her. As their eyes met, he watched the seriousness of her gaze change as she focused on him. He stood in front of her, her large eyes holding steady as she returned his stare, the flashing blue of the police lights reflected in her dark pupils. It was a moment he would remember forever as he watched her eyes change into a smile, if it is possible for eyes to smile. He took her hands and she leaned against his chest and another train rumbled over the bridge and disappeared towards the centre of London.

'I don't want you out of my sight again,' he said into her hair. 'It's too complicated.'

She was quiet, the shaking he had felt when he first embraced her slowly subsiding. He kissed the top of her head and marvelled that the bizarre circumstances that surrounded him, a body lying in the main road behind, in a part of London entirely unknown to him, amongst a throng of people, some of whom were staring at them, should appear so perfectly normal, as if all his life had been leading to this point.

She looked up at him and he knew with absolute certainty that the magical combination of shapes that made up her face was the perfect reflection of the way she was, fierce, determined and utterly beautiful.

'Giacomo Baldini,' she said, their faces almost touching, 'perhaps it was always meant to turn out like this. I think you saw it before I did.'

'No,' he said, 'you saw it a long time ago. You made it happen. When you stole the painting you set in motion our meeting. It was fate and I can say to you now that from the first moment I saw your face, I fell in love.'

She brought her lips against his and in the warmth of their touch she felt an enormous safety, which was only partly physical. She knew that she didn't have to explain herself to this man, that somehow he knew her, accepted her for what she was, and in the safety of that knowledge she felt her shoulders drop and her body shape itself against his as though it was fluid.

Chapter 38

She looked at the picture of them both, which must have been taken outside the register office, her head turning, her eyes on him and her smile matched by his own, an exact encapsulation of their mood. She read the story beneath the photograph, under the headline:

Security Chief Marries Thief

Habiba Popals, twenty-three, yesterday married Giacomo Baldini, thirty, in a brief ceremony at Kensington Register Office. The day before she had been released from Holloway Prison, having served a six-month sentence for stealing a small Messina painting from the National Gallery. Giacomo Baldini, then the director of security for the gallery, led the investigation into the theft. The painting was quickly returned to the gallery, although Baldini resigned his position shortly afterwards. In the court case that followed, Habiba Popals revealed that she had stolen the painting as part of an elaborate plot to expose Sean Dunmore, who, she alleged, had raped her. Sean Dunmore had been a security officer at the gallery; he was later killed in a road accident at Shepherd's Bush when being chased by the police. Subsequently, several other women have come forward to allege assault at the hands of Sean Dunmore. It appears that Baldini fell in love with Popals during the course of the investigation and he spoke in her defence during the court case. 'If there is an excusable crime, this is it,' he said, 'although I understand my views put me in an intolerable position. I don't believe Habiba Popals should go to prison.' The judge was sympathetic, citing slow-burn provocation as a mitigating circumstance and Popals was given a token six-month sentence. Speaking after yesterday's marriage ceremony she said, 'I wanted to swap a bad marriage for a good one,' but refused to elaborate further. Our medical correspondent writes, 'This is a peculiar twist in the Stockholm Syndrome, a phenomenon where a strong relationship develops between a criminal and his or her captor. Such incidents can have a profound effect on personality resulting in unexpected behaviour.'

She tossed *The Times* across to Giacomo, who was drinking coffee, the remains of breakfast scattered on the round table between them.

'It appears we are victims of the Stockholm Syndrome,' she said, laughing. 'Perhaps you'd like to comment.'

She was wearing a pale pink, silk camisole which came down to just below her knees, with two narrow straps over her wide shoulders. The garment suggested the body beneath, the shape of her breasts and her hips lightly touched by the fine material as she rose to kiss him, leaning over the cluttered table.

They were in Paris and the day before she had taken him to see *The Origin of the World* watching him, smiling, as he surveyed the picture.

'You're not going to steal this one, as well?' he had said, leaning forward towards the raised pudenda. 'I'm not sure where we would put it.'

She thought of how they had made love, a few days after the death of Sean Dunmore. He had been wonderfully careful, approaching her as he might a wounded animal and she had responded to his gentle caresses. She had carried a residue of apprehension, uncertain of the mental scars that had been left in the wake of the assault, but these dissipated like a morning mist and she lost herself in the extreme physicality of what followed. Afterwards she remembered lying, exposed, the sheets jumbled around her, just like the Courbet picture, watching him look at her. He had run his hands up her leg, lightly over the mass of hair and down the other leg to her foot, where he slowly felt each of her toes, gently separating them and sliding his fingers in between. She had remained absolutely still, but the sensation of his hand lightly gliding over her swept through her from the base of her spine to the top of her head.

'I want to take you to Paris to show you something,' she had said. 'Perhaps we could go for our honeymoon.'

She recalled his face now, the smile spreading across it, wider and wider.

'Excuse me, Ms Popals. Where I come from, it is the man who proposes to the woman.'

'Ah, Signor Baldini, and where exactly is it that you come from?'

Her spell in prison had been nothing in comparison to the entrapment she had felt in the years after the assault, the walls of fear and anger that had proscribed her life. Giacomo saw her every day and they planned the marriage for as soon after her release as they could. Her confinement seemed part of the whole, another stage in the distancing of Sean Dunmore and the welcoming of Giacomo Baldini.

'So what's this about bad marriage,' he said, raising his eyebrows and looking at her over the paper. 'Is there something you have to tell me?'

'Oh, yes,' she said, raising her own eyebrows. 'There is so much to tell you.'

And she felt, in the comfort of that moment, the past lives of Anam, Noreen, Kiran and Jamila fade into the background and take their place like distant hills, shapes in the far distance. This was her life, in the here and now, and the remote echoes of other worlds slowly receded to leave her at one with the present.